Praise for Kyoko Mori's previous novel, SHIZUKO'S DAUGHTER

"A jewel of a book, one of those rarities that shine only a few times in a generation . . . A work of art."
—*The New York Times Book Review*

"Beautifully written . . . Yuki's life is buoyed by the legacies that her mother bequeathed her: a love of art, nature, and her aging grandparents. In the end, she forges a new life and even a sweet and happy romance."
—*Los Angeles Times Book Review*

"Lyrical . . . A beautifully written book about a bitterly painful coming of age."
—*Kirkus Reviews*

"Quietly moving . . . An emotionally and culturally rich tale tracing the evolution of despair into hope."
—*Publishers Weekly*

"Poetically crafted . . . Mori has a fine eye for details. . . . Her characters, especially Yuki, are well realized and clearly drawn."
—*Booklist*

By Kyoko Mori
Published by Fawcett Books:

SHIZUKO'S DAUGHTER
ONE BIRD

Books published by The Ballantine Publishing Group are available at quantity discounts on bulk purchases for premium, educational, fund-raising, and special sales use. For details, please call 1-800-733-3000.

ONE BIRD

Kyoko Mori

FAWCETT JUNIPER • NEW YORK

A Fawcett Juniper Book
Published by Ballantine Books
Copyright © 1995 by Kyoko Mori
Excerpt from *Shizuko's Daughter* copyright © 1993 by Kyoko Mori

http://www.randomhouse.com

Library of Congress Catalog Card Number: 96-96498

ISBN 0-449-70453-X

This edition published by arrangement with Henry Holt & Company.

Printed in Canada

First Ballantine Books Edition: October 1996

10 9 8 7 6

For my childhood friends:

Naoko Yamaguchi Miki, my first shinyu *(best friend),*
Naoko Murao Dalla Valle,
Tadashi Kuzuha,
and
Makoto Kuzuha

Acknowledgments

The author wishes to thank the following people who helped her learn about birds:

Dave Willard, bird specialist: Chicago Field Museum.

Mike Reed, curator; Mark Naniot, ranger technician; Liz Burrows and Jim Skaleski, volunteer rehabilitators; Terri Wusterbarth and Maureen Parks, animal care interns: Bay Beach Wildlife Sanctuary, Green Bay, Wisconsin.

Tim Berkopec, veteran bird-watcher.

Chuck Brock, who gave up his spare room for use as a nursery for orphaned and injured songbirds.

The rehabilitation of birds and other wildlife in the United States is regulated by the United States Fish and Wildlife Service and various fish and wildlife departments in individual states. Only licensed rehabilitators are permitted to care for wildlife.

1

A Game of Tag

"Tell me the truth," I insist while my mother keeps shoving sweaters into her suitcase.

Though she is kneeling on the floor just a few feet away, she won't look up at me. Frowning, she pretends to examine the sleeve of her gray cashmere pullover, as if she had found a hole or a stain that demanded her attention. I sigh loudly and start pacing in front of her.

On the windowsill behind her, the late-afternoon sun is hitting the four plastic containers in which she had planted her spring seeds two weeks ago. The rectangular containers are large but shallow, holding just a finger of dirt around each seed. Half the plants have sprouted, their heads bent down with the cracked seeds stuck on top like tiny helmets: pansies, spring chrysanthemums, impatiens. The lavenders and the petunias are taking their time, their slow-germinating seeds hidden in the soil. My mother has covered the containers with clear plastic and placed them on heating pads, with a spray bottle ready for their daily misting. As long as I can remember, she has coaxed seeds to grow in the middle of winter and has had the seedlings ready for her garden in early March. But not this year, or ever again. I know she is not coming back.

In late November, when Mother first mentioned spending the winter with her father in their old home in a small village north of Kyoto, I knew right away that something was wrong. The more she kept explaining her reasons, the more I knew that she wasn't telling the truth. "Grandfather Kurihara has a difficult time managing alone," she said. "I want to help him get through the winter. I'll write to Grandmother Shimizu in Tokyo. She won't mind staying with you and your father until I come back." Grandfather Kurihara is old, and he has been alone since my grandmother's death almost three years ago, but he is strong and healthy. My mother—or anyone's mother—would not leave her own home to take care of her father unless he were sick. Besides, if Mother were leaving to help him, she would have left right away, back in November. Instead she has waited till now, the last week of January. Winter is already half gone.

Mother has put away the cashmere sweater and is now reaching for her wool skirt. I kneel down beside her. Without a word, she stops what she is doing.

Putting my arms around her shoulders, I try to reason with her. "It's easier for me if I know. You don't have to pretend in order to spare my feelings. You didn't have to start up the plants to fool me." A whining tone creeps into my voice, so I pause and take a deep breath. At fifteen, I am too old to cry or to speak in the sad, nasal voice of a child.

Slowly, my mother leans forward and hugs me. "I wish I could take you with me, Megumi," she says into my hair, each word warm and distinct, her wish ending with my name. Megumi means "God's blessing."

"The day you were born was the happiest day of my life," Mother has told me many times. "I knew that God had given me the most important blessing ever." Thinking about that makes me miss the old times—the two of us drinking hot chocolate in the winter and looking at the

2

pictures in my album, laughing about what a fat little baby I used to be, wondering how I ended up big-boned and thin. My mother keeps holding me tight. I wish this afternoon would go no further. It's four-thirty; the sunlight is bright and orange, the way it gets an hour before sunset. If I sit still and say nothing more, maybe the day will pass without anything happening. But on my way home from school, I promised myself that I would speak nothing but the truth on our last afternoon together. "I'll be honest," I said over and over as I walked past the bare branches of the cherry and maple trees planted along the sidewalk; when the leaves come out in March or April, they will be reminders of my promise. By then, Mother will be long gone, living with Grandfather in their quiet home far from here. How can she leave me if I really am the greatest blessing of her life? Was she lying to me even back then?

I drop my arms from around her shoulders and pull myself out of her embrace.

"It's no use wishing," I tell her. "I know you can't take me. I'm not stupid."

Without a word, she looks down at the floor.

I stand up and start walking around the room again. Mother has often said that when a woman leaves her husband, the children must stay with their father, especially if the woman's parents are poor. The woman must go to live with her parents for the rest of her life, giving up her children until they are old enough—full-grown adults— to visit on their own; the father usually does not allow any visits. The children, she said, would be better off with the father: Growing up poor and fatherless means growing up in shame, being despised by strangers and neighbors alike. She had been talking about other people when she said these things—people we had heard or read

3

about, since no couple we know in Ashiya or Kobe has been divorced or separated—but I always understood she meant us. She has been preparing me for a long time, warning me of what would happen if she were to leave my father.

Still, that is not the same as telling the direct truth. Mother has never said anything about not coming back; for nearly three months, she has been pretending that she is going for a short visit rather than giving me up and returning to live with her father for the rest of her life. Even now, she hasn't said anything except a halfhearted wish to take me with her. I stop pacing and look at her as she smooths her black wool skirt with her fingers, getting it ready to be packed. Though she is taking only two suitcases, everything in her room has been put into boxes. If I had been dumb enough to believe her story about taking care of Grandfather, I would have guessed the truth when she started packing all of her belongings. How could she think that I would be stupid enough not to notice? All my life she has told me how smart I am.

"You didn't have to lie to me," I mutter.

She looks up, her face drawn tight and her large eyes wide with hurt.

Immediately, I want to take back my words; I want to apologize and insist that I didn't really mean it, I was just upset. But I can't. It would have been better if Mother had told the truth. No matter how upset we might have been, we could have made plans for the future. I would have helped her pack, hard as it might have been. Anything would have been better than standing around like this, pretending that the worst thing in my life was not about to happen.

Mother is staring at me, saying nothing. Staring back at her pale cheeks and thin lips, I wish she would cry. I want to see tears trickling down from her eyes as she opens her mouth to admit, "I'm sorry I lied." That would make me feel if not better, then less bad. But if she said she was sorry, how could I respond? "That's all right. I understand"? No. I don't understand.

The two of us continue to face each other in silence. When the doorbell rings, I almost jump.

"I'll go get the door," I say, darting out of the room.

Mrs. Kato, my mother's best and oldest friend, is standing in the doorway with her son, Kiyoshi, slouching behind her in his navy blue school uniform. Nobody smiles or says "Good afternoon." Mrs. Kato heads straight toward Mother's room without taking off her winter coat, which is the same gray as the hair around her temples.

Kiyoshi and I step into the hallway, glancing at each other but saying nothing. It's just like when we were children and one of us had done something wrong. I see him every week at church, but in his school uniform he doesn't look like himself. The starched white collar and the heavy jacket make him seem older, more serious. Christian Girls' Academy, the private, all-girl school I attend, has no uniforms. In my blue jeans and fuzzy red sweater, with my long hair pulled back in a ponytail, I must appear childish. He has grown a little taller than I in the last few years, and I cannot get used to having to tilt my head up to talk to him. His face has changed, too. His jaw and nose have gotten larger and thicker, though his eyes are the same as when we were children—narrow eyes that crinkle into little half-moons when he smiles, which he doesn't do very often anymore.

Inside the bedroom, Mother and Mrs. Kato are speaking in low voices. Mostly it's Mrs. Kato talking. She comes out after a while, carrying both suitcases. In the

5

hallway, she nods to us and points her chin toward the front door. She doesn't have to say anything. Kiyoshi and I file outside and stand on the driveway, where the Katos' white Toyota is parked. The sun is sinking fast over the western mountains.

My mother steps out of the house while Mrs. Kato is putting the suitcases in the trunk. Empty-handed, not even carrying a purse, Mother leans on the passenger's door. She has put on a dark blue jacket over her white blouse and blue skirt. Her long black hair, wound up in a bun, is unraveling around her pale, oval face. She has gotten so thin in the last year, almost gaunt-looking because she is tall. The jacket hangs loose on her shoulders. She blinks and takes a deep breath, as though the walk to the car has exhausted her. Leaning back, she lifts her head a little toward the sky—she looks completely lost and alone.

I run up to her and embrace her. When she hugs me back, the bulky wool of her coat bunches up around my head and shoulders. Though I am only an inch or so shorter than she, I feel small, wrapped tight in the thick sleeves through which I can scarcely feel her arms.

"I need to go away so I can see you again someday," she whispers. "Do you understand?"

When I nod, the fabric rustles against my ears like a thick cocoon of leaves. Her voice sounds muffled, far away.

"If I don't leave your father now," she continues, "I can't bear to live long enough to see you grow up."

I nod again.

"I'm sorry," she whispers, and lets go.

Stepping back, I see her face set hard with sadness and resolution—her lips drawn tight, her jaw clenched. She

6

has made up her mind and she is trying to be brave. She wants me to do the same.

"It's all right," I manage to say. My voice comes out weak and shaky. "Please don't be sad." *Take me with you,* I want to beg. *Please. I'll do anything.* But I suck in my breath and clench my teeth, drawing my lips as tight as hers. Mrs. Kato is standing next to us now. Short and plump, she seems so sensible, businesslike. Mother and I stand like two ghosts hovering over her.

"I want you to go with Kiyoshi to our house," Mrs. Kato tells me. "I won't be back till late, but my husband will be home. You should stay with us until your grandmother is here. It's all right with your father. I already asked him."

"He's not coming home for a while, is he?" I mumble.

Mother and Mrs. Kato quickly glance at each other and then down at the ground. My father won't come home till his mother is here to take care of me because, unlike Mrs. Kato's husband, he has never cooked supper or cleaned the house for himself. Besides, our house is not the only place he considers home—where a woman is waiting to care for him. Though we all know these things, Mother and Mrs. Kato are still embarrassed to be reminded. They would rather I pretended not to know about my father and his girlfriend; they want me to play dumb. Mrs. Kato looks at me, her broad, square face wrinkled with a frown. I am being rude, I know, by not thanking her for the invitation to her house. She is only trying to be kind. But I can't stop being angry. Everybody knew the truth about today—my father, Pastor Kato, even Kiyoshi—and nobody would admit it to me.

My mother hugs me one more time, but I don't hug her back. She scarcely seems to notice. Letting go of me, she opens the car door and slides into the passenger's seat.

7

Mrs. Kato is walking over to the driver's side. This is the last moment in which I could ask them to stop. I could start to cry and scream. I could stand in front of the car, pound my fists on the windshield and beg them not to go. But I was never one to throw tantrums, even when I was very young, so I just stand next to Kiyoshi on the driveway, saying and doing nothing. I can't wait for this moment to pass, for the whole thing to be over with, so I can be alone.

The car backs out of the driveway and then glides down the street. Mother twists around in her seat to look back, but she does not wave. Neither do I. Waving is for a happier good-bye, like those times when she and I were leaving her parents' village after our summer visits, back when Grandmother Kurihara was alive. We waved and waved; it was a way of saying "We had a wonderful time even though we are sad to go. We'll be back next summer." Now Mother is going there and never coming back.

When the car disappears around the corner, I go back inside and run upstairs to my room. Kiyoshi follows me but stays in the doorway, looking in. I pull some clothes out of my oak dresser, throwing a few T-shirts and jeans down on the floor, followed by some socks.

"You'll see her again soon," Kiyoshi says abruptly while I am kneeling on the floor with my backpack.

"No, I won't. My mother is not coming back."

"You'll go visit her, then."

Instead of answering, I stuff my gym shoes and pajamas into the backpack. The next moment, he is in the room; he kneels next to me and says, "Come on, it'll be okay. You'll see her soon."

"No, I won't. Father won't let me."

"I'm sure you are wrong. He will." Kiyoshi picks up my T-shirts and holds them out toward me.

I grab the shirts and yank at them, hard; Kiyoshi flinches as though I had swung at him. "Don't touch my things!" I yell.

"I was trying to help." He shrugs.

"Get out. I don't need your help."

He stands up and takes a few steps backward.

"I want to be alone. Leave my room." Clenching my socks in my fist, I wind up my arm and take aim. The socks hit him in the stomach, but his blue uniform is thick and stiff. He only jumps a little.

"Okay, okay." Kiyoshi backsteps all the way to the door and disappears into the hallway.

But as soon as he is gone, I wish I hadn't lost my temper. It doesn't make me feel better at all to be alone. Kiyoshi must be standing at the top of the stairs, listening for any little sound. He must think I wanted to be alone to cry. I can almost see his thick eyebrows and big nose, wrinkled into a worried frown. I quickly throw my things into the backpack and get up, not wasting a minute. The last thing I want is his pity.

In the hallway, I nod my head and point to the stairs. Our footsteps make hollow noises as we go down.

At the bottom, he turns and reaches for my backpack before I can put my arms through the straps. I *can carry it myself*, I want to say. *I'm not weak or sick.* But I'm too mad to even say that or to argue, so I shove the backpack at him. He takes it and puts his arms through the straps.

In silence, we walk out the door and down the hill toward the church rectory where his family lives. The sun has disappeared behind the mountains. It's getting dark fast and the air is chilly. We keep walking, both of us taking big, sullen steps, coming down hard on our heels. He glances sideways at me now and then, maybe waiting for me to say something, but I'm in no mood to make small talk, much less to apologize. Even in the dusk he looks ridiculous, with my pink backpack stuck to the back of his navy blue uniform. At any other time I would have laughed.

As we turn the last corner onto his block, the streetlamps light up, as if our steps had turned them on. The lamps bloom pale yellow in a long row along the sidewalk. Suddenly, I remember my mother's seedlings on the windowsill.

"I forgot something," I blurt out. Before he can reply, I start running back up the hill.

A few blocks past the commuter train station, I dodge businessmen with briefcases on their way home and women my mother's age bringing home their groceries in baskets or shopping carts. It's only two miles from the Katos' house to mine.

In the dark, my house looks large and squat—a square stucco building with shiny blue tiles on the roof, Western-style, like the houses of most of our neighbors. Pulling the keys out of my jeans pocket, I unlock the door and go straight to Mother's room on the first floor. I switch on the white overhead lamp. In the empty room, even the brown carpet looks sad. On the windowsill, the sprayer is still half-filled with water. My mother had left the plants just the way they were, expecting me to care for them.

How could she do that? I wonder, as I walk up to the sill and reach for the containers. She knew I was staying with the Katos until Grandmother Shimizu could come from Tokyo. Did she think I would come back to the empty house every day just to mist the plants? Did she expect Kiyoshi and me to carry the planters down the hill

10

to his house? No. More likely, she didn't care what happened to them.

She had no reason to care. She must have planted the seeds only to fool me.

I quickly unplug the heating pads and stack the containers together, crushing most of the seedlings. The containers are unwieldy and wobbly; it's hard to hold on to them. I keep walking, sidestepping down the narrow hallway into the kitchen, then out the back door into our fenced-in yard.

In the light spreading out from my house and our next-door neighbors', I walk past the maples and elders to the very back of the yard where Mother had planted three Russian olives and two camellias in a row. I stop between the two camellias and put down all the containers but one. Stepping up to the taller camellia, I turn that first container upside down. Clumps of moist soil fall to the ground, making a faint sound like a sigh. I toss the container aside and pick up the next one, empty it, and then the next and the next.

When I have emptied all of them, there is a small heap at the root of the tree. Crushed seedlings are scattered in the soil like small threads dropped on the floor of a sewing room—pulled-out stitches and discarded thrums.

The seedlings are better off this way. I have not inherited my mother's way with plants. Even cut flowers wilt after a day in my vase because the water I put in is always too cold or too warm. The potted plants I sometimes receive as gifts—geraniums, miniature azaleas, cyclamens—shrivel up on my desk because I water them too much or too little. Mother often took the plants I nearly killed and coaxed them back to life, giving them just the right amount of water and light, pinching back their growth to keep the leaves thick and healthy. She

11

should have known better: Without her the seedlings would dry up and die or be drowned in water. She shouldn't have started them in the first place.

I kneel down and smooth out the mound of dirt, spreading it over the grass at the root of the tree. Two summers ago, we buried our canaries under the other camellia, the smaller one. The canaries died because Father had forgotten about them while Mother and I had gone to stay with Grandfather Kurihara. We came home late at night to find Father gone and the birds hunched down at the bottom of the cage. Their seed dish held nothing but cracked hulls, and the water in their water dish had dried up. The canaries would not touch the seeds or the water Mother and I offered. They sat listless, their beaks opening up now and then, straining for breath. When I got up in the morning, meaning to call a veterinarian, the canaries were already dead. Their bodies were yellow puffs that looked like dried flowers and weighed almost nothing.

Father came home the next night and explained that he had been suddenly called away on business in the last few days. He would not apologize.

"Small animals are very delicate," he reasoned. "You have to accept that they die easily."

"But they didn't just die," I protested. "You killed them by forgetting about them. Their being fragile had nothing to do with that."

"If you cared so much about them, you should have given them to someone else to watch. I had other important things to worry about."

"I wanted to give them to Kiyoshi. Don't you remember? But you told me not to bother because you meant to be home every night."

Father shrugged and walked out of the room. A few

nights later, he came home late, as usual, while I was sleeping. I woke up and saw him standing on my chair, trying to reach the hook over my desk where the canaries used to be. It must have been one or two in the morning. Outside, everything was dark and quiet. Inside the bamboo cage Father was holding, small birds were whirling around, making beeping noises.

"I don't want new birds," I said. "I want an apology."

Father stepped off the chair, slammed the cage down on my desk, and walked out of my room. He stomped down the stairs, out the front door. In the cage, the birds were shrieking, battering their wings against the bars. I could not see how many there were. Covering my head from their noise and the light Father had left on, I went back to sleep.

In the morning, the birds were sitting on their perch and making their beeping noises. There were four—little white finches with black markings and pink beaks. Father wasn't home. I got dressed and walked to the nearest pet store and put the cage on the counter.

"These birds aren't from our store," the old man behind the counter said.

"Take them anyway," I told him. "I don't want a refund." I turned around and left while the man stared. All the way to the door, I could hear the finches fluttering and beeping.

Now, kneeling in the backyard, I remember the daffodil bulbs my mother had put in that fall, over the canaries' grave. She planted daffodils because their petals would be the same color as the birds' feathers; she was hoping that the flowers would give me some small comfort. The daffodils survived the winter and bloomed last spring, and this year, too, some leaves are already up—curled tight, smaller than my thumb. They are delicate as

13

bird wings and beautiful, but they do not cheer me up. Not in the least.

I stare at the leaves and remember the last thing I said to my mother when we were alone: "You didn't have to lie to me." The look on her face when she heard my words was the same look she had when Father called late at night to say that he wasn't coming home. Each time he called, she seemed stunned, in spite of the other nights when he had acted in exactly the same way. In silence, she would throw out the tea leaves that she had carefully measured into his teapot, clean the kitchen counter, and go to her room. Some nights I could hear her crying. Though she tried to stifle her sounds with her pillow, I heard the quick, sharp breaths she took between her sobs. Maybe she never got used to my father's thoughtlessness. But my father isn't the only thoughtless person in our family. When I had accused my mother of lying, I didn't care if my words hurt her; I wished she would cry. I have just destroyed her seedlings—seedlings she must have started for the same reason that she planted these daffodil bulbs, to give me something beautiful. It was unfair of me to think they were just part of her lie. Whatever her faults, my mother is considerate. Even when she was upset, she would try to cheer me up. I can't think of the last time she said an angry or unkind thing to me. Unlike my father and me, she would rather cry than make other people cry because of her.

Looking over the pile of dirt and dead plants, I think of other ways in which I am just like my father. Neither of us can be quiet for long. Quick and jumpy, we sit impatiently drumming our fingers on the table, or rocking back and forth in our chairs. My father's mother, Grandmother Shimizu, is always scolding me for having no poise, although she never criticizes my father. Being rest-

14

less, she says, is not as serious a fault in a man as it is in a woman. But Grandmother Shimizu is a very nervous woman herself, always picking at the tablecloth with her fingers as she sits drinking tea, her thin neck held tight as a knotted cord. Maybe my father's family has given me their meanness and restlessness. I am nothing like my mother, who is quiet and gentle, who makes plants thrive.

"Megumi," someone calls from behind.

Kiyoshi comes running across the yard, still in his uniform. He doesn't have my backpack anymore. I am not sure how long I have been gone.

He stops a few feet away, his big shoulders moving with his breathing. I scoop up a handful of dirt. "My mother's seedlings," I explain. "I put them out of their misery."

Because the lights are behind him, I can't see his face very well as he stands there. He is not one to talk when worried or upset. He could stand there saying nothing all night, waiting for me to go on.

I open my hand and let the dirt drop through my fingers. Kiyoshi once told me that his earliest memory is of sitting with me in the sandbox in the church playground. We were sticking our hands into the hot sand, stirring it around, having fun, when suddenly, I grabbed a handful of sand and flung it at him. I don't recall throwing the sand at him, but I was happy to hear him remember that. I am five weeks older than he; I was always the tougher of us two.

But now this memory makes me sad. We have known each other all our lives, fifteen years—more if we counted the months when our mothers and their other best friend, Mrs. Uchida, were three pregnant women, sitting side by side on a big couch and knitting baby

15

sweaters, as in the pictures all of them had in their albums. I used to imagine Kiyoshi, me, and the other boy, Takashi, teasing and challenging one another on that couch, about which one of us would be the first to make our appearance. Kiyoshi and I go back a long, long way. And still, there is nothing he can say to make me feel better. It isn't his fault. He had nothing to do with my mother's leaving.

"I'm sorry I was irritated," I offer, even though my voice still sounds begrudging. "I know you were just trying to help."

"It's all right." He kneels down next to me and hesitates, as though he were thinking about patting me on the shoulder or ruffling up my hair—which he would have done when we were younger, back in grade school. He doesn't now. We are grown-up. He leans forward a little and says, "Are you all right?"

I nod.

"Let's go home," he says. "My father's making us spaghetti for supper. He just got back from his hospital visits."

"Did Pastor Kato know what was going to happen today?" I ask. "You can tell me the truth."

"Yes, he knew."

"And you?"

He nods.

We stand up and start walking toward the house. Halfway there, I stop, so he has to, too. "Promise me something," I say.

"What?"

"Don't tell your mother I did that." I turn around and point toward the camellia tree where I have left the dead seedlings and the empty containers.

He narrows his eyes a little, hesitating. Even more than

16

I, Kiyoshi is a stickler for telling the truth, the whole truth.

"She'll just worry about me. Or feel sorry for me."

"She already feels sorry for you."

His bluntness takes me aback, but I don't get upset. At least he is being honest.

"Then I don't want her to feel sorrier."

"Okay," he agrees. "I won't say anything."

We go in the back door, quickly walk through the house, switching off the lights, and then leave by the front door. The key turns hard.

Good-bye, I want to say to the house. I almost imagine its square outlines sagging. Upstairs in my room, the three windows are completely dark. I used to love my room, especially in the fall, when all the trees in the yard were yellow and red, the colors of sunset; sitting on my bed, I would pretend that I was floating in the sky, that my room was a balloon sailing through the sunset clouds. How could I have been so happy when, downstairs, my mother was waiting for my father, who never came home? How could I imagine sailing on a silly balloon while she was making up her mind to leave me forever? "If I don't leave your father now," she had said, "I can't bear to live long enough to see you grow up." She was saying that her unhappiness had almost killed her. How could I be happy in my room while she was feeling so bad? I turn away from the house, feeling cold and dizzy.

But Kiyoshi hasn't noticed. He is already several steps down the sidewalk, his stiff, uniformed back toward me. Long ago, we played a game of tag in which we tried to step on each other's shadows. The person whose shadow was stepped on had to turn around and become the chaser, trying to step on other kids' shadows. Now there is no moon out, and the streetlamps cast only weak gray shadows. All the same, I charge after Kiyoshi and stomp on his shadow's blurry head.

"You'll never catch me," I taunt as I sprint past him. I concentrate on the sound of my shoes hitting the pavement and try to think of nothing else. In a few seconds, Kiyoshi's footsteps come clonking down after me. Ahead, in the cold, my breath streams out white and hovers like the thought balloons in the comic books we used to read. Weaving my way through the broken shadows of trees, I chase my blank thoughts as they shoot up to the sky.

2
Distant Crickets

Downstairs, in my mother's old room, Grandmother Shimizu is practicing her samisen. The strings make harsh pinging noises that echo up the stairwell. She is playing much louder than she did last year or the year before. Although she would never admit it, Grandmother is losing her hearing. "Don't mumble. Speak up," she often hisses at me through her gritted teeth.

"Grandmother Shimizu is a good person," my mother used to claim. "She just has a gruff manner."

Mother wasn't completely wrong. Three years ago, when I came down with the flu during my visit to her house in Tokyo, Grandmother Shimizu was like a different person. Every time I woke up, she was sitting by my bed, her back bolt upright, her bony hands gripping the edge of my blanket. She looked sick herself: Wisps of iron gray hair stuck out around her skinny face, and her small eyes were puffy from not having slept. Once I was better, she brought me herb tea and broth she had made from old Chinese recipes; she did not scold me if I had no appetite. "That's all right. Go back to sleep. Don't worry," she had said, her voice sounding soft and kind. But as soon as I was well, she was back to her old self—criticizing me for speaking too much and too fast, for not sitting still, for almost any little thing.

The way she scolded me was nothing compared to the way she found fault with my mother.

"How can my son enjoy being home if you don't keep house better than this?" she would yell if she found a single crumb on the table, a drop of water splashed on the counter and left to dry. Though Grandmother is short and frail-looking, she made my mother cower with her angry words and silent stares. Often during Grandmother's visits, my mother had red, swollen eyes in the morning, so I knew that she had been crying in bed.

Even then, Mother would insist, "Grandmother Shimizu is strict because she loves us. She is from a different time. Correcting us is her old-fashioned way of showing love."

After having that flu at her house, I could see some truth in what Mother said. Maybe Grandmother loves me but can only show it by being gruff and critical. But that's only true about her and me. Grandmother never loved my mother; anyone could see that from the look in Grandmother's small beady eyes—a cold, dead-fish look. I wish my mother had not tried to make our family sound happier than we really were. The way she talked all winter about visiting Grandfather Kurihara, it was almost as if she had believed the lie herself, even while packing all of her possessions.

Grandmother continues to practice her samisen. It's only eight-thirty on Saturday morning, too early to be playing any kind of music. I have been up since six o'clock trying to work on my essay for school. I crumple another piece of paper and toss it into the wastebasket. How can I concentrate with Grandmother making so much noise downstairs, her fingers twanging and buzzing the angry strings? Besides, the topic is silly and far too broad: What is it like to be a high school student in 1975?

The essay is for the time capsule project sponsored by Sumitomo Bank. In the vault of the bank's Osaka office they are keeping a locked trunk, to be opened in the year 2000. It will contain newspapers, magazines, books, movie posters, photographs, and one essay chosen to represent each of the area schools. At our school everyone who is starting tenth grade or higher in April is supposed to submit an essay. The deadline is the end of this school year, the second Friday of March. That is only a week away.

In the year 2000, I will be forty; my mother, seventy. I cannot imagine what we will be like then. Will we visit and write to each other, exchange flower bulbs and knit each other sweaters, just as my mother and Grandmother Kurihara used to? Or will I be like my father, who spent little time at home even during Grandmother Shimizu's visits—going on business trips and leaving Mother and me to entertain her? Will my mother and I ever get over our years of separation? When I am forty years old, will I still be angry at her for leaving me?

Mother has been gone for only a month and two weeks, but it seems like a long time. As soon as Grandmother Shimizu arrived and I came back from the Katos' house, Father and Grandmother sat me down in the kitchen and told me: Just as I expected, I am not to see my mother as long as I live in my father's house. That means at least until I am done with college, seven years from now. Seven years is almost half of my life so far. My mother has left me, knowing that we will not see each other again till I am twenty-two.

I stare at the blank paper on my desk. What can I possibly say about myself or about high school to people in the future? Who am I to speak for my entire high school, anyway? I am one of the four girls at Christian Girls'

Academy—nine hundred girls, from seventh to twelfth grade—who does not live with both her parents. Everyone knows who we are. The other three girls have one parent each because either their mother or father passed away a long time ago. I am the only girl in my school whose parents are alive but not together. How can I write an essay to represent our school, to tell people in the future what it was like to be a high school student in 1975?

I pick up my pen and then put it down. In the past I had always been good at writing; every time there was a contest, I could count on getting an honorable mention at least, and often better. But this time is different. I have nothing to say.

I look out the window, trying to think. But soon I am not really thinking of the essay, or anything in particular. Beyond the white wire fence that separates our two yards, my neighbor Keiko Yamasaki is sitting on her patio. Dressed in her fluffy white angora sweater and a gray wool skirt, she is sipping coffee from a large black cup. Nowadays, even when she is alone, Keiko behaves as though she were being admired or photographed. If I had binoculars, I could see her perfectly painted face—blue eye shadow, dark mascara, rouge, cherry red lipstick outlining her mouth in the shape of tiny angel wings.

Keiko and I are the same age; we used to be close friends. We walked to elementary school wearing matching hats, mittens, or shoes that we had begged our mothers to buy. I brought her to church so we could spend our Sundays together. Several times I punched Kiyoshi because he had teased Keiko and made her cry.

We don't go to the same school now. She is finishing up at the public junior high school down the street and in April will be going to the big senior high school a few miles to the west. Since seventh grade I have been at

Christian Girls' Academy—my mother's and Mrs. Kato's alma mater—which has junior high school, senior high school, and college all on the same campus. But that's not why we are no longer friends. It's because ever since seventh grade, Keiko has been two different people.

On weekdays she is a studious girl, walking to school in the blue uniform, her hair in tight braids; on weekends she looks like the girls on magazine covers, her face heavily made up, her hair in big curls. The few times we went shopping together in downtown Kobe, more than two years ago, Keiko smiled and made eyes at the clerks at record stores, young men in blue jeans and white shirts. The giggly and nervous way she talked to them was nothing like the quiet, stuck-up manner she had with the women clerks in dress shops. As we walked down the street, she was constantly fidgeting and whispering to me. "Don't look now," she would titter breathlessly, "but that boy over there? He's watching us. I wonder which one of us he finds so fascinating." I stared straight ahead, pretending not to hear. I had to grit my teeth to keep from hissing, "Shut up. You are embarrassing me." Oblivious to my irritation, Keiko kept giggling even though there was nothing remotely funny.

That wasn't all. If it had been just her silliness, I might have gotten used to it in the end. I know plenty of girls at school who are silly out in public where there are boys. I can learn to ignore that, especially if the girls are considerate and smart when we are alone together. But one Sunday, Keiko came over in a tight black T-shirt and a red miniskirt, her face made up and her nails painted a bright red. When I came home from church, she was sitting in the living room with my father while my mother was preparing tea in the kitchen. Keiko was talking to

23

Father in that overly sweet, giggly voice she used with the young men at record stores. She hadn't gotten up to help my mother or insisted that Mother, too, sit down. I was so mad I almost asked her to leave, right then. If I had gone over to the Yamasakis' house and Keiko had been out, I would never have sat down with Dr. Yamasaki as though I were an important guest while Keiko's mother worked in the kitchen like a maid. That afternoon, in my room, Keiko said, "For an older man, your father is quite good-looking. No wonder he is so popular with women." "Where did you hear that?" I asked, my voice going sharp. "Oh, everyone knows," she said, waving her manicured hand like what she'd said was nothing.

I never asked her over again, and when she called, I always had an excuse ready. She caught on before long and started giving me the cold shoulder, too. Now we don't even say hello to each other in front of our houses.

Putting down the coffee cup, Keiko stretches her arms over her head in an exaggerated gesture. Maybe she is pretending to be a bored, pretty actress. I look away; my eyes hurt from scowling.

Turning back from the Yamasakis' yard to ours, I catch a glimpse of something fluttering on the grass. A cluster of leaves, I think, or a dried-up flower head from last fall. But this thing keeps moving in the same place—back and forth on the grass and then upward a little. I step over to the window, shading my eyes with my hand. Soon I can see what it is—a bird, greenish brown and bigger than a sparrow. He keeps hopping on the lawn and trying to fly up to one of the forsythia bushes Mother had planted along the fence. Every time he reaches a branch, he falls off, his wings beating hard. His legs must be hurt; he can't hold on.

24

In a few minutes, that bird will be too exhausted to get up. Outside, it is warm enough for Keiko to sit on the patio in her sweater, but too cold for a small bird to lie on the damp grass. I wonder if Keiko sees him from her patio, much closer than I am to the fence. But it won't do the bird any good to be seen by her. Keiko was always a big coward about any living thing—equally afraid of butterflies and spiders, little rabbits and garden snakes. I once made her cry by showing her a rubber tarantula; she couldn't touch it even after she knew for sure that it was a toy. She would faint if she had to touch a wild bird. That bird would be dead in twenty minutes, half an hour, if Keiko were the only person around.

I turn away from the window and walk back to my desk. Pulling open one of the drawers, I grab the shoebox in which I have been keeping the three letters Mother sent to me in care of the Katos. Quickly, I dump the letters back into the drawer, punch holes in the lid with my pen, and run downstairs with the empty box in my hand.

Keiko is still on the porch. We stare at each other briefly but say nothing. I run to the forsythia bush just as the bird lands on a low branch. Immediately losing his balance, he hangs upside down with one foot, his wings going wild and a brown crest standing up stiff on his head. His feathers underneath the crest and on his chin are ink black. I know what kind of bird it is—a Japanese waxwing. Mother and I used to see flocks of them swarming around the Russian olives and camellias in our backyard in late winter and spring; they flew only a few feet above our heads and darted in and out of the trees, eating the buds, flower petals, and even new leaves. I glance at the line of trees in the back but see nothing.

On the ground, the bird is hopping on one leg; the other one folds up and down, with the toes curled into a

25

tight ball. He begins to pump his good leg and to flutter his wings, getting ready to fly to the branch again. Every few seconds, he makes a thin, lisping sound, like a barely audible whisper.

I am only five or six yards away, but the bird seems too intent on his jump to notice me. I begin to crouch down, slowly and quietly. *What if he bites me?* I think as I take a small step. Immediately, I am ashamed to be such a coward. The waxwing is barely larger than my hand. If he bit me with all his strength, he couldn't hurt me.

Taking a deep breath, I swoop down on the bird just as he is flying up. My timing is right. I close my left hand around his back, my fingers holding the wings shut. The bird gives out a sharp screech and turns his head, his mouth opening to screech again and again. I slowly bring my right index finger to his mouth, and he does bite me, but his mouth is soft. It doesn't even pinch. I bring him up closer to see. There are splashes of red edging his wings and tail, and just for a second, I think of blood. But that is another foolish thought. The red spots are his markings, like the black patches on his throat and under his crest. The bird's heart is beating fast against my fingers, his legs pumping hard. There is nothing broken or cut, no blood, no bones sticking out. Whatever is wrong with the bird, he isn't going to die, at least not right away. Still, my heart begins to beat faster, too. "Small animals are very delicate," I remember my father saying in his calm, reasonable voice. "You have to accept that they die easily." The bird screeches; his voice is high and shrill like a whistle saying *Hurry! Time is up.* Quickly, I slide him into the box, close the lid, and run across the yard. Keiko is openly staring at me now, but it's no time to worry about her.

The bird begins to make dry, scratching noises inside

the box, his wings beating against the cardboard. Even through the lid, I can hear his cries.

"I'm only trying to help," I tell him. "We're going to get someone to look at you."

Carefully I walk around the outside of the house. Grandmother is still at her samisen, singing along with the tune now. Her voice is more like a croak, partly because that is the style of singing, but also because she has a low, choked-up voice. Father is staying in Hiroshima, working at an out-of-town branch of his insurance company, which is based in Kobe. More and more he gets assignments to work in Hiroshima and is gone even on weekends. Both Grandmother and I know why. His girlfriend, Tomiko Hayashi, lives in Hiroshima, upstairs from a bar she owns. Father stays at her place almost every night; now that Mother is gone and Grandmother has come to care for me, he has no reason to spend time here. But just like my mother, Grandmother would never mention Father's girlfriend to me. Instead, she twangs her angry music on the samisen and scolds me every chance she gets.

If Grandmother knew what I was doing now, she would be mad. "Animals," she would say, squinching her eyes in disgust, "are full of fleas and diseases. Don't ever touch that bird. Just let him die." In her house in Tokyo, she used to set little live traps for mice, only to drown the mice in a bucket of water and throw them into the trash. Whenever I stayed with her, I got up early every morning to check the traps; if there was a mouse in any of them, I took the trap to the farthest corner of the yard and turned it upside down. The mouse scurried away and disappeared in the grass or under rocks, spared from Grandmother's bucket at least for another day. If we had mice in our house, I'm sure she would kill them in the same

27

way. She used the live traps only because they were easier to clean than the kind that broke their necks.

Carrying the shoebox, I walk as fast as I can. I know just where to go, and it isn't far. About half a mile up the hill from my house there is a veterinarian who takes care of wild birds. Everyone in Ashiya knows about her from the occasional newspaper articles in the summer, when she takes care of the baby swallows, sparrows, and thrushes that people find on sidewalks, apparently having fallen from their nests. Bird Woman, as people call this veterinarian, is a spinster and the only daughter of a well-to-do family. Though I have never visited her clinic, my mother and I used to walk past it on our way to the woods that border our city to the north.

Running up the last few blocks, I arrive at her clinic in a few minutes and stand in front of a black iron gate, over which hangs a sign, MIZUTANI ANIMAL HOSPITAL AND WILD BIRD SANCTUARY. The white stucco building inside the gate has two stories and rose-colored slates on the roof; it's a little bigger than our house. Bird feeders hang from hooks outside every second-story window.

No one comes out after I ring the bell. The doctor may be gone because it's Saturday. The waxwing is still rustling around inside the box, but he has stopped screeching. Maybe he is getting weak and tired. I ring the bell again and again.

Because I am so intent on the door, I don't see the woman who must have come out of the side gate of the house next door until she is standing a few feet from me.

"Looking for me?" she says, smiling. She is a thin young woman dressed in a white linen blouse and blue jeans, her hair very short, almost like a little boy's bowl-shaped cut. Her bangs, trimmed straight across her fore-

28

head, emphasize her large brown eyes and straight nose. Long silver earrings dangle from her earlobes. "Are you here to see me?" she asks again.

"No. I've come to see Dr. Mizutani."

The woman laughs, tipping her head backward, not covering her mouth with her hand the way other women do. Her silver earrings are shaped like parrots with long tail feathers. "So you don't think I'm Dr. Mizutani," she says, still laughing, narrowing her eyes. Her small, delicate-looking mouth stretches into a grin.

I can't stop staring. This woman is too young to be a spinster, or a doctor for that matter. She looks more like a college student, though she must be a little older than that. Reading newspaper articles about her, I always imagined her to be forty-five or fifty, short and fat, dressed in sensible brown suits like many of my teachers at school. I never thought she would be a young woman—maybe twenty-eight or thirty at the most—thin, long-legged, pretty. The doctor stops laughing and raises her left eyebrow. "What can I do for you?" she asks.

Feeling stupid, I stick the shoebox into her face and say, "Here. I've found a bird. A Japanese waxwing. Something is wrong with his foot."

Dr. Mizutani takes the box in her hands. Her fingers are long, her nails cut short and left unpolished. She is wearing a silver ring, but not on her ring finger.

"Let's go inside and take a look," she says, opening the gate.

I follow her through the waiting area, past the small examination rooms, and into a back room that holds shelves of bottles, a large double sink, and a long counter where the doctor places the shoebox. She turns on a bright white light.

"Is the bird going to fly out of here?" she asks, her hand on the box lid.

"He might. There is nothing wrong with his wings, nothing I can see anyway. But his foot is hurt. He kept falling off the forsythia branches in my yard." I pause and then add, "I live just down the hill."

The doctor opens the box with one hand and scoops up the bird with the other. Gently turning her small wrist, she holds him upside down to look at his legs. His injured foot stays curled tight while the other curls and opens. The doctor coaxes open the injured foot with the tip of her little finger and keeps looking, squinting slightly. After a while, she holds the bird out to me. He has not screeched the whole time. His mouth opens and closes, but no sounds come out, except for a barely audible hiss.

"See this foot? It's swollen a little, redder than his right. There is a small cut between his toes, and he's lost one of his nails. Can you see that?"

I nod.

"He must have gotten his foot caught in something. Some kind of wire."

Most of the houses in my neighborhood have white wire fences, like the one between our house and the Yamasakis'. One of them, maybe even ours, must have hurt the bird. "Will he be all right?" I ask the doctor.

"I hope so." Dr. Mizutani takes a cotton ball, dips it in water, and cleans the bird's cut. "It doesn't look too bad. It'll probably heal."

"What if it doesn't?"

The doctor shifts her hand so the bird is right side up, his crested head peeking out from between her thumb and index finger. His brown eyes look alert. "Aren't you a little too young to be so pessimistic?" the doctor says

30

and smiles. A faint line appears on the left side of her mouth.

"I'm fifteen," I tell her.

The doctor raises her eyebrows, as if to say, *So?* "Birds can live with one good foot. Once in a while, you'll see pigeons and doves with some of their toes frozen off—one of their feet will look like a stub. Those birds can still perch so long as they have one good foot. Of course, it's a strain on that foot, so I'd prefer to see this bird use both of his. His cut doesn't look so bad. He should be all right if he doesn't get an infection." She pauses, as if to make sure I am paying attention, and then goes on. "Birds usually don't get infections because their body temperature is so high—they can easily fight off bacteria—but we'll give this one some antibiotics to make sure. It won't hurt him." The doctor rummages on her shelves to find a small bottle. She turns back to me, the bird still in her hand—almost as if she had forgotten it, in the way someone will forget about a favorite bracelet she wears all the time.

"Are you going to take care of this bird until he gets better? You can take him home if you want to."

"Me?"

"You found him. I'll show you what to do. It won't be hard."

"But I'll just kill him," I protest, "I mean, by mistake. I can't even grow houseplants."

"This is a bird, not a plant," Dr. Mizutani points out, as if that explained everything. "Are you right-handed or left-handed?"

"Left," I reply, surprised to be asked. People usually assume that everyone is right-handed.

"Give me your right hand, then. You'll need your better hand to hold the syringe."

I reach out. She opens up her palm slowly. I close my fingers around the bird's back, holding the wings shut.

"Good." The doctor mixes a drop of the medicine with two drops of water and puts the mixture into a syringe, which she holds out to me. I take it in my left hand. "Now, make sure his head is between your thumb and index finger of your right hand, so you can steady him if you need to."

"Okay."

"Put a drop of liquid on the side of his beak. You see, right at the corner where his beak starts, it looks almost like he has lips?"

"Yes."

"Put a drop right there."

I squeeze the syringe carefully and see the liquid bead up. The bird begins to drink, scarcely opening his beak. I know he is drinking because his black throat flutters. He blinks a couple of times.

"Give him the rest of it, one drop at a time. There should be only two or three more drops."

The bird continues to drink, fluttering his throat, not at all struggling with me now. I can't believe that I am holding a wild bird, making him drink from a syringe. The doctor watches me. After I am done, she says, "Great job. You have a natural touch."

I put down the syringe but keep holding the bird, his feathers smooth and silky against my palm.

"You don't have to give him any more medicine until tomorrow morning," the doctor says. "He only needs a drop every day, so you could put it directly into his mouth, but it's better the way I showed you."

"Why is that?"

"You have to be very careful when you put water in birds' mouths. A drop too much could drown them."

"Birds can drown in the water in their own mouths?"

"Yes, but you don't have to worry about that. This bird isn't going to open his mouth for you anyway. He's not a baby." The doctor goes into another room and comes back with a plastic pet carrier, its bottom lined with a paper towel. "I don't use metal bird cages for wild birds," she explains. "The wire is hard on their wings." She opens the door of the carrier for me to put the bird inside. I reach in and slowly open up my hand. Leaning on one leg, the bird hops to the back corner and stands there, tilting his head to one side.

"Let's go find some food for him." The doctor leads the way out of the clinic, down the flagstone path between her clinic and the big Japanese-style house next door with black *kawara* slates on the roof.

"How do you know I can take care of that bird?" I ask as I follow her. "Why don't you keep him?" My voice sounds shrill and worried. There is no way I can take that bird home. My grandmother will never allow it.

Stopping and turning around to face me, she says, "I usually would. I don't trust most of the people who bring me birds. But you are different."

"But you don't know me. Maybe I'm careless. Maybe I won't take good care of him."

"I already know that you are not careless," she says, starting to walk again. "Most people come and say, 'I found this bird. It's hurt. It won't fly.' That's about all they would notice. You could see the injury was on his foot and not his wings. You seemed perfectly comfortable about picking him up."

I don't say anything. She looks back.

"Is something wrong?" she asks. "Are you still worried?"

How can I tell her the truth? *I can't take the bird home because my grandmother will kill me.* If I say that, the

33

doctor will ask why I'm worried about my grandmother instead of my parents. I will have to tell her more: *My mother left me, and my father really doesn't live with me, either. He's always in Hiroshima with his girlfriend, so I'm alone with a grandmother who hates animals.* I can't tell her anything like that. She will think of me as a pitiful girl, not the attentive and observant person she imagined.

"No, nothing," I say, shaking my head.

"It's okay if you're worried a little," she says, smiling. "Caring for any living thing is a big responsibility."

She seems so cheerful and confident that I try to smile back. She tilts her head a little to the side; the parrot earrings dangle and shake. I can see why people call her Bird Woman, although they may not mean it in a completely flattering way. No one would criticize her openly, of course, because she is a doctor and the daughter of a rich family, but people always sound a little begrudging when they talk about someone who is a spinster. Maybe calling her Bird Woman is like speaking behind her back. But the name fits her, too. She is like a flamingo or a crane—slim and lively, pretty in a slightly odd way.

Inside the large kitchen of the house next door, an old man and an old woman are seated at the table. They are having miso soup and rice—a standard breakfast for people their age. They put down their bowls and chopsticks when we come in.

"My parents." Dr. Mizutani sweeps her hands toward them in a somewhat comical way. "Professor Mizutani, of the Classics department of Osaka University, and Mrs. Mizutani, teacher of flower arrangement." She grins and tilts her head, as if to say *I'm exaggerating, don't be scared of them.* "And I forgot to ask your name."

34

"I'm Megumi Shimizu."

The old couple smile and bow slightly without getting up. They are dressed the same way Grandfather and Grandmother Kurihara dressed around the house—the man in a casual black kimono, the woman in a gray housedress.

"Megumi Shimizu, a girl who knows her birds," the doctor announces, walking past the table and opening the refrigerator. "Megumi brought me a waxwing with an injured foot. She's going to take him home and care for him for a week," she tells her parents over her shoulder while pulling out a box of strawberries, a bunch of green grapes, a few nectarines. After washing them in the sink, she cuts them up; it looks like she's making a fruit salad, only the pieces are smaller.

"Would you like some breakfast?" Mrs. Mizutani asks me, already getting up.

"Oh, no, thanks."

"Don't be polite." The old woman smiles. She is bony and thin, like Grandmother Shimizu, but her voice has the soft, gentle tone Grandmother Kurihara's had.

"Mother." Dr. Mizutani shakes her head. "A young girl isn't going to have miso soup and rice for breakfast. Even I don't eat that. Megumi is only fifteen, half my age." Scraping the cut-up fruit into a jar, the doctor returns to the refrigerator and brings me a container of strawberry yogurt. "Here, you take this."

"For the bird?"

"No," she laughs, "for you. My mother will get you a spoon. Sit down and wait for me."

Mrs. Mizutani is already handing me the spoon and then sitting down. Her daughter disappears to another part of the house while I sit down and begin to eat the yogurt.

35

"So you are a young woman who knows about birds," Professor Mizutani says in a deep voice. His eyes wrinkle up when he smiles, the lines around them spreading like a cat's whiskers.

"Not really," I answer. "Dr. Mizutani is being kind, I'm sure."

"Oh, no, not our daughter." The old man widens his eyes and tilts his head toward his wife. "Kumiko is never overly kind in her comments about people, wouldn't you agree?"

Kumiko—*forever beautiful*. I wish my name meant something like that, instead of *God's blessing*.

"I won't say that Kumiko is unkind," Mrs. Mizutani offers, "but no, she doesn't pay idle compliments."

Dr. Mizutani returns with two flowering peach branches. "Mother, we are taking these for the bird. I'm sure your students can do without them. They'd be perfect for the bird to perch on."

Mrs. Mizutani shakes her head, smiling at the same time, as if to say *What's the use of saying no?*

"Megumi, you can bring that jar of fruit."

I jump up, take the spoon and the yogurt container to the sink, and grab the jar.

"It was a pleasure meeting you," the old man says.

"Yes. Come back and visit us again," his wife adds.

"Thank you."

Dr. Mizutani is already going out the door. I have to run to catch up.

Inside the pet carrier, the waxwing is still sitting in the back corner, leaning on his good foot. The injured foot is folded up halfway.

"Birds perch on one foot all the time," the doctor tells me. "But normally, the other foot would be folded all the

36

way up to his body, not halfway like that." She trims a few inches off the peach branches and hands them to me. "In a few days, when he seems a little better, put these inside the carrier and see what he does. If he still can't perch, you should take them out and try again later. No need for him to get tired out from trying too hard."

I nod, still wishing I could tell her that I can't take the bird. But how can I? She has even told her parents that I would care for him.

"When you get home," she goes on, "give him some of the fruit in a small dish, and also some water in a shallow container. You can clean the cage by changing the paper towel. He won't be too much trouble." She hands me the bottle of antibiotics, a syringe, and another small bottle. "Vitamins. You can sprinkle a few drops on his food."

"All right."

The doctor puts the bottles and the syringe into a paper bag. "Bring him back next Saturday, and we'll see if he can fly and perch. Of course, you should call me if you have any questions or problems." She jots down her number on a piece of paper and drops it inside the paper bag. "Don't be shy about calling. I don't care what time it is, and you won't wake up my parents because they have a different number. I have a room in their house, but usually I sleep in one of the upstairs rooms here."

"What if the bird gets out of the cage?"

"That's a good question. Do your windows have blinds?"

"Yes."

"Keep the blinds closed, then, so he won't fly into the glass. How about any mobiles or wires that could hurt him?"

"I don't have anything like that." As soon as the words are out of my mouth, I wish I had said that my room was

37

full of mobiles. That would have been a good excuse, but it's too late to change my answer.

"It should be all right, then. If he gets away, you can catch him. Wait." She goes back to another room and returns with a net, the kind children use to catch butterflies. "Here, you can borrow this."

"That?"

Tipping her head back, she laughs. "Waxwings are great fliers, but they aren't that hard to catch. Besides, you are a very competent person. So long as you keep the door closed so he stays in your room and doesn't fly all over your house, you'll have no problem. If you want to, you can let him fly around to get exercise, once his foot is better."

"No, my grandmother would be very upset." The words come out before I can stop them. My heart sinks, and I wait for the doctor to question me about my family.

But she doesn't seem to notice anything odd about my having a grandmother. She shrugs and says, "Tell her that the bird can't hurt her. I know people worry about birds getting stuck in their hair and all kinds of nonsense like that. Tell her she's wrong."

She must think that I have a normal grandmother who just lives with my family. I don't know what to say. How can I tell her that my grandmother is all I have, that she drowns mice?

"Is something wrong?" the doctor asks me.

"No, nothing," I reply. "But I'd better go home."

"I'll give you a ride."

"That won't be necessary. I can carry everything."

"Of course you can. I want to give you a ride all the same."

She doesn't wait for my answer. Picking up the pet carrier and the butterfly net, she heads out of the clinic and into the garage, where she opens the door of a red truck. She puts the pet carrier on the seat and waits for me to climb in before closing the door. We sit with the bird between us, the butterfly net and the paper bag on the floor. The moment the doctor puts the key in the ignition and the engine turns over, the waxwing hops forward and trills one sharp whistle. He stands cocking his head to the side for a while; then, straightening out his neck, he stares ahead with his beak slightly raised, looking like a pilot about to take off.

"I don't know why," the doctor says, laughing. "Birds always do that in cars. They look straight ahead, as if they want to drive."

I'm laughing, too, just looking at him. He seems so serious and comical at the same time. My cheeks and mouth feel strange—I haven't laughed much in the last month and a half.

"Tell me where you live."

"Just down the hill and then a few blocks to the west."

Halfway there, the doctor asks, "How did you know this was a Japanese waxwing?"

"The crest, the black markings, and the red band across the tail. They don't look like any other bird."

"Of course not. But I meant, how did you know that?"

"My mother," I answer. "She used to tell me the names of birds. She didn't want me to grow up knowing only sparrows, crows, and swallows. It bothered her that people didn't know the birds, trees, and flowers around them, so she used to take me on walks, to show me things."

"Used to?" The doctor takes her eyes off the road momentarily to glance at my face.

Looking straight ahead, I explain what I was hoping I wouldn't have to. "My mother doesn't live with me anymore. She went back to live with her father. She had to leave me behind because my grandfather is too poor to support both of us. He lives north of Kyoto, in a little village, and has an embroidery workshop. He's poor because people use machines now for the work he does by hand." I pause and add, so as not to sound completely pitiful, "My mother wanted to take me with her, of course. She only left me behind because she thought I would be better off with my father and his mother, here in Ashiya." I say nothing about how my father is never around and how my grandmother scolds me every day.

Dr. Mizutani is silent for a long time. Then, in a very gentle voice, she offers, "I'm sorry. That must be so hard."

Suddenly, my eyes fill with tears. I wish her voice didn't sound so kind. Turning my head to the side window, I blink and pretend to be looking at the scenery. But a few more teardrops come out before I can stop. Dr. Mizutani's hand reaches across the truck toward me, over the bird cage. She is holding out a tissue. I take it and dab at my eyes.

"I never know quite what to do," the doctor says, "because everyone is different about crying. Are you someone who wants to be consoled, or should I pretend you aren't even crying?"

"You should pretend," I answer right away. "I hate crying in front of people."

"Me, too," she says. "I hate that more than anything." She pauses and adds, "I hate crying even if I'm alone." Her voice drops a little, as if she were remembering something sad, but maybe she is just being sympathetic and trying to spare my pride. She doesn't seem like a person who ever cries, alone or in front of people.

We don't talk until we are driving the last block to my

house. Dr. Mizutani puts one hand on top of the pet carrier and steers with the other. "This bird is lucky to have met you," she says. "If you hadn't found him, he would have died from exhaustion." She parks her truck in the driveway and turns off the engine. "Can I help you carry things?"

"No, thank you. I can manage," I reply quickly. The last thing I want is for her to meet my grandmother and hear her yell at me.

"I expect to see you in a week, then. Call me if you have any questions."

"Okay." I open the door and pick up the carrier, the net, and the bag.

"Listen," she calls when I step down off the truck. "I really enjoyed meeting you."

"Thanks."

Before I can think clearly enough to say, "I enjoyed meeting you, too," the truck is already backing out of the driveway. I watch for a while and then walk to the front door, feeling sick to my stomach at the thought of my grandmother.

Grandmother Shimizu is right inside the door, sweeping the hallway with a broom. Her dark brown kimono reminds me of withered leaves. She is just like a shriveled-up plant, frail and bony, her face full of wrinkles. I shouldn't be scared of her. She is shorter than I am, so I can see the top of her head, where her iron gray hair looks brittle and thin. Even so, I feel as though she were towering over me. I begin to cower, just like my mother used to.

"Where have you been?" she asks in a sharp voice.

"Dr. Mizutani's, up on the hill," I answer, making sure to speak up clearly so she won't accuse me of mumbling.

41

But she is no longer worried about where I have been; she is staring at the pet carrier and the net.

"I brought a bird to the doctor, and she gave it back to me to care for," I explain. "A waxwing. I'll have him for a week in my room."

Grandmother doesn't start yelling right away. First, she fixes me with an icy stare. This is how she used to scare my mother, too; she's trying to build suspense before her first angry word, giving me time to feel bad even before she speaks. I have been dreading this moment all along, but now that it's here, I'm suddenly more angry than scared. The way she tries to intimidate me is so obvious. She must think I am too stupid to see her tactics. But she has no right to try to scare me. Why should I have to explain and apologize for everything I do? I can never please her, anyway. No matter what I say, Grandmother will be upset. The whole time I was gone, she was sitting here imagining the things I might be up to, none of them good. She always assumes the very worst about me, just like she did about my mother. That is wrong and unfair. I shouldn't have to pacify her about every little thing. This is my house. What I do in my room is none of her business.

I take a deep breath to steady my voice and say, "It shouldn't make any difference to you if I bring this bird to my room. You won't have to see him again unless you come snooping."

About to say something, she changes her mind and snaps her mouth shut. Her jaw is clenched, and she is scowling hard. I can feel her mind working, searching for something mean and cutting to say to me. I'm not going to wait to hear it.

Without a word, I start up the stairs to my room. I half expect her to come running after me, but she doesn't.

She must know that she'll never catch me. She has bad knees and complains about backaches all the time. I hurry up the stairs, go into my room, and close the door, my heart beating very fast the whole time. I listen for Grandmother's footsteps, until I am sure that she is not coming up.

Once I am convinced, I walk up to the desk. I know she will be especially mean to me for the rest of the day and even all week, but for now I am safe. Setting down the pet carrier on the desktop, I put some of the fruit in the small dish Dr. Mizutani has given me and push it inside the cage door. Immediately, the bird comes hopping, one-legged, and pecks at a cut-up grape. He swallows the piece whole; his head goes down again into the dish. By the time I get some water from the guest bathroom across the hallway, the bird has eaten several pieces of fruit. The tip of his beak is red from berry juice. I hang the pet carrier from the hook on the ceiling where my canary cage used to be. My grandmother, too old and unsteady on her feet to stand on the chair, won't be able to reach the bird. The best she could do, if she ever came into my room, would be to stare at him and feel mean, like an old and feeble cat.

On my oak dresser, the owl-shaped clock is ticking. The clock was my mother's present to me on my seventh birthday, the year I learned to tell time. The owl's yellow eyes shift from side to side every second, and every hour the clock makes the right number of hoots. For years, my mother and I laughed to hear that sound. I must have just missed its eleven hoots. I don't have much time to work on the essay. In less than two hours, I am supposed to meet my friends downtown to see a movie. Sitting down at my desk, I pull out another blank sheet of paper.

"I am not sure," I write in ink, "what it is like to be a
43

high school student in 1975. I only know about myself. My family is nothing like anyone else's, and that makes me different from all the other girls at my high school."

As I continue to write, the waxwing begins to make a thin, lisping sound, a wavering voice like the distant crickets in late summer and fall. His voice reminds me of the field of pampas grass behind Grandfather Kurihara's house. Long ago, before my mother began crying herself to sleep and making secret plans to leave me, I used to walk in the pampas field every August, holding hands with my mother and Grandmother Kurihara, listening to the crickets in the grass and the cicadas in the trees above. Our footsteps stirred up the green grasshoppers, which spread their iridescent wings and flew up in long arcs all around us.

"Listen," my mother would whisper.

The grasshoppers' wingbeats whirred like tiny springs inside a watch. I would hold my breath and be absolutely quiet so I could hear them amid the chirping of the crickets and the buzzing of the cicadas. The arcs of the grasshoppers' flight were like waves rising and falling, while the wind whistled through the pampas.

Maybe in the year 2000, my mother and I will stroll in that pampas field and hear the grasshoppers again. I will be almost as old then as she is now, and she will be the age Grandmother Kurihara was. Maybe by then I won't have to miss her or be angry at her for leaving me with a lie. Our time apart may seem like a long-ago, sad memory to reminisce about, the way old people often talk about the bombs and the famine during the war. "We'll think of this time and laugh about it later," Mother used to say when I was upset or sad as a young child. "No bad time lasts forever." She would smile, comforting me, trying to believe it, I think now, herself. Maybe the two of

44

us will be laughing in the year 2000. Anything is possible, I suppose; all kinds of things, good as well as bad, could happen in twenty-five years. But for now, I wish for the past, not the future. I would give anything to go back to my childhood, when I could stand in the field between my mother and grandmother, and all I had to do was listen.

3
On the Mountain Path

The moment I walk up the rectory stairway into the Katos' kitchen, I know that they have been arguing. Mrs. Kato jumps up from her chair and asks, "How about some tea?" Her voice sounds too chirpy, her smile looks too bright. Before I can answer, she is turning on the stove and measuring the tea into a small pot. Brushing her short, graying hair away from her square face, she smiles at me again.

Pastor Kato puts down his bowl of rice and nods absent-mindedly toward me. He goes back to eating, dipping his chopsticks into the miso soup to scoop up bits of *wakame* seaweed. Kiyoshi won't meet my eyes. The three pieces of toast on his plate are dry and cold. He is wearing blue jeans and the brown T-shirt he got at the Bible camp in Shikoku last summer, where he decided that he believed in God and wanted to go through confirmation. The front of the T-shirt has a picture of a big mountain with footprints all over it; on the back, the word *Rejoice* is written in rainbow colors above the New Testament passage—printed in white letters—about spreading the good news.

While I reach out for the cup Mrs. Kato offers, Kiyoshi stands up abruptly, scraping the chair legs against the floor. The sound of his footsteps fade down the hallway toward his room. The door closes slowly but firmly.

"How is school?" Pastor Kato asks me as I sit down in Kiyoshi's chair. Pushing his reading glasses down to the tip of his nose, he peers at me across the table. He is tall and gangly. Dressed in a plain white shirt and baggy brown pants, he looks much older than my father. The round bald spot on the top of his head has been getting a little bigger every year.

"School is already over for me," I tell him. I don't know why he forgets that our school always gets out earlier than the public schools. "Yesterday was the last day. I still have to turn in my essay for the time capsule contest, though. My teacher gave me some extra time."

"I'm sure your essay is worth waiting for." Mrs. Kato chimes in.

"I don't know. This essay was hard to write. I finished it last night but I don't like it."

"Always so hard on yourself," Mrs. Kato says, frowning. That's what she used to say to my mother. "Chie," she would scold, her soft voice saying my mother's name, which means "blessed with wisdom." "Don't criticize yourself so much. Don't be so hard on yourself."

"My mother didn't write back, did she?" I know the answer from the expression on Mrs. Kato's face.

"No. Not yet," she says, forcing a smile. "But I'm sure she will soon."

Mother has written only three times since she went away in January. Her first letter was full of apologies. She was sorry to have left me, to have kept me in the dark about her real plans until the last day; she wished she could see me or at least call me. "I miss you terribly," she wrote, "but I know this was the only way I could live long enough to be with you in the end. Your father and I

47

made each other very unhappy. I could not go on living in his house without feeling that I was being false to both myself and him, that I was living a big lie. He and I were always angry at each other; we could no longer feel kindness or love. Although your father and I were not married in a Christian wedding because he has never been a believer, I know that God does not intend any marriage to be like ours. Mrs. Kato and I talked and prayed together for nearly a year about what I should do; I consulted Pastor Kato, who also prayed with me. They both agreed with me in the end. My leaving was the only way—God will forgive me and keep you in His loving care. Of course, not being able to see you is the hardest thing for me. But, Megumi, you and I will live to be old women. Seven years is nothing. Let's endure the hard times ahead. Even if I am not with you, I will be thinking of you day and night. Please try to forgive me for leaving, for lying to you about coming back in the spring."

In that letter, Mother was more honest than she had been in a long time—admitting her unhappiness and saying that the years ahead will be hard. Though I didn't feel better, the letter made me want to forgive her. I wrote back and said that I understood, that I would try very hard to go on alone and be strong until we were able to see each other again. I meant that then, but I'm not so sure now. In the next two letters, my mother went right back to her pretending; she gave news about the early spring weather, Grandfather's embroidery business, the neighbors—she made no reference to sadness or unhappiness, as though she were writing to me while on a vacation. It's just like Mrs. Kato offering me tea in her cheerful voice when Pastor Kato and Kiyoshi must have been having one of their angry arguments about religion. Until last year they fought because Kiyoshi was not a believer; now that he is, they yell at each other just as much. Kiyoshi doesn't think his father's faith is strong enough, while Pastor Kato claims Kiyoshi's beliefs are extreme, too unforgiving. If I were Mrs. Kato, I would be sick of the arguments by now. Still, that's no reason to ignore them. Kiyoshi and I have been noticing this for a long time: Our mothers often pretend that our families are perfect and happy. Our mothers, who are Christians and profess to be truthful, should not care so much about keeping up appearances.

I sip my tea slowly, listening for any noise that might come from Kiyoshi's room. There is nothing. A few years ago, he used to slam his door and then play his rock music loudly enough to shake the hallway outside his room. Now he sulks in silence. Pastor Kato picks up the morning paper and continues to read, leaving Mrs. Kato to bring his dishes to the sink. He is a pastor, and he can cook; all the same, he does not pour his own tea or wash his own dishes when Mrs. Kato is around. Mrs. Kato rinses the dishes and sits back down to drink her tea. None of us says anything for a long time.

"I'd better get going," I say.

"Wouldn't you like something to eat?" Mrs. Kato asks.

"No, thank you." I bring my cup to the sink, leaving Kiyoshi's uneaten toast on the table.

"I'll see you at church tomorrow," Pastor Kato says, looking over his papers.

"Yes. Thank you for the tea, Mrs. Kato." There is no sound from Kiyoshi's room. For a second, I consider going to knock on his door, but I don't. It was rude of him to leave the table when I came in, including me in his angry silence as if I, too, were to blame. It isn't my fault if his mother wants to speak to me in a cheerful voice. I didn't ask her to pretend.

49

I run down the stairs into the empty churchyard. There is no wind today. Under the maple tree, the three swings look like a row of minus signs floating in the air.

As I walk up the hill to my house, I wonder why Mother has not written. In my letter a week ago, I asked if I could call her on the telephone from the Katos' house once a week. "Of course, Father has forbidden me to speak with you," I wrote. "But he said I couldn't write to you either and you agreed to write to me at the Katos' house. If I called you from there, it would be the same thing. I shouldn't have to obey Father when his orders are so unreasonable. I don't think it matters about being strictly honest. Even Pastor Kato knows the whole situation and does not mind your writing to me at his house."

I wish I hadn't made such a stupid case. I should never have reminded Mother that we are already lying to Father in a way by writing to each other. Mother might have thought it over and decided that we should stop writing. This very moment, she could be trying to compose her last letter to me, her last letter for the next seven years. Maybe she hasn't written yet because that final letter is so hard to write.

I cannot imagine never hearing from her again. I would rather that she wrote twenty letters that made me angry, letters full of lies and pretending. When I was in grade school I used to get into fights with friends and say to them, "I'll never speak to you again," and they would say the same to me. But within two hours, we'd be talking again, even if it was only to call one another names or whine and complain about one another's faults. It's almost the same thing with my mother. No matter how angry I am with her, I can never say that I want to stop writing or speaking to her.

Shivering, I turn up the collar of the purple spring jacket Mother sewed for me last year. The houses I pass have pots of pansies, spring mums, and yellow daisies in their windows and on the patios. There are no flowers at my house. Grandmother Shimizu has brought her bonsai trees from Tokyo: three pines with roots knotted and swollen out of the shallow soil like hardened hearts. She keeps them on a low table in her room. Once a month, she trims them, looking at the diagram in her book about how to keep them small, how to make them last. The bonsai remind me of the kind of person my mother did not want to become—shrunk and old, living with my father in bitterness. I have to admit, if I thought I were turning into such a person, I would have left, too. I would have done what my mother has done.

Father is in the kitchen, eating his breakfast of salted fish, rice, and miso soup. He is wearing a navy blue jogging suit in which he sometimes practices his golf swings in our yard. He came home from Hiroshima late last night and is still here, for a change. I wonder how long he will stay.

Just like Pastor Kato, Father is reading the morning paper propped against his dishes. Unlike the pastor, though, he doesn't have to wear reading glasses, and his black hair falls thick and shiny over his dark eyebrows. His eyes are sharp glints in his angular face. He is tall, but not in the gangly way Pastor Kato is. "You are lucky. Your parents are such a good-looking couple," people used to tell me. "No matter which one you take after, you'll be good-looking, too." I never was happy to hear that. To me, it was obvious that my mother, with her oval face and large eyes, was by far the better-looking of the two.

Grandmother Shimizu coughs and clears her throat but says nothing. She has had breakfast already. Every morning, she rises before six and eats a small bowl of rice, nothing else. Now she is hovering in the kitchen in her gray kimono, filling Father's teacup every few minutes, straightening out the countertop.

"Did you have a nice walk?" my father asks me over the newspaper.

"Yes," I reply, standing in the doorway to the kitchen. "It's a warm day. I walked down to the river." I can't believe how easy it is to lie to him, to not tell the whole truth. Lying to him doesn't bother me anymore, and that's the sad part. With everyone else, at least it troubles my conscience not to be completely honest.

"So what will you do during spring vacation?" He puts down the paper momentarily and gives me a stiff smile, his "Now we will have a conversation" smile.

"I don't know." I shrug. I try to keep my face blank, but my heart sinks at the thought of vacation. My friends are going out of town with their mothers, brothers, and sisters—mostly to visit their mothers' families. What will I do alone?

"Megumi should be studying," Grandmother cuts in. "She should be thinking about transferring to a public school—if not this April, certainly next year."

I clench my fists; my fingernails dig into my palms.

"It's not even too late to transfer this year," Grandmother continues. "The sooner she does it, the better. Her school gives her no real discipline. The public school children study twice as hard because they have to take tests. They are not guaranteed a place in a college the way she is at that school. But many of them will end up at national universities, while she can only go to a mediocre women's college."

"Christian Academy College isn't mediocre," I say.

"It certainly is," she snaps back. "You are transferring

52

to a public school soon and studying to go to a national university, just as your father did."

Father rustles his paper. "Mother," he says, "I'm sure there is plenty of time to think about Megumi's schooling. We don't have to make decisions this morning." He glances at me and nods slightly. *You know your grandmother,* he seems to be saying silently. *Just let her talk.*

I glare back at him, wanting to stomp out of the room. How can he sit there and say nothing more in my defense? It's his fault that I have to live with Grandmother. My mother would be here if he hadn't made her so unhappy. Even if she had left, he wouldn't have needed Grandmother to take care of me if he knew how, if he wasn't planning to practically move to Hiroshima the moment Mother was gone. The least he can do when he is here is to tell his mother to shut up, to stop nagging me.

Grandmother stretches her thin neck and smirks. She knows, and I know, too, that my father would never talk back to her. He might as well just move to Hiroshima and never come back, for all the help he is to me.

"I don't want to hear any more about my school being mediocre," I say to Grandmother in the iciest voice as I can manage. "I'm not going anywhere else, and you can't make me."

Grandmother Shimizu purses her lips and squints, tilting her head a little to the side. She looks like a crafty old woman, a witch from one of the fairy tales my mother used to read to me.

"Why should your father pay a high tuition to send you to a private school he didn't choose? It never was his idea."

"It wasn't just my mother's idea. I want to go there myself," I protest. I want to sound calm and reasonable,

53

but my voice gets shrill. Grandmother is a shrewd talker. She knows just how to make people feel afraid and confused so they doubt themselves and believe that she is right. She might convince my father to stop paying my tuition. She might force me to go to a public school where kids wear blue uniforms and take exams instead of art and writing classes.

Father puts down the paper and sighs in an exaggerated manner. "I've been working very late every night. It's Saturday. Can't we all stop arguing and get along?" He tries to smile, first at me and then at Grandmother. "I'm sure we can talk about this another time."

His thin-lipped smile reminds me of the times he and Mother used to argue. Right after making her cry, he would go out and come home with some special gift for me—a toy, a necklace, a tin of cookies. He had that same smile on his face when he offered me those gifts, before I ran to my mother and he stormed out of the house again.

"No, we can't talk about it another time or ever again," I yell at him now. "I refuse to go to any other school." I turn around and stomp down the hallway. In the kitchen, Grandmother turns on the faucet. As I climb the stairs to my room, I imagine her squinting into the steamy dishwater as if she wanted to scrutinize each individual germ she was killing off.

Perched on a peach branch inside the pet carrier, the waxwing is making his cricket noises. He has eaten half the fruit I put in this morning. His hurt foot is grasping the branch almost as firmly as the other foot, though he is missing one nail. When I put in the branch three days ago, he immediately hopped onto it and stayed perched—before proceeding to strip off all the buds and the blossoms. He shredded and spat out most of them but ate some. Now he is rubbing his beak against the bark like someone sharpening a knife.

It's time to bring him back to the doctor. I take down the cage from the hook above my desk; then I leave through the front door without saying good-bye to my grandmother and father.

"The bird looks very good," Dr. Mizutani says, peering into the pet carrier. "We should let him go."

"Will he be all right?"

The doctor opens the cage and pulls out the bird in one quick motion. Flipping him over, she examines his foot and nods. "His foot is almost healed," she declares as she puts the bird back in the carrier. "If he were still curling his toes and dragging them behind, I would have asked you to keep him another week. We would have taped his foot around a little ball of tissue to hold his toes in the right position. That usually works. But he doesn't need any more help. Did you see him fly?"

I nod. "I let him fly around in my room after all. He landed on the windowsill and pecked at the wood."

"Your grandmother didn't mind?"

"She doesn't have to know everything I do."

Dr. Mizutani smiles. "How did he fly?"

"He was very fast. Sometimes he stopped in midair and changed directions or swooped down, like an airplane doing tricks."

"He's ready to go, then. I'm glad we don't have to keep him another week. Soon it'll be time for him to migrate to Siberia."

"Siberia? That's so far away." Perched on one of the peach branches, the bird is preening his feathers. I cannot imagine how many millions of wingbeats it would take him to cross the ocean.

"From here to Siberia is a very short migration for birds. This bird was born in Siberia. He's already made the same trip at least once. But I want to give him plenty of time to find other waxwings. Birds migrate in flocks, not alone."

Over the ocean, there would be no place to rest, nothing to eat for miles and miles.

"I don't like to keep birds longer than I absolutely have to," the doctor continues, "especially if they are alone. Birds don't do well alone, not for long."

"Why not?"

"They lose interest in living. I wasn't very worried about this one, since he's an adult and it was only going to be a week or two. But if I have just one baby sparrow or thrush, I can't always get them to live. When they are all alone, some baby birds stop opening their mouths for food. They don't want to eat or live. They just give up. I have no other explanation."

The waxwing hops down from the branch to peck at a piece of melon. He swallows and begins to whistle again.

"You are not sad to see him go, are you?" Dr. Mizutani asks.

"No." I shake my head. "I'm glad he's better. I'm only worried a little."

"What are you worried about?"

"How will he find the others?"

"Hear that? The way he's calling? That's how birds find each other. He'll keep calling to the others, and he'll listen for them, too. Besides, we'll bring him to a place where other waxwings are likely to come. I know a good place."

"I'd like to come along."

"Of course. You nursed the bird. You have to be the one to let him go."

* * *

I follow Dr. Mizutani on the narrow path through the woods that border our city to the north, where my mother and I used to walk. I have not been here since she went away. The loose dirt and gravel crunch under my feet. The air smells of pine needles and cedar bark, moss, and wet leaves from last fall. The waxwing is quiet inside the pet carrier, perched on a branch and looking straight ahead.

"Here," Dr. Mizutani says when we come to a small clearing.

I set the pet carrier on the ground.

"See those?" She points to a dozen chokecherry trees about twenty yards away. The leaves have not come out yet. On the bare branches, last year's cherries are left like small black bells. "Waxwings are nomadic, so they're hard to predict. They appear out of nowhere, eat, and take off. But I've seen them every spring, eating those dried cherries. They'll be here again."

"Are you sure?"

"Trust me, I know these woods. Every week, I spend hours walking here. I must have seen almost every bird that came through here in the last five years." She pauses, a slight frown on her face, and then goes on in a brighter voice. "Anyway, your bird is familiar with this area. He was probably flying around these woods before he came down the hill to our neighborhood and got hurt."

"All right," I tell her. "I'm ready."

The doctor lifts the pet carrier onto a flat rock on the side of the path. "Go ahead," she says to me. "You open the door and let him go."

I unlatch the door and pull it open. The bird cocks his head as if contemplating the possibilities. After only a few seconds, he flies out and makes straight across the clearing toward the chokecherries. For a short while, I can follow him with my eyes as he soars from branch to branch, making his thin, lisping calls. I watch him until he flies out of the cherries and disappears in the cedars above. Without speaking, Dr. Mizutani and I head back, me carrying the cage and leading the way this time.

"Good job," Dr. Mizutani says, coming up next to me where the path widens, closer to the road now. She lays her hand on my shoulder for just a second.

We don't speak for a while more, till she says, suddenly, "I almost forgot to tell you. My father knows you."

"I don't think so. We've never met before."

"Not in person," she explains. "But aren't you the girl who won an honorable mention for the peace essay contest last summer?"

"The one the city sponsored, back in August?"

"Yes. My father was one of the three judges. He was so impressed with your essay that he remembered your name, though he didn't think of it till you were gone. He's getting a little old. Your essay was about your uncle, he said."

"He remembered that?"

"He was really moved by what you wrote. If it had been up to him, you would have won first prize. The other judges liked your essay, too, but preferred the two that discussed politics more directly. My father was angry at them for not seeing that your essay was much stronger, more sincere, for being so personal."

Walking in these woods where my mother taught me the names of birds and trees, I think of her and her older brother, Susumu, who was killed in Manchuria during the Second World War.

"My mother still regrets his death," I wrote in the es-

58

say. "The last time she saw him, they had a terrible argument. My mother was opposed to the war, while Susumu was determined to fight. They were both angry when they said good-bye. Now she will never be able to make peace with him. But what makes her sad, more than anything, is her belief that he died for a wrong cause."

Listening to the sound of our footsteps, I remember the things my mother told me about the war.

"Soldiers in Manchuria did not spare the people there," she taught me when I was thirteen. "They killed women, children, old men and women. They burned down villages. I can't say that my brother never did anything wrong. He, too, might have killed someone's sister, someone's child or grandmother. At the very least, he must have watched other soldiers kill defenseless people. He didn't try to stop them. That doesn't mean that he deserved to die, of course. Still, it's wrong to think of him as a hero. Your grandparents would be furious to hear me say these things to you. They insist that Susumu was just another victim of the war, like the people who died from the firebombs dropped in Kobe. But the Bible says the truth will make us free, and I believe that. Susumu was a soldier. He went to war, prepared not only to die but to kill. He was not like the firebomb victims, who were not soldiers, who never killed anyone. I wouldn't be honoring my brother's memory if I lied and made him out to be a hero or an innocent victim. Nobody is completely innocent in war—even those of us who stay home and support it or don't oppose it hard enough."

For a moment, I want to sit down on the path and cry. I have been unfair to my mother, thinking of her as a big liar. Just like Mrs. Kato, she liked to make believe that our family was perfect when it wasn't. But when she pretended that Grandmother Shimizu was a kind person, that

59

her own going away for seven years was like going on a vacation, she was just telling me what she wished she could believe. That is not the same as an out-and-out lie, and besides, she didn't always pretend. She told me a big, painful truth about her own brother—he might have killed innocent people in the war.

Dr. Mizutani and I leave the woods and begin walking on the paved road, only a few blocks away from the clinic. Behind us, the cedar trees stand tall, casting shadows. My scalp prickles as if the dark green shadows were pulling at my hair. I have not said a word in a long time.

"I would never have written that essay without my mother," I announce, trying to keep my voice even. "She taught me a lot."

"That doesn't have to stop." Dr. Mizutani hesitates for a second and then adds, "I'm afraid this is none of my business. But why shouldn't you be able to see her even if she doesn't live with you?"

"My father and grandmother would never allow that," I explain. "They say that my mother gave up the right to be with me when she decided to leave. She has already made her choice."

The doctor shakes her head. "How could they say that? Your mother didn't have much of a choice." She is frowning; her voice has a sharp edge.

I shrug. What she says is true, but that makes no difference.

"Will your father and grandmother reconsider if you keep asking to see her?"

"No." *The doctor has no idea,* I think with sudden irritation. *She thinks my father and grandmother are normal, nice people like her parents. She doesn't know what she's talking about.* To be fair, she doesn't know because I haven't told her anything about my father or grandmother. Still, I can't help being annoyed. I don't want to talk about my family, with her or anyone.

"What if you absolutely insisted?" she goes on.

I shake my head and say nothing more, hoping that she will get the hint and drop the subject.

"I don't mean to press," Dr. Mizutani says instead, "but will you let me help you if I can?"

"Why?" I ask without thinking. It's rude to ask people why they are offering to help. All the same, it *is* none of her business whether or not I see my mother. Maybe, being a doctor and having rich and kind parents, she thinks there is a solution for everything and she can help anyone. She's wrong. My family is beyond help.

"Why do I want to help you and your mother?" she repeats the question.

I nod.

She hesitates for a second. "I was married once. I didn't have children. But if I did, I wouldn't want to give them up just because I wanted a divorce. That isn't fair."

I stare at her and nearly drop the empty pet carrier. With her eyes narrowed and her lips downturned, she looks serious, even upset. I remember her comment last week about not liking to cry in front of people or alone. I imagine her walking in the woods for hours by herself— just as my mother did last spring while I was at school; my mother's shoes were drenched and muddy every afternoon from her solitary walks.

"Don't look so shocked," Dr. Mizutani says, trying to take a light tone. But her voice sounds shaky as she says, "It isn't inconceivable, is it—that I was married?"

"Oh, no, not at all," I say quickly, looking away from her. I don't want to think that Dr. Mizutani ever cried herself to sleep or spent hours walking on a muddy path, feeling lonely.

61

"I wasn't married for a long time," she shrugs, finally managing a little smile. "Three months to be exact. I'll tell you about it sometime."

I don't know what to say, so I stay quiet. We keep walking.

Soon we are back in front of her clinic. I hand over the pet carrier. "Thank you very much," I say, feeling stupid and clumsy. I turn to go.

"Wait," she says. "I want to ask you something. I need some help. In a month or so, people will start bringing me baby birds. I can't take care of them all. I need an assistant."

"You're asking me?"

"You won't have to be here a lot. You can take the birds home and take care of them. If your grandmother doesn't mind, that is." She stops and peers into my face.

The way I've been talking she must think I am a completely spineless person. "I don't care what my grandmother says. What I do in my own room is my own business."

"Good for you." Dr. Mizutani beams, looking cheerful again. "I'll pay you, of course."

"That isn't necessary."

Pursing her lips, the doctor shakes her head in mock admonishment. "Never turn down money when it's offered to you for honest work."

"Okay."

"It's settled, then." She holds out her right hand. "I'm going to northern Japan for a few weeks to see the migrating birds. But I'll be back. I'll call you then." She pauses and adds, with a big smile, "A lot of birds migrate through the forests and grasslands in the north. It's a trip I love to make. I go every year. It's fantastic to be in the woods, alone with flocks and flocks of birds. But it'll be nice to come back and see you."

"Thank you." We shake hands before saying good-bye.

Watching her go into the house, I stop thinking about her walking in the woods in our city. Instead I imagine her driving up a narrow mountain path in her red truck. Alone behind the wheel, a map spread over the empty passenger's seat, she would smile and hum a tune, knowing exactly where to find the rare birds.

The next day, Sunday, I take the commuter train and walk up the hill to my school. The teachers' mailboxes, where I'm supposed to turn in my essay, are in the same building as the chapel. On the lawn in front, a crowd is gathering for the high school graduation. The girls who just finished the twelfth grade are wearing their best dresses, mostly black, navy, or dark red. Some of the fathers, wearing black suits, are smoking cigarettes. The mothers, in formal black kimonos with family crests embroidered on the back, are fussing over their daughters with combs and handkerchiefs. Though most of the girls will be going to Christian Academy College to study music or literature, they seem as excited as if this were their last day here. Their happy chatter is broken up once in a while by a few girls bursting into loud laughter or calling to one another.

I duck into the building in my gray T-shirt and blue jeans, drop the essay in Mrs. Fukushima's mailbox, and run down the hill. The early forsythias and camellias are budding already, the buds appearing on leafless branches.

In three years, I will be at my graduation, the only girl without a mother. Grandmother Shimizu will never set foot here, not even for the ceremony. Until the very last day of my high school, she will nag me to change

63

schools, to study for the entrance examinations to get into a national university. She hates Christian Girls' Academy because she considers it foreign (it was founded by American missionary ladies at the turn of the century) and because my mother went here. Most likely, I will be all alone on my graduation day. My father will feel too awkward to come, the only unaccompanied father. He will say that he is too busy, that graduation is just a formality. He will spend the day in Hiroshima with his girlfriend, whom he can never bring to a graduation ceremony: My father, a rich and important person, cannot come to his daughter's school with a woman who makes a living by serving whisky and sake. No matter how much he prefers Tomiko to my mother, he will still be married to my mother, if only in name: he believes—as does my grandmother—that people from good families don't get divorced.

It makes me happy to think of my father's girlfriend as someone not good enough to come to my school, much less to marry my father. But the satisfaction doesn't last more than a few seconds. Maybe I am turning into a stuck-up person, just like Grandmother Shimizu. I have many reasons for disliking Tomiko Hayashi, but what she does for a living shouldn't be one of them. She probably can't do anything to change *that*. I don't want to be like Grandmother Shimizu, who always looked down on my mother for coming from a family who used to be well-to-do before the war but became poor afterward. Though most people in the kimono business lost money after the war, Grandmother Shimizu always made it sound as if my mother's parents didn't work hard enough. Despising Tomiko Hayashi because of the bar is the same kind of unfairness. But how can I help but hate everything about her?

Walking past the gate of my school into a residential neighborhood, I envy all the families living in the houses I pass. Each house must have a mother, a father, one or two children. No one is as alone as I am.

Birds never do well alone, Dr. Mizutani said. Sometimes, a lone bird that falls out of a nest will just give up and die. Maybe I am like a lone bird. My mother and I were two baby birds in the nest, and now she is gone. I can think of her only in that way—as another helpless baby, not as a mother bird returning with food in her beak. If my mother wasn't the mother bird, who would be? "God," Pastor Kato would answer. He would remind me that we are all baby birds that God provides for: Not one sparrow falls, the Bible says, without God's knowledge. But where is the comfort in that? If God knows about the sparrows falling, why doesn't he keep them from harm? Maybe God isn't there watching at all. I've been thinking that for a long time now.

Waiting for the train at the station, I remember another thing Dr. Mizutani told me: Birds can drown in the water in their own small mouths, as if a few drops of water contained a whole ocean. My mother is a bird whose mouth has become a big sea of tears. She had to leave me to keep from drowning.

The train is coming. I hear it first—a slight whistle of vibration, then a rattle and a roar as the cars come around the bend and stop in front of the platform. As I rise from the bench and step into the nearest car, I am thinking of that waxwing, alone in the leafless chokecherry tree, making his sad cricket noise, calling to the others that he could not see. It is a long way to Siberia, and he cannot migrate alone. I wish I could have heard the call of the flock answering him. Though each bird's voice is thin and sad, a whole flock would sound entirely different, their voices ringing like a huge chorus of tin whistles. It's been a whole day since I let my bird go. Maybe by now he has found the others and is eating wild cherries, mountain ash and oleaster berries, storing up strength for the migration. On the train, my eyes closed, I try to see him among a migrating flock. He will take the loneliness of my room on his long journey; each whistling note he makes will be a little of my sadness falling over the ocean, to be swallowed in the clash of the waves and the commotion of many birds flying.

4

Southern Constellations

Mrs. Kato has decorated the altar with hothouse flowers—dark pink roses, blue delphiniums, baby's breath, and asparagus ferns. The colors remind me of tropical fish, of blue and pink cichlids among green algae. Rising with the rest of the congregation to sing the communion hymn, I imagine the church filled with water instead of air. I am trying to breathe under a blue current while fish swim overhead, their bodies glittering in the sun.

Behind me, old men and women are singing half a beat slower than the organ's accompaniment. Their voices quaver, thin and holy. Next to me, Kiyoshi's tenor notes rise like perfect balloons of sound. Only two or three years ago, when his voice was changing, he croaked in a raspy whisper and mouthed the words in church without singing. Now his voice is better than before, lower but more resonant. My voice has remained high, reedy and childish as ever. I wish I were a boy—to be given a new voice at thirteen, like an important gift.

After the final verse, I mouth the word "Amen" but do not sing it. *Amen* means "so be it." How can I say that when I won't be participating in Communion? I am not eager to accept God's gifts, the way the hymn says. I glance sideways to see if Kiyoshi has noticed my omission. His face turned straight forward, he doesn't notice anything but his own eagerness for the holy supper.

The folding chairs squeak and scrape as we sit down. Mrs. Wada and Miss Fujimoto go up to the altar, take the silver tray Pastor Kato has blessed, and begin to pass it back and forth down the rows of chairs. When the tray comes to me, I hold it in my lap for a second. Though only a dozen people take Communion every month, Mrs. Wada has prepared at least thirty doll-sized glasses of grape juice and a mound of bread, cut into thumbnail-sized cubes. The bread reminds me of the crumbs my mother used to scatter on the back porch for the birds. Only sparrows were bold enough to come so close to the house; still, we never tired of watching them, especially in the spring, when the birds brought their babies and fed them beak to beak. Fat and fluffy, the babies fluttered their wings as if to stay balanced, just as swimmers move their legs and arms to keep afloat. The sparrows grew fast. By June we could not tell the young birds from the rest of the flock; by then, every bird ate alone, minding his own business.

Passing the tray untouched to Kiyoshi, I watch him pick up a piece of bread and put it in his mouth. His throat moves when he swallows, his mouth closed tightly. Lifting the tiny glass to his lips, he drains the few drops of juice. I imagine his soul—a small sparrow flying inside his chest, wings fluttering against his rib cage. Last Christmas, while Kiyoshi declared his faith in front of the congregation and was confirmed, I sat in the back applauding and trying to feel sincere. I wanted to be happy for him, but I was embarrassed more than anything. As the pastor blessed Kiyoshi, I could feel the older people in the congregation wondering why I wasn't up there with him. Even my mother, who was sitting next to me at the service, seemed a little sad. Watching Kiyoshi up there, she must have thought about when he and I were babies.

In my album, there is a picture of Kiyoshi, Takashi Uchida, and me wrapped in identical white baby shawls for our baptismal blessings. The same picture must be in the boys' albums, too. Our mothers often told us that Kiyoshi and Takashi cried when Pastor Kato sprinkled water on their almost-bald heads, while I gurgled with laughter, as if I were delighted to be blessed. Kiyoshi turned out to be the one to renew those blessings by choosing the Lord on his own, as an adult. Sitting next to my mother at the confirmation service, I couldn't help wondering if she was disappointed in me. Though I hadn't been sure about God for years, I never said anything to her. She had more than enough things to be sad about. I couldn't make her stay awake at night, worrying about me not going to heaven with her and the Katos.

Kiyoshi bows his head for a moment, offering a silent prayer. Miss Fujimoto is leaning over to take the tray from him, to pass it to the people in back. She glances into my eyes; immediately I look down. Miss Fujimoto used to teach Bible study classes at Christian Girls' Academy—she was once my mother's, Mrs. Kato's, and Mrs. Uchida's teacher. She was also my Sunday school teacher a few years ago. Her favorite Bible story was about Jesus leaving his ninety-nine sheep to go and look for the one sheep that was lost. Every time Miss Fujimoto sees me at church these days, she must think of that lost sheep. She doesn't know what I really think. If I were that sheep, I would tell Jesus and the rest of the flock *Go on your way and don't mind me. I like being on my own.*

As Miss Fujimoto moves on down the aisle, I look up

at the hothouse flowers. My mother, who used to arrange flowers for church, would never have used these. In April, she would have chosen budding branches of cherries, pansies and jasmine from her own garden, a large bouquet of white tulips. Mother always found something natural and appropriate to the season. Flower arrangement, she told me, was all about being in harmony with the seasons, with the natural world. Last year, in the middle of February, she brought bare cherry branches and a handful of peacock feathers shed in autumn. The bright green and blue eyes floated among the dark branches like planets suspended in the sky. If she could have stayed with us and kept bringing flowers, I might have been able to believe in God. I might have felt more hopeful when the pastor talked about the beauty of the world and the grandeur of God's plans.

After the service, I follow Kiyoshi across the churchyard and up the steps to the rectory. In his family's kitchen, he hands me my mother's letter. While I am opening the envelope, he goes to the refrigerator, pours a tall glass of milk, and tips it toward his face.

"Do you want some milk?" he asks, already finished with his.

"No, thanks." No girl would pour and drink her own beverage before offering some to a friend.

Kiyoshi stands by the table, wiping his mouth with the back of his hand. I unfold my mother's letter; my hands are beginning to shake. This is her first letter in more than a month—ever since I asked her if I could talk to her on the phone. The words run top to bottom in the old style, written in black calligraphy ink on white paper. There is only one page. My eyes skim through the brush strokes, looking for bad news.

Dear Megumi,

I hope you had a good spring break and started the new school year feeling well rested. You must be excited about your new classes. Whatever you do, though, please be careful not to overwork yourself. I have always been proud of how well you do in school. But remember, your health is more important than any achievement. Try to study in moderation. I worry about you.

Everything is fine here. My father has gotten some substantial orders for wedding gowns. He and I are busy embroidering every day. He has hired back Mrs. Toda because his fingers are getting too stiff for some of the detailed work. His designs, however, are as beautiful as ever. I especially like his cranes, pine groves, and peony blossoms. We wish you could see them.

My father and I think of you every day. I am praying that God will comfort you. My father prays at the Buddhist altar, asking the spirits of your grandmother, my brother, Susumu, and all our ancestors to watch over you. I used to think that I had disappointed my parents by turning away from their religion, but these days, I feel at peace. In a way, my father and I are praying to the same God even though we have different names for Him. We respect each other's form of devotion and know that you are in good hands.

Now I must give you my answer, which I know you will not like. About your calling me on the telephone—my answer, I'm afraid, is no. Megumi, I cannot bear to hear your voice when I know we cannot see each other. I know you will feel the same way. Writing letters is another matter, since we can collect our thoughts in private and compose letters that encourage each other to be strong. If we were to talk on the phone, we would not be able to remain so calm. We would both cry and be more miserable than before. Trust my judgment on this.

I apologize that this letter is so late in coming to you. I wanted to write immediately and give you my answer, once and for all, about the telephone calls. But I couldn't. I kept thinking of how disappointed you would be, and I could not make myself write. I thought about it over and over, and prayed, too, for guidance. My answer is still the same. Forgive me. Please know that I am thinking of you day and night, that I miss and love you.

Good-bye for now. Please send my regards to the Katos.

Your mother, Chie

I fold up the letter and stick it in the pocket of my skirt. "I'd better get going," I say, my voice sounding weak and unhappy. My mother is a coward. She is afraid to talk to me on the telephone because we might cry. She couldn't answer my letter right away because she was afraid of upsetting me. By waiting she has only wasted her time and upset me even more. If she was going to say no, she should have said it right away, instead of keeping me in the dark for a month and starting her letter with unimportant news. Why doesn't she understand that I would rather know the truth—even if it's bad news— than be pacified with lies?

"This is a terrible letter," I blurt out while following Kiyoshi down the steps. "My mother won't talk to me on the phone because she thinks it will make us sad. But she can't even come out and say that right away. She has to first go on about embroidery and tell me to study in moderation because my health is more important. How could she write such a stupid letter?"

Kiyoshi stops in the middle of the stairway and whips around to face me. "I'm sure your mother means well," he admonishes, frowning. "She wants to say only the positive things. She doesn't want to hurt your feelings. It's selfish of you to blame her for that."

I am too surprised to speak. My friends at school would have said, "That's awful. I'm sorry to hear your mother's being so unreasonable," or "I'm sorry. I would be upset, too." Though their remarks may mean little, I would have been comforted by their sympathy. Why can't Kiyoshi, too, say something kind? I would have been happy to know that he cared about me and worried about my feelings even if he doesn't understand everything I'm going through. I know for certain that no girl would criticize me when I am already feeling bad. Kiyoshi didn't always do that, either. But in the last year or two, he has often contradicted me when I have been upset with something or somebody—going out of his way to take the other person's side and insisting that he was trying to be fair, that he only wanted to tell the truth.

"What do you expect her to say?" he presses, in a loud, angry voice.

"I don't know. Something other than platitudes."

He shakes his head. "You shouldn't be so judgmental. You know your mother feels lonely. Why not be more sympathetic?" He spins around and runs down the steps before I have a chance to tell him that he is the one who's being judgmental.

Following him down, I'm glad I have not told him anything more about Mother's letter, that she thinks being a Christian is the same as being a Buddhist. Kiyoshi would be appalled to hear that. Pastor Kato would assume that Mother was losing her faith, and even Mrs. Kato would be shocked. Whatever Mother really meant by her words, I know I should never tell anyone. Lately, my mind is filled with things I cannot tell anyone. No matter how much my friends care about me, almost everything I think about is beyond their true understanding. The best they can do is to offer small consolations.

Outside, the sun is shining on the white gravel of the parking lot. A few cars are left. Some old people must still be drinking tea in the fellowship hall, downstairs from the rectory. When Kiyoshi and I were in grade school, there were other children at our church—boys and girls whose mothers, like ours, had converted to Christianity in their school days during the war. But the women have stopped coming, and so have their children. Every year our congregation is smaller. Now it is mostly old people and a few high school and college students who come for a few months and then stop, to be replaced by others like them.

"Come on," Kiyoshi says at the gate. "I'll walk you home."

Don't bother, I want to tell him. *I can walk by myself.* But if I said that, he would think I was sulking because he was right and I was too proud to admit it.

He is already walking out the gate. I shrug my shoulders and quicken my steps to catch up.

From the gravel path by the Ashiya River, the water looks low, as it has been for the last few years. It's hard to imagine the floods and tidal waves we learned about in our civic history classes. A kingfisher skims the surface and then flits out of sight. Up on the hill to the northeast, our old grade school juts out of the green pines. The

74

small windows glitter in the sunlight against the cream-colored facade.

"Your neighbor Keiko Yamasaki is in my biology class at the new high school," Kiyoshi says as we walk side by side on the path.

"What?" I say, hardly concealing my surprise. Kiyoshi and Keiko had gone to different public junior high schools. I had forgotten that they would both be attending Ashiya North for senior high. "How is Keiko?" I ask, trying to sound casual. I have never told Kiyoshi the particulars of our falling-out, though he must have noticed that I never mention her anymore.

"Very well. She says she started going to church again recently—a small church in Kobe that emphasizes studying the Bible."

"That's good." I wonder if he notices the sour note creeping into my voice.

"We decided to be lab partners," Kiyoshi continues. "Our teacher said we could choose anyone."

"I didn't think you and Keiko would remember each other so well. You only knew each other because of me."

"Of course we remember each other. Don't be silly. Anyway, we already had a lab session, on the second day of school last week."

"What did you do?"

"We tested our blood types."

I wince in spite of myself. We did the same lab work last year at my school, during the winter term. While Mr. Sugimoto, our teacher, was handing out the clean needles, I started feeling queasy. Still, I cleaned my right index finger with the cotton ball and held the needle in my left hand, trying to work up my courage. I didn't want to be squeamish or silly, but I couldn't help the icy, numb feeling that made my fingers curl up tight. I

75

thought about the sharp tip piercing through the skin, digging across a few millimeters of flesh, and then making a tiny hole in the wall of my vein. My hands began to shake, and I felt hot and cold at the same time. When I finally pushed the needle in, though, no blood came out. So I had to prick my finger again, then again—three times—before I saw a tiny speck of blood through the skin. My ears started ringing with a sound that reminded me of faraway waterfalls. It was impossible not to think about rivers of blood. Taking a deep breath, I squeezed my finger in spite of the sick feeling that was starting in my chest and stomach. Blood slowly beaded up like the heads of the fancy dressmaker's pins in my mother's sewing box. Next thing I knew, I was in the nurse's office, unable to remember how I had gotten there.

"You think too much," my lab partner, Mieko, laughed when I tried to explain why I had fainted. Mieko is one of my two best friends at school. She is a sensible person, but she was wrong this once. "I wouldn't have been able to do it, either," she said, her round face dimpled with laughter, "if I had thought about every detail the way you did. You should have just taken a deep breath and pushed the needle in. It was easy if you didn't think."

What she said made no sense at all. I can't blank out my mind the same way I would clear off my desk. It's one thing to stop thinking about something that happened a long time ago or something that might happen in the future. If I try very hard, I can even take my mind off an annoying incident from yesterday or a worrisome event scheduled for tomorrow. But how can I, or anyone, not think about something that is happening right at the present moment? That is simply impossible.

"I hated that experiment," I confess to Kiyoshi. "I fainted."

"Keiko was afraid at first, too," he says, smiling. "I told her that I would poke her finger for her if she didn't want to do it herself. But she wouldn't trust me. In the end, she could overcome her fear because—this is what she said—she thought about Jesus. When she remembered how much Jesus had to suffer on the cross, she realized that pricking her finger was nothing."

Without thinking, I burst out laughing. "What a silly idea," I say.

Kiyoshi shoots a sharp glance at me. A hard line forms along his big square jaw. "What's so silly about that?"

His brown shoes are coming down flat and hard on the path. They are too tight across the instep, and they look wrong for his black pants and pale blue shirt. I am suddenly sick of the way he is dressed, and the way I am dressed, too—in my pleated blue skirt and white blouse, clothes I wear only to church.

"I don't think there is anything wrong with thinking about Jesus at school, do you?" Kiyoshi presses. "God isn't just for Sundays, at church."

For me, I want to shout, *God isn't for any day of the week. I don't believe anymore. I keep coming to church out of habit, or just to get out of staying home with my grandmother.* But the words shrivel up in my throat and refuse to come out. Maybe this is how Kiyoshi felt when his voice was changing and he could only speak in whispers and croaks. My throat hurts as if it were sticky and full of lumps, crammed shut with words that had been stuck there for years.

In silence, we walk away from the riverbank, toward the commuter train station. Most of the houses we pass in this stretch were built before the war. They have new additions in the back or over the garage, the shiny stone and concrete stuck on top of old wood.

77

"Keiko says that the pastor of her church is touched by the Holy Spirit," Kiyoshi announces after a while. "He can speak in tongues."

I nod but say nothing.

"Keiko is asking the Holy Spirit to touch her. She wants the gift of speaking in tongues someday."

How can Keiko be a religious person? Only two weeks ago, she was sitting on her patio in a flimsy spring dress, vain as ever.

"My father doesn't believe in the gifts of the Holy Spirit," Kiyoshi declares.

"That's not true. Your father is always talking about the Holy Trinity. Every Pentecost Sunday, he preaches about the Holy Spirit descending on the disciples."

"But he doesn't think those gifts are for us. He said people who try to have visions or speak in tongues are wrong. They are asking God to prove His existence through signs rather than believing without seeing. He was mad at me for bringing up the subject. We had a big fight." Kiyoshi sighs, shaking his head. His small eyes are scrunched up, looking tired and sad.

"That's too bad," I offer, trying to speak in a soft and comforting voice. "I guess Pastor Kato can be a little stubborn sometimes. He shouldn't get mad at you for wanting to talk about your faith, even if you two don't always agree."

Kiyoshi holds his head up higher and stiffens his back. "I'm not saying that my father is a narrow-minded person or a hypocrite. He is a very good minister." He turns sideways and scowls into my face, his big nose turned up and his eyes looking very cold.

What is wrong with him? He is actually getting mad at me, when I was trying to take his side and console him. He keeps giving me a cold look, his mouth drawn thin

78

and hard. If we were children, I would punch him and run back home alone. Why did he decide to walk with me? He should have stayed home if all he was going to do was pick fights with me and talk about what a great Christian Keiko is.

We proceed past the train station and then down a street lined with bakeries, delicatessens, boutiques. Neither of us speaks. At the end of the block, Kiyoshi stops abruptly in front of a bar that has a lavender-painted door. THE ORCHID JAZZ CLUB, the sign above the door reads.

He stares at the sign as if to evaluate it and then starts walking again. "Toru and Takashi Uchida are back in town," he says.

"They are?" I ask. "How do you know?"

"I saw Takashi at school. We have a gym class together."

I haven't seen or heard from the Uchida boys for almost five years, since they went to live with some relatives in Tokyo following Mrs. Uchida's death.

Kiyoshi glances back and points at the jazz bar. "Takashi said Toru works there."

"At the bar?"

He shrugs. "They don't go to church anymore. They stopped being Christians when they moved to their grandparents' house."

That wasn't what I meant. I was thinking that Toru would not be old enough to work at a bar, but maybe he is. He is more than five years older than the rest of us. He would be twenty or twenty-one, a few years out of high school.

"My father says that's the problem with families where only the woman is a Christian," Kiyoshi continues. "It's hard for the children to keep up their faith. If he had a daughter, he wouldn't want her married to a nonbeliever, the way your mother and Mrs. Uchida were."

We turn the corner and start climbing the steep hill of my neighborhood. Toru and Takashi must have come back to live with their father because they are finally old enough to take care of themselves and not be a burden. If Grandmother Shimizu had not agreed to rent out her house in Tokyo and come to stay with us, I might have been sent to live with her for a few years until I was old enough to keep house for Father. It makes no sense—that I am supposed to give up my mother, who can take care of me, and live with Father, who cannot even keep house for himself and is never home. "That isn't fair," Dr. Mizutani said about women having to leave their children. She is right.

"My father was worried about you," Kiyoshi says, "right after your mother went away. He was afraid that you might stop coming to church."

Though Kiyoshi looks sympathetic for the first time all morning, I am too stunned to answer. What a petty thing for Pastor Kato to worry about. He should have been concerned about me feeling lonely. Instead, he's been watching my church attendance. It's no use saying any of this to Kiyoshi, so I just look up at the sky. An airplane is flying overhead, trailing a jet stream like a white river. When we were in kindergarten, every time one of us spotted an airplane all the kids would run to the window, pointing and shouting. There must have been fewer planes flying over Ashiya back then. Seeing one used to be a special occasion.

"I'll see you tonight," Kiyoshi says in front of my house. "You're coming to the Bible study meeting, aren't you?"

"I'll try. I may not if my father is home. He doesn't like to see me going to church twice a day."

"Well, that's his problem," he says, already turning away.

The house is locked, with nobody home. My father came home late last night, only to leave early in the morning to play golf with his friends from work. Grandmother must have gone to the store, carrying her small woven basket in the crook of her arm. While other women from our neighborhood bring their shopping carts and return with at least a few days' groceries, Grandmother goes every afternoon with her tiny basket. Then she complains about how she must walk several blocks to the store every day, how her back aches from walking up and down the hill. She could make her work simpler if she wanted to.

I unlock the door and run up to my room to put away my mother's letter in the desk drawer. It feels good to take off the church clothes and change into my jeans and T-shirt. Putting on my sneakers, I run out the door and up the hill to Dr. Mizutani's.

A crow is making a racket inside a large pet carrier, cawing and screeching. His right leg taped around a splint, he staggers a step or two and almost falls over when he opens his ragged wings. He slouches down in the corner, his wings drooping shut. He reminds me of an old, beat-up umbrella.

Dr. Mizutani puts on leather gloves that go up past her elbows. "He's not a happy bird," she says. Opening the carrier, she grabs the bird by the legs and stuffs him inside the cardboard box I am holding open. We hoist the box up onto a scale that hangs from the ceiling. Frowning, the doctor watches the needle swing.

"Not too bad," she says. "His weight is pretty good, considering." She takes down the box and pulls out the bird, who seems temporarily dazed. "But he's not eating much on his own. Let's feed him."

We go over to the counter, where I have thawed and cut up some meat—from what sort of animal, I don't want to ask. The first day I came to work, two weeks ago, I opened the freezer and discovered a bag of frozen rats, all of them with paws curled up and teeth sticking out in sinister smiles. I almost got sick right then. I tried not to let on. Dr. Mizutani must have seen my face, all the same. "We don't use those very often," she said. "And if we do, I won't make you cut them up."

"Okay," she says, grasping the crow by the legs in one hand and holding his wings shut with the other. "I've got him. He can't jump out and bite you. Go ahead."

Picking up a small piece of meat with the tongs in my left hand, I walk up to the crow and place my right thumbnail in the corner of his mouth. Bristly black feathers cover the bottom quarter of his beak. They are thick and iridescent. His beak is the only part of him that looks completely healthy; it is solid and glossy black, slightly curved, like a handle of a treasure chest. Slowly, I insert the tip of my index fingernail in the other corner of his mouth and press until his beak opens up.

"Great job." Dr. Mizutani nods.

Holding the bird's mouth open, I shove in the first piece of meat, as far down his throat as I can, and quickly pull back the tongs. Then I hold the beak closed inside my fist so the bird cannot open his mouth and spit out the food.

"Stroke his throat so he has to swallow."

With the smooth part of the tongs, I stroke his throat and neck. His small shiny eyes watch me warily.

82

"I think he likes you," the doctor says.

I feed him five pieces of meat, until the bird opens his beak after the throat-stroking and spits back the last piece he had somehow been holding in his mouth. He caws and hisses at me.

Dr. Mizutani laughs. "I guess he's had enough." She places the bird back into the carrier, where he caws for a while and then is quiet.

"Is he going to be okay?"

"I hope so. He looks bad, I know. But I want to give him a chance."

"What happened to him?"

"Sit down. I'll tell you." She points to one of the hard-backed chairs along the counter. "A woman called me Thursday morning, right around dawn," she begins, pacing back and forth in front of my chair. Even in her loose-fitting white lab coat, the doctor looks thin, though not exactly frail. "I was just waking up. I could hardly hear the woman; she was whispering. She kept saying something about bad luck. As it turned out, this crow was caught in a leghold trap in the woods, set for some other bird—owls, maybe, or hawks. People trap them illegally and mount them for decorations." She crosses her arms, hugging herself as though she were cold. "The trap must not have been pinned down very well. The woman's house was right next to the woods. So the crow came into her yard, dragging the trap. The woman's husband was outside trying to kill him because he thought crows bring bad luck. The woman thought so, too—only she thought killing the bird would bring worse luck, so she called me. Imagine that." Dr. Mizutani uncrosses her arms and flings them down. "She only wanted to save him because she was superstitious, not because she was appalled by her husband's cruelty. I jumped out of bed, got dressed, and drove over. The house was only a mile west of here. I got there in no time."

"You went up to the woman's husband and told him to stop?"

She nods. "He wasn't alone. A few other men had come from the houses in the neighborhood carrying rakes and brooms. No one had a gun. The men were trying to hit the bird, to beat him to death, but he was putting up a good fight. He was screeching and hissing at them, and every time he moved, the metal trap made a terrible clonking sound. Lucky for him, the noise must have scared the men. Maybe they were superstitious. No one wanted to be the one to kill him. But they did hit him a few times. When I examined him later, I found some swelling on his back—that isn't from the trap. He's lucky they didn't hit him in the head or break his wings."

I try to picture the doctor, this thin young woman, walking up to a group of men she had never seen.

"I told the men they'd better back off. I threatened to call the police. People can't kill wild birds in the city. Cruelty to animals is a crime. What I really wanted to do was to grab one of the rakes and hit back. I didn't, of course. I put the bird in the carrier and left as soon as I could. I wasn't sure if I would be able to do much for him. If not, I wanted to put him out of his misery as quickly as I could. Now, I don't know. He isn't as bad as I first thought he would be. He only had one leg caught in the trap. That leg is broken, but it's a clean break so it might heal. He must not have been in the trap for more than a couple of hours, so he wasn't starved and dehydrated. I saw another bird last year, an owl, also caught in a trap. His feet and legs were crushed and he was almost starved to death. I put him down. This crow is in pretty good condition compared to that. Still, I hope I'm not just prolonging his suffering."

Inside the carrier, the crow is cawing again. His voice sounds sad, full of complaints. *You were a lucky bird,* I want to tell him, *to meet a kind and brave woman.*

At four-thirty, back at my house, the telephone rings while I am reading in my room. Grandmother is busy cooking in the kitchen. I run down the stairs into the front hallway to pick up the receiver.

"Hello," Father says. There is music playing in the background—a symphony. He must be at the clubhouse of the golf course. "How was your day?" he asks, his voice cheerful, in a forced way.

If we were face-to-face, I would just shrug and not even answer. But we are on the phone, so I have to say something. "Fine," I mutter.

"You're not in a sulk, are you? Are you upset about something?" he asks, half laughing.

I *am* upset, about all kinds of things. I can't talk to Kiyoshi anymore without one of us getting mad; it bothers me that he has been so easily taken in by Keiko's new piousness. I'm mad at myself, too, for not having told him the truth about my loss of faith. As though that weren't enough, my mother has written another letter full of platitudes, and she refuses to talk to me on the phone. And all over my city, people don't care about animals— men try to kill an injured bird with garden rakes. But how can I tell Father about my unhappiness when he is the biggest cause of it all? If it weren't for him, Mother wouldn't have had to leave me or lie to me. If he hadn't made her so unhappy, maybe she wouldn't have become such a coward, afraid of hurting other people's feelings—so afraid that she cannot be honest.

In silence, Father waits for my answer, as though he really cared about my happiness.

"No, I'm not upset," I say through gritted teeth.

He doesn't notice the tone. "Good," he says in his cheerful voice. "Is your grandmother home?"

"Yes. She is in the kitchen."

"Let me speak with her."

After handing over the phone, I stay around in the hallway listening. Grandmother says very little except, "Yes," "That's fine," "All right." Though their voices sound nothing alike, she says the same things Mother used to say.

As soon as she hangs up, I ask, "Father isn't coming home, is he?"

She makes a sour face. "He played golf later than he was planning to. He has an early morning meeting in Hiroshima, so he decided to go there tonight and take a hotel room. That way he doesn't have to get up early and rush off."

Just like Mother, Grandmother Shimizu reports Father's lame lie without comment. He has planned all along to leave for Hiroshima from the golf course. He must have left this morning with his overnight bag packed—unless he has clothes and shoes at Tomiko Hayashi's. That's more likely. Father must have a closet full of belongings at her apartment by now. I imagine a cramped tatami room above a bar, his clothes and hers crammed together inside a cheap dresser.

Without speaking, I follow my grandmother into the kitchen, where she has been preparing the broth for the seafood stew Father likes. The broth is made by simmering dried fish heads and chopped vegetables for hours. No one likes the stew except him.

In silence, Grandmother Shimizu begins to strain the

86

broth, putting the liquid into a plastic container to save for another day. She empties the strainer into the garbage pail, tap-tapping it over the edge. The shriveled fish heads tumble out into the pail and clonk against the plastic.

"Grandmother," I call.

She looks up, her eyes tired, almost sad.

"I can make supper, if you'd like. It's just the two of us. We could have something simple."

Immediately she stiffens; the muscles of her thin neck stick out as she tightens her lips. She snorts, a *humph* noise blowing through her nose. "There is no reason not to have a proper supper just because your father is too busy." Without another word, she opens the refrigerator and begins to rummage.

"Would you like some help?" I ask.

Instead of answering, she grumbles, "Don't you have some homework?" She doesn't even turn around to look at me.

My mother would have smiled sadly and accepted my help. When Father called at the last minute and stayed out, I made her supper or we went out to eat, and she was particularly nice to me, trying to listen to my chatter and laugh at the jokes I told to cheer her up. Maybe that was part of her being a coward—her pretending everything was all right when it wasn't. Still, there is a big difference between her and Grandmother Shimizu or Father. Whatever Mother did wrong, she has never blamed me or been mean to me like Grandmother Shimizu, who won't even let me cheer her up. Her back still turned to me, Grandmother picks up a head of lettuce and puts it down. I can imagine her face without seeing it: She is scowling at the lettuce as though it had intentionally disappointed her. It was stupid of me to try to cheer her up.

She doesn't want to feel better; she'd rather stay mad—just like she prefers to go to the store every day so she can complain about her aching back.

I stand around for a few seconds and then go up to my room, leaving Grandmother to chop off the heads of carrots and tear up the green leaves of lettuce. I wish she were just a mean old woman and not my grandmother.

I start back for the church after supper. It's six-thirty; the streets are dark though the sky over the mountains is still red with the afterglow of the sunset. The Bible study meeting begins at seven, in the living room of the rectory. There will be only six or seven people—two older women, a few college students, Kiyoshi, and me. With Easter coming up next week, we have been studying the Gospel passages about the Passion. Last week, we read the chapter in the Gospel According to John, about Pontius Pilate questioning Jesus. The last thing Pilate asked was, "What is truth?"

"What do you think of *that* question?" Pastor Kato asked, sliding his reading glasses off his nose to peer at us from his big stuffed chair. "Why didn't Jesus answer him?"

Everyone, sitting in the various chairs and couches scattered around the room, fidgeted for a long time. Finally, I said what seemed obvious from the start.

"According to the Bible, Jesus is the truth, so Pilate's question was stupid. He was standing right in front of Jesus and asking what the truth was, as though it were somewhere else. Jesus didn't answer because the answer was obvious."

Pastor Kato beamed at me, nodding his head so vigorously that his thinning hair—what's left of it—bounced up and down on his head. "That's right. The Gospel According to John, the rest of you might want to remember, starts with a reference to the one true word that was always with God. That true word, of course, is Christ."

After the meeting, a college girl who had been confirmed with Kiyoshi came up to me. "You are so smart," she said with a sigh. "I read the Bible every day, but my understanding is nothing like yours."

I stared at the girl's high forehead and horn-rimmed glasses, wishing I could tell her the truth: Answers like that come easily to me, but they mean nothing.

Walking down the hill now, I am irritated to remember her serious face. I'm tired of people telling me how smart I am. I hear that at school, too. "But you're different," many girls—though not my best friends—say to me. "You are smart." Then they shrug in a halfhearted way, as if they had given up on themselves and had chosen me to go on being smart all by myself. In almost every class, these girls sit silently, waiting for me to give the right answer. The teachers call on me when no one speaks. I used to love raising my hand both at school and at church, waiting to be called on. Not anymore. I sit silently, knowing that sooner or later I will be singled out to give the answer.

Though Kiyoshi seldom answers his father's questions, he gets mad at me for holding back. Ever since he was confirmed, Kiyoshi has been irritable about religion. For years before that, we talked to each other about our faith, our doubts. Now he doesn't ask me about when or if I plan to get confirmed. Maybe he already knows that I don't believe anymore. I should just tell him the truth instead of pretending to believe week after week, month after month. I am the biggest hypocrite, I think, as I trudge down the hill. How can I accuse my mother of being a liar and a coward when, by waiting and pretending, I am doing exactly the same thing she did?

Halfway to the church, I walk down the street in front of the train station. The neon sign is lit up above the jazz club Kiyoshi had pointed out to me. Green vines and purple flowers flicker on and off above the lavender door.

"They don't go to church anymore," Kiyoshi said about Toru and Takashi, his face looking smug.

How can you be so quick to pass judgment? I should have demanded.

A faint tune is coming through the door. I take a few steps toward the music. Kiyoshi must be helping his mother clear the dinner table right now, while his father goes to sit alone in his study to look over his notes. I can almost feel the scratchy wool fabric of the couch where Kiyoshi and I will sit side by side. Every week, we sit in the same place, as if Pastor Kato had given us assigned seats.

"My father was worried you might stop coming to church," Kiyoshi said, "when your mother went away."

I wonder what my mother is doing this moment, so far away from me. I try to picture her sitting on the tatami floor of the embroidery workshop, her thumb and finger around a silver needle piercing a shiny silk fabric. She might be embroidering a flock of cranes on a bride's gown, each stitch bringing out the luminous white glow of the wings. Whatever she meant by saying that she and Grandfather had the same God, I will never find out. I wasn't able to tell her about my loss of faith even when she lived with me. How can I question her about her beliefs when we can only talk to each other through letters? She will never return to the Katos' church to decorate the altar or to sing hymns or to listen to sermons. She is far away making beautiful designs on someone else's clothing.

Suddenly I feel so sorry for myself that I could cry. Taking another step toward the door, I almost stumble and fall over, like that sick crow trying to flap open his wings. I lean forward a little, eyes closed. The music is still going on inside. It sounds muffled and distant, like a faint music-box tune.

With my eyes still closed, I remember Toru Uchida's face in church, at the funeral service for his mother. We were singing the last hymn as Toru, Takashi, their father, and uncles were carrying the coffin down the aisle. Our voices went up higher and higher, trilling words about how great God is, how our hearts sing His praises. Mid-breath and singing, I caught sight of Toru's face streaked with tears. He wasn't even trying to stop or hide them. The moment our eyes met, my mouth clamped shut. I couldn't sing anymore. Soon, Toru was walking past me, and the two of us shook our heads exactly at the same time. *I won't sing the rest of the hymn,* I was trying to tell him with my eyes, *out of respect for you.* I'm sure he understood. His eyes were saying *Thank you. I know it.* That was the very last time I saw him. Though I looked for him after the service, his family had already left to drive to the cemetery, and he and Takashi took the train to Tokyo that evening.

That moment in church was the beginning of what I know now. Because of what happened during that service, I started thinking that God either doesn't exist or doesn't care. It wasn't just Toru's tears. Pastor Kato had said in his sermon that we could not always see God's plans. "Some people," he preached, "are called upon to

91

suffer on the hospital bed so that the pastor who comes to the bedside can witness to their families and the Gospel may be spread through their suffering." My mother, who was sitting next to me with tears brimming from her eyes, winced when she heard those words; I heard her draw in a quick, small breath. The pastor was saying that Mrs. Uchida had suffered and died from cancer so that Mr. Uchida and his family could hear the Gospel. Even back then, I knew that was wrong—as wrong as singing about how great God was while Toru wept. How could I have kept on going to church since then, for five years?

I step back and look at the blinking neon sign. Toru must be inside this bar, mixing drinks, listening to the music I can barely hear. He might not remember me, or he might not want to. I have changed a lot since we last saw each other, and he must have, too. Maybe he would not like me now, just as I no longer like Keiko, who was my best friend five years ago. But I want to believe that it isn't always too late to start talking to an old friend. I am planning to see my mother in 1982, seven years from now, after not seeing her or talking to her at all except in letters. If I can't get up the courage to speak to Toru now, I might as well forget about her, too.

I put my hand on the door, lean with my shoulder, and push my way in. The door swings shut, leaving me in the dark interior of the bar. I panic for a moment, but it's too late to turn back. I have to keep walking toward the empty counter.

Above, the small ceiling lights remind me of the planetarium, where I used to sit long ago with my mother while a woman's voice took us on an imaginary journey down to the Southern Hemisphere. That was our favorite part of the whole presentation—that long, imaginary trip. Our faces upturned, my mother and I leaned back in the dark, staring at the domed ceiling that flickered with the Southern Cross, Hydra, Centaurus—stars and constellations we would never see in our lives together, or apart.

5
The Map of Light

On the racks behind the counter, wineglasses hang upside down like melting icicles. The bartender looks up from the dishes he has been washing. For another second, I hear the whoosh of the water hitting the stainless steel sink; then it is quiet except for the piano solo from the stereo.

Toru has grown tall and lanky. If we were to stand side by side, I would come up only to his chest. His face, except for being thinner, looks the same. His eyes are dark brown and long; he still has the thick eyelashes we used to tease him about. His left cheek, but not his right, dimples as he smiles and takes a step toward me.

"You look all grown-up, with long hair," he says, wiping his hand on the white apron he is wearing over his white button-down shirt and blue jeans. "The last time I saw you, your hair was shorter than mine. You were such a tomboy." He extends his hand over the counter.

"Kiyoshi Kato told me you worked here." I shake his hand, which is warm from the dishwater. "I wasn't sure if you would recognize me."

"I was just thinking about you this morning." He lets go of my hand but keeps smiling. "Sit down. I'll be right back."

Reaching overhead, he pulls down two of the wine-

glasses and tilts a wine bottle over them; the glasses
bloom red against his white cuffs. He comes around the
corner and brings the wine to the two women sitting at a
table in the corner. The only customers in the bar, the
women are wearing thin spring dresses and high heels.
They must be twenty-eight or thirty, about the same age
as Dr. Mizutani, though they look nothing like her. One
of them pulls a cigarette out of her pack. Toru takes a
lighter from his pocket and holds it out. The woman
leans toward him, her head bowed over the flame. She
says something I can't hear. Toru steps back, a polite
smile on his face.

"Kiyoshi saw your brother at school," I say when he
comes back and stands across the counter, opposite my
stool. "He said they were in the same gym class."

"I know," Toru laughs. "I can just see the two of them
together. I don't know about Kiyoshi, but Takashi never
stopped being clumsy. He's not much of an athlete."

"Neither is Kiyoshi. I can still outrun him from his
house to mine."

When we were children, Toru wouldn't play a game
unless he and I could be on the same team. We always
won. At the beach, the two of us would swim out until
our feet didn't touch bottom. Treading the deep water,
we taunted Kiyoshi and Takashi, who splashed around in
the shallows. "Cowards, cowards!" we would shout,
laughing while the waves crashed over our voices. All
our three mothers waved from the beach, their faces tight
with worried smiles.

"Are you still a tomboy?" Toru asks.

"I don't know. I played volleyball on the school team
two years ago, but I didn't try out last year."

"Why not?"

"I made a girl cry at the city tournament. She was the
95

weakest defender on the other team. I had a very mean roundhouse serve, and I kept aiming it at her. She missed four in a row and had to be taken out of the game. I could see her sitting on the bench, crying. That was the last game I played. I quit."

"Because you made her cry?" Toru tilts his head.

"Not just because of that. When she started falling apart after the first couple of serves, I never thought of stopping. I was happy. I kept thinking, 'Great, one more point, one more point.' That girl could have dropped dead right there and I would have kept aiming my serve at her. Everyone was glad—my coach, the other girls on the team. But I had to quit, because I didn't like how happy I was to see someone falling apart."

Toru bursts out laughing and then shakes his head. "I really missed you while I was in Tokyo. I don't know anyone quite like you."

"Are you making fun of me?"

"No, not at all." He leans forward, his elbows on the counter. "When we were young and our mothers brought us together, I never liked playing with my brother or Kiyoshi. They were too young for me. But you were different—you were bright and quick. I could play with you." His hair, which is parted on the side, falls over his left eye; he pushes it back with his fingers.

The piano solo has stopped. One of the women walks up to the stereo, which is against the wall, and puts on another record. She walks back slowly, looking over her shoulder toward us while a big band starts playing a dance tune. On the table, both women's glasses are more than half full.

"Do you see a lot of Kiyoshi?" Toru asks.

"I see him at church. We don't go to the same school. You know he's at Ashiya North, the same as your

96

brother. I've been at our mothers' old school since seventh grade." I stop, suddenly worried about mentioning his mother. But Toru is still smiling.

"So you and Kiyoshi aren't boyfriend and girlfriend?"

"Oh, no."

"You can tell me the truth." He winks.

My face feels hot as he continues to smile. "I've never had a boyfriend," I tell him, "but if I did, it sure wouldn't be Kiyoshi. No way."

"Why not? What's wrong with Kiyoshi? Poor guy. He might be crushed to hear you say that."

"But I've known him all my life."

Toru raises one eyebrow. "So? Lots of people date and even marry their childhood friends."

"Not me. I don't want to date or marry someone I've known since we were babies. I would feel like nothing new ever happened to me, like I made no progress from the beginning to the end." I stop, embarrassed. I have known Toru all my life, too. I don't want him to think I am being rude or stupid. "I don't mean that people I've known all my life are not good enough for me, to be friends with," I start to explain, my face feeling hotter by the second. I am throwing my arms around, waving my hands like a crazy, nervous person.

Toru reaches out and takes my wrist. His long, thin fingers can easily go around my sharp wrist bone that sticks out. He squeezes my hand lightly and then lets go. "I was just teasing you," he says. "I know exactly what you mean about not making any progress. I feel strange living with Father in our old house, after all these years. The house looks the same, we even have the same furniture, so it's hard for me to remember that I'm grown-up now. Seeing the same person all your life would be just like that. I want no part of it, either."

The back door opens while I'm thinking of what to say. A middle-aged man saunters in, walking past Toru behind the counter to the cash register on the other end. Toru shrugs and goes to talk to him.

On the big-band album, the brass section starts playing. From the way the man keeps glancing in my direction, I know he is talking about me. He doesn't look like anyone I have ever seen—he is dressed entirely in black, his graying hair tied in a ponytail.

"That's my boss," Toru says when he comes back.

"I thought so."

Leaning over the counter, he whispers, "He doesn't want you to stay here because you look too young. Don't be insulted. He's just nervous."

"I'm not insulted. I *am* too young. You have to be eighteen to be in a bar."

"I told him we were childhood friends and we haven't seen each other for so long. So he's letting me off for a while. Sunday nights are always slow. He doesn't need me now."

At the other end of the counter, the man is reading the newspaper and paying no attention to us.

"Do you want to go outside and talk?" Toru asks. "Or I can give you a ride if you were on your way someplace? What do you want to do?"

I jump off the stool, though unsure of what to say.

Toru is already taking off his white apron. "Let's get out of here first and then decide. Come on."

As I follow him to the door, the two women look up from their drinks. Both are wearing bright red lipstick, their mouths carefully outlined and then filled in, the way children paint flowers or trees. The music grows faint as the door swishes shut behind us.

Outside it is already dark. Toru points to a blue car in

the parking lot, its paint chipped in places, the front fender bent in. "My grandfather's old Honda," he says. "I drove it back from Tokyo when Takashi and I came back. Grandfather is letting me keep it. He's eighty and doesn't see well enough to drive." Opening the passenger's door for me, he asks, "Were you on the way somewhere?"

By now, Pastor Kato must be well into his lecture. Everyone is sitting in their usual almost-assigned seat—everyone but me. "I was," I tell Toru when he comes around and sits behind the wheel. "But not anymore. I changed my mind."

He turns his head toward me, his eyes narrowed.

"I was going to the Bible study meeting at church, but I don't want to go after all. Not tonight, and maybe not ever again."

"Okay," Toru says, shrugging his shoulders. "Shall we go for a drive, then?"

"Sure."

"Can we see our old school? I haven't been there since I moved back."

"That sounds good. I haven't been there, either, though I see it every day, up on the hill."

Toru puts the key in the ignition; the engine turns over with a noise like a dry cough. As we pull out of the parking lot and head north, he asks, "How do you like going to our mothers' old school?"

"I like it." I picture my grandmother's sour face. She has not given up though it's April and I am still at Christian Girls' Academy. At least once a week, especially if my father is home, she brings up the subject again and insists that I should transfer to Ashiya North next April. Sometimes Father changes the subject or placates her by saying, "We'll talk about it some other time." Other times he lets her talk on. I don't know if he is ignoring her or if he is beginning to agree with her.

"Is everyone as religious as our mothers were?" Toru asks.

"No, not at all. We have chapel every morning before classes and Bible study twice a week, but most of the girls aren't Christians. They and their families chose the school because it's a good private school and we don't have to cram for exams."

"I guess that's how it was for our mothers, too," Toru says. "They didn't come from Christian families, either. They converted while they were going to school."

"That's true."

"How about you? You still go to church, right?" Toru looks at me for a second and then turns back to the road.

"I do, but it's more out of habit. I didn't get confirmed last Christmas when Kiyoshi did. I don't believe in God anymore. I should just stop going to church." I pause and peer at Toru's face, wondering if he remembers how we both shook our heads in the middle of the hymn at his mother's funeral. Maybe he is hearing the hymn trilling in the back of his mind right now, the echoed phrases praising God's greatness. I want to tell him that my doubts began when his mother died and I saw him cry at the funeral. I want to let him know that I was offended by Pastor Kato's sermon. But something—maybe some kind of respect—prevents me from saying it.

We are at an intersection. "I stopped believing a long time ago," he says, turning to me. "Of course, that doesn't stop me from waking up in the middle of the night in cold sweat, worried that God is going to punish me after all and send me to hell. But I get over that in the morning. Daylight makes a big difference."

The traffic light changes, and we proceed up the hill.

The steep incline makes me lean against my seat, my shoulders tilted back as though I were somersaulting backward down the hill. *A couple of backsliders,* Kiyoshi would call us. I picture Toru and me tumbling down a long green hill toward a blue lake, laughing all the way while Kiyoshi stands at the top, his face worried and afraid at the same time. It's just like when he and Takashi could not swim out to the deep water.

In a few minutes, we pull into the parking lot of the school. After Toru turns off the headlights and cuts the engine, we sit looking down at our city. Beyond the coast, which is lit up, the dark water stretches out in the shape of a bow.

"Our hometown." Toru sweeps his hand in front of him in an exaggerated gesture.

"Are you happy to be back?"

Turning sideways, he leans back on the door so that he is completely facing me. "I don't know." A slight frown appears on his face—just a tiny wrinkle between his thin, arched eyebrows. "Takashi and I came back because Father wants us to go to college, get married, and settle down in this area, not in Tokyo. He doesn't know that I'm not planning to do any of those things."

"You're not?"

"I didn't go to college two years ago when I graduated from high school. I'm not going now."

If I were to work at a bar instead of going to college, my father and grandmother would disown me. It would make no difference that Father has been seeing a woman who owns a bar and lives upstairs from it. No girl from a respectable family could work at a bar. A few of the eleventh and twelfth graders at my school wait tables during the summers to earn extra spending money, but only at lunch places downtown that serve coffee and sandwiches, where the customers are usually well-to-do older women taking breaks from their shopping. It's different for boys. My friend Mieko's older brother waited tables last summer, at a place that served cocktails; he was even allowed to work at night. Mieko's parents would never let her do that. I have noticed this for a long time: Boys are allowed to do more things than girls are—to come home later, to take trips just with their friends during the summer. Still, even if I were a boy, my family—and I'm sure most of my friends' families—would be very upset if I refused to go to college.

"What about your family?" I ask Toru. "Didn't they mind your not going to college?"

"Of course they minded. Both my father and grandfather were very, very angry at first. But what could they do? They couldn't *make* me go."

"But they could. They could threaten to kick you out of the house or even disown you." If my grandmother and father disowned me, my life would be completely changed. I would have to live with my grandfather and mother and be a burden to them. They would blame themselves for being poor, for not being able to give me everything that my father can. The kids from my grandfather's village don't go to high school. They quit after ninth grade to work for their parents on their farms and in their weaving cottages. A village girl my age would already be working, spending hours bent over crops or threading looms in dimly lit rooms. Most of them marry young and go to live on another farm or in another cottage just like the one they left. I wouldn't even be able to do that: No one would marry me if my father disowned me.

Not knowing my gloomy thoughts, Toru tips his head back and laughs. "My father and grandfather did threaten

102

to disown me," he says. "My grandfather said I couldn't live in his house if I didn't go to college. That didn't bother me. I had a few older friends who lived in rooming houses, so I arranged to move in with one of them. Grandfather came home one night from his chess club and saw me loading my friend's car. He asked what I was doing, and I said I was moving out. He just stood there with his mouth hanging open. I guess he wasn't expecting me to take him at his word. I lived with my friend for a month, and then my grandfather and father backed down. I returned to Grandfather's house because I felt sorry for Takashi, being there alone. I came back to Ashiya for the same reason. I didn't want my brother to be stuck living with Father all by himself. I want to stay around for a while and make sure he's going to be all right."

I wish I had an older brother who would worry about me like that. I don't mention it, though, because I don't want to sound self-pitying.

"I'm not going to stay too long," Toru continues. "I'm already anxious to get out of here, and it's only been a few weeks."

"What will you do?" I have no idea what people do if they don't go to college or settle down to work.

"I don't know. Travel someplace. I've always wanted to go to South America, and maybe India. I want to travel for a while and not be responsible to anyone else."

No one else I know has ever thought of traveling so far away. If I were to leave my father's house, I would have no place to go except my grandfather's, no way to earn a living as Toru does. He is older and more resourceful than I, but he is luckier, I'm sure, in being a boy. Even an older girl does not live away from her home except in a dorm or a rooming house that her parents have found for her. If I left my house, I wouldn't have a friend to move in with, the way Toru did. Traveling to a foreign country alone is unthinkable. Most women—my mother, for one, and Mrs. Kato, too—would never step out of their houses alone except to go grocery shopping, to take a walk, or to go to church or school. They go together just to shop downtown or to see a movie or eat lunch. Dr. Mizutani is the only woman I know who has traveled anywhere all by herself. I can easily imagine her going to South America or India if those places struck her fancy, but she is definitely the only one.

"I try not to think too much about the future," Toru says. "At the present, I'm living with Father and Takashi because Father thinks we are old enough to take care of ourselves. We know how to cook and wash our clothes and clean the house, maybe better than he does. And while I'm here, I hope you and I will have a lot of chances to talk."

"I would like that." *There is so much you can tell me*, I think but don't say, for fear of sounding pushy.

"Let's get out and walk," he says, opening the driver's door.

The empty schoolyard is lit by a few white lamps. The old playground equipment is still here—the seesaws, the slide, the monkey bars, the swing set, all of them painted the same pale green as before. Far off in the north corner, they still have the blue platform where our principal stood to give his short lecture every morning at the school-wide assembly. When I was in first grade, Toru, who was in sixth, was our student council president. Every Wednesday he stood on that platform to give his report, just as I would five years later, when I was the first girl ever to be elected president.

"Did you know I became student council president in

104

sixth grade? I stood on that platform every Wednesday, just like you used to. You and Takashi were in Tokyo by then."

"I had no idea." He turns to me and takes my hand. "We're going to stand up there again," he says, already beginning to run.

Hand in hand, we sprint across the yard, our shoes kicking up the white sand. At the platform, he lets go of my hand. We climb up the steps and stand side by side on the top. In the dark, I try to imagine the faces of kids and teachers looking up at us. A year ago, I heard that one of our old teachers had died from a heart attack. Now I can't help thinking about his ghost floating around in the dark. There are hundreds of people, I'm sure, who had once gone to this school and have since died. We could be addressing a huge assembly of ghosts. The tall trees on the edge of the schoolyard begin to close in on us. I imagine them waving their branches, moving toward us. Shuddering a little, I turn to Toru. Our eyes meet, and suddenly, we burst out laughing at the same time.

"You try and catch me." Tapping him once on the shoulder, I run down the platform, across the yard, to the swing set. He catches up and sits down on the swing next to me, both of us still laughing.

Down the hill, I survey the city lights, looking for Toru's neighborhood, a few miles south of my house. It's easy to find—a cluster of white-and-orange house lights near a large, keyhole-shaped forest that is dark. We used to walk with our mothers around the periphery of that forest, which is fenced off because an emperor's son was buried there in the fourth century. When I was very young, I thought that the whole forest was his tomb; I imagined the prince's knees under the pine trees, a meadow growing over his mile-long legs. People must

105

have been bigger back then, I assumed. I didn't think there was anything strange about that. In the Old Testament stories we heard in Sunday school, people often lived to be thousands of years old. Though the Bible stories were set in Egypt and Israel, I believed that all over the world, people had lived much longer back then. No wonder they were bigger, too, I thought, since they had more time to grow. When my mother discovered my mistake, she laughed, but not in a mean way. She laughed the way Toru did at the bar when I told him why I had quit the volleyball team. Their laughter said that there was something about me they liked very much, even though—or maybe because—I had strange ideas.

Toru is moving his swing back and forth. The chains creak. Overhead, bats are flying—zipping out of the pines and cherry trees and swooping near the lights to gobble up some moths.

"My mother went back to live in the country," I say over the creaking of the chain.

He puts one foot on the ground to stop the swing.

"Did you know? She left in January."

"I knew. When my brother met Kiyoshi at school, he asked how you were. Kiyoshi told him."

"He did?"

Toru nods. "I thought about calling you. I drove in front of your house a couple of times last week—I was hoping that somehow you would be out in the front and you would see me. I didn't ring the doorbell because I felt shy about seeing your father or your grandmother. I'm sorry I didn't stop. I was just thinking about you this morning."

Leaning back on the swing, I stare upside down at the school building.

"You must have felt terrible."

I straighten up and turn to Toru. In the dim white light of the lamp, his eyes look kind.

"Yes," I reply. "I was lonely. I still am." Tears are starting, pricking the back of my eyes like little needles. Squeezing my eyes shut and stopping the tears, I get off the swing and walk to the parking lot, with my eyes only half open. Toru's footsteps follow behind me. I stop in front of his car and lean back on the hood. Standing beside me, he puts his hand on the small of my back.

"I wanted to see you because I understand. I know how you must feel."

I nod in silence.

He draws me closer and leans forward to hug me. My cheek pressed against his collarbone, I can smell a faint whiff of soap or shaving cream. He rubs my back slowly, his hand going up and down along my spine, and touches his lips to my forehead before letting go. I step back. My pulse is fluttering in my neck, my heart beating as if I had sprinted a hundred yards. I want to hug him back, stand on my tiptoes to brush my lips against his cheek. I have never felt quite this way about him, or anyone else, before. But my eyes still hurt from pushing the tears back inside, and I am so sad about everything that has happened since I last saw him.

Down the hill, our hometown glitters in the dark. We grew up looking at this same view; we stood on the same platform, sat in the same chairs, learned the same lessons five years apart at this school. I can easily imagine him waking up in the middle of the night now, afraid of God—missing his mother, too. If there was no God, where would Toru's mother be? What is the sense of her living or dying? How can he stand the thought of her being nothing but specks of dust? I want to say something to break the sadness we both know, but no words come to

107

me. It's getting late. Soon he will turn to me and tell me that we should get going, that he has to get back to work.

I close my eyes and say the first thing that comes to me when I open them. "Thank you for coming back." My voice catches in my throat and comes out thin and shaky.

He steps closer and takes my hand.

"I didn't mean," I add quickly, my face feeling hot. "Of course you didn't come back because of me. I didn't mean to sound presumptuous. I just wanted—"

"It's okay," he says, lacing his fingers with mine. "You don't have to explain. I'm glad to be here for you." Reaching over with his other hand to pull me closer, he wraps his arm around my shoulder.

As I raise my arm and circle it around his waist, I remember how we used to walk around like this a long time ago, kidding around, pretending to be a four-legged monster chasing Takashi and Kiyoshi in the dark. Even back then, Toru was a head taller than I. He will always be taller and older; I can never catch up.

The wind begins to rise as we stand in silence. The city lights flicker and shimmer below. When I close my eyes, I can see the white dots on the inside of my eyelids, as if a small map had been imprinted in my memory to bring me back, always, to this moment.

6
A Mother's Spell

On Wednesday night, I sit at my desk trying to write to my mother. *The spring term is going well. Dr. Mizutani and I are taking care of a crow. The Uchida boys are back in town.* One by one, I cross out the sentences and squeeze the paper into a tight ball in my fist. My words sound newsy and cheerful, just like my mother's. It isn't how I feel. *I know you worry about me,* I want to write, *but you are worried about the wrong things. School is not my problem. I am not overworking. You are my problem. You won't even talk to me on the phone. You keep pretending that nothing is wrong.* But I remember how gaunt my mother's face looked on the day she left me. I imagine her lying on her thin futon in her room at Grandfather Kurihara's, unable to sleep because of my letter. She would get up with dark circles under her eyes, the tiny wrinkles around her mouth a little bigger and deeper.

I take out another sheet of paper, but no words come to me. Elbows on the desk, I lean forward, pressing my eyes into the heels of my hands. My head feels like a terrible burden. It's as if I had turned into a girl from one of the stories my mother used to tell me at bedtime, back when I was six or seven. A long time ago—the story began—there was a girl whose mother was dying. In the last few days of her life, the mother put their family treasures in a huge earthenware bowl and placed it upside-down on her daughter's head, completely covering her face. Then the mother cast a spell to make the bowl stick. After her mother died, the girl went to work as a humble maid, despised by everyone for her strange appearance. Even small children threw stones at her or chased her with sticks. One day many years later, when the girl was crossing a busy street while running away from the people who tormented her, a prince's carriage came speeding around the corner and almost knocked her down. The prince jumped out to make sure she was all right, and being a kind man, he apologized as courteously as if she had been the richest, most beautiful princess instead of a poor crippled girl. His kindness broke the spell. The bowl cracked and fell to the ground, scattering many golden coins and gems. Her wealth, however, was not what impressed the prince. Astonished by the girl's beauty and gentle manners, he fell in love. In this way, the girl who wore a bowl on her head became a rich and beautiful princess.

I open my eyes and stare at the blank sheet of paper in front of me. I wish my mother had never told me such a stupid story. How could a mother cast a spell on her daughter and turn her into a crippled monster? If the girl had only met cruel people, she would have stayed a cripple for the rest of her life. Her mother should have come up with a better spell—one that didn't rely so much on chance. There was no guarantee that the girl would ever meet a kind person or that the person who broke the spell would be a prince rather than a sick old man. Things could have gone wrong even if she had met a perfect prince. What if he hadn't fallen in love with her? He might have politely apologized for the near accident and gone on his way, leaving the girl alone on the street with her scattered treasures.

Just about all the stories Mother told or read to me, I think now, were depressing and unfair. We had several books, big glossy books with beautiful pictures—*Japanese Folk Tales, The Brothers Grimm, Hans Christian Andersen, The Fifty Famous Tales*. If I hadn't been fooled by the pictures, I would have seen the unfairness of the stories right away. They were almost always about children whose parents had died; or worse, children whose parents left them in the dark woods because there wasn't enough food to go around. These children had to do big, heroic things—kill witches, find treasures, become kings or queens—before they could come home to their father or mother or grandparents, who were finally happy to see them. The children who weren't so good—those who went dancing behind their parents' backs or stepped on the loaves of bread their mother had baked—had to have their feet cut off or else they sank into marshes. How could my mother read these stories of punishment when she was always telling me to forgive my friends for breaking my toys or calling me names, because we were Christians? Nothing she said made sense, even back then, though I didn't notice it so much.

I'm glad I don't have those books she used to read to me. When I was in third grade, my mother and I donated them to a small town in Kyushu, where a typhoon had destroyed the school and the library. I was so proud of myself. I used to imagine boys and girls sitting on rafts amid rising rivers, reading my books and smiling. How could I think that anyone would be comforted by those stories? I should have sent comic books and funny stories, something to make the children laugh.

By second or third grade, my mother and I weren't

111

reading many fairy tales. Instead we studied the Bible together every night, going through the Gospels, the Acts of the Apostles, and then Paul's letters. The stories in the Bible were no better. If I acted like the five wise bridesmaids in one of the parables, everyone would be disappointed in me. When the bridegroom was delayed and the lamps belonging to the other five bridesmaids—the dumb ones—started going out, the five wise bridesmaids refused to share their extra oil. That didn't seem fair or particularly Christian. "Always be considerate to people": I have been taught at home, at church, at school. "Share your possessions with others." In the Gospels, there is a story about Jesus cursing a fig tree because it didn't have any fruit when he was hungry. The tree withered. That story makes no sense, either. Maybe the tree had no fruit because it wasn't the fig season or because the tree was too young. What kind of person would expect trees to have fruit every time he got hungry?

"You are too smart for your own good," Mother used to tell me when I said that the stories made no sense. "You think too much."

How can a person think too much? Most people don't think enough. My mother should have thought more before she left me with my father and grandmother—two people she could not bear to live with herself.

I pick up my pen, but put it down again. I don't know what to say to my mother in a letter when I can't see her or even talk to her for seven years. In the fairy tales, the good children could come home after years of dragon slaying and other heroic deeds, to be welcomed by their parents, who were overjoyed to see them. There were big feasts and grateful tears and living-happily-ever-after. But that's just make-believe. Nothing like that will happen to my mother and me. No matter how many letters

112

we write, we may have turned into strangers by the time I am twenty-two.

The telephone is ringing downstairs. My grandmother must be in the laundry room, washing my father's shirts. I can hear the water running. She doesn't seem to hear the phone ringing, so I go downstairs and pick up the receiver.

"Hello," a woman's voice says, high and trembly. "Hello, this is Tomiko Hayashi from Hiroshima." She sounds like she is on the verge of giggling.

"Yes, I know," I say, making my voice sound low and serious, not high in the cheap way hers is.

The woman laughs though there is nothing funny. "Is your father home?"

"No, he is not."

"He must be working late, I suppose."

"I don't know whether he is working or not. But he is not here." *You know better than I do!* I want to yell. My father came home late last night, unpacked his suitcase, and went right to bed. I didn't even know that he was planning to come back here tonight.

The woman laughs some more. "Will you tell him that I called, then?"

"Yes. I will tell him."

Tomiko hesitates. I imagine her lips close to the receiver. They would be painted bright pink or orange. In the only picture I have seen of her, Tomiko Hayashi was wearing a yellow kimono with designs of red fans, her face heavily made up. She was standing next to Father, her small, chubby hand on his shoulder. In spite of the makeup, she had beady eyes, a flat nose, and a huge, grinning mouth, and was not pretty in any way. Behind them, I could see the sign over a bar: TOMIKO'S INN. My

113

father had left this picture on his desk in his study a few years ago—carelessly or on purpose, I'm not sure.

Tomiko stays on the line, as if she meant to spy on my thoughts by listening to me breathe. "Good-bye." I slam down the phone and hope that the sound will give her a terrible earache.

Back in my room, I plop down on my bed and stare out the windows at the blue-purple sky. The water continues to run downstairs. My grandmother must still be washing the shirts, scrubbing the collars and the cuffs by hand as she always does. Does she consider the shirts to be extra dirty, poisoned even, because my father had brought them back from Tomiko's? My mother never put my father's clothes in the washing machine with any of ours. I wonder, now, if it was for that same reason. With my mother, I was always on her side: her clothes and mine together in the washer, my father's in a different pile. My grandmother is different. She doesn't want me on her side. Even without looking, I know the face she is making right now as she scrubs my father's dirty clothes; her pinched look says that she is disappointed in everyone, especially in my father and me.

About an hour later, my father comes home. I hear the front door rattling as he opens it; then he is in the foyer taking off his shoes. I could run downstairs right away to tell him about the phone call, keeping it a secret between the two of us, but of course I don't. I wait until he is sitting down in the kitchen with Grandmother, drinking the bitter green tea she has prepared for him. By then, he is dressed in baggy long underwear and a black kimono jacket he wears around the house. Every night when he comes home, Grandmother has his change of clothes and tea ready, just as my mother did. After he comes out of

114

his room, his clothes changed, she goes in and puts away the suit, shirt, and tie he has left in a crumpled pile. I have not left dirty clothes on the floor since first grade, when my mother showed me how to hang up my skirts, fold my sweaters, and put the rest in the dirty-clothes hamper. My father has never done that for my mother or grandmother.

stand in the doorway outside the kitchen, watching him reading the evening paper and drinking tea. Grandmother is sitting across the table, waiting for him to talk to her. He doesn't say anything. These are the times I feel sorry for Grandmother. Her face has a watchful and anxious look. She wants so much for him to talk, to tell her about his day.

In the shadow of the newspaper, my father's face looks gray. There are dark circles under his eyes. His clenched jaw and thin nose give him a grim and unhappy expression. "Your father is tired because he works so hard for us," my mother used to tell me. "He can't help feeling irritable." That was her explanation for why he often snapped at her and made her cry. I suppose she wasn't just pretending. My father does work hard. He is an important person at his insurance company; he makes good money. "We should appreciate all he does for us," my mother used to say. She must have been trying to convince herself instead of really believing it, but she did have a point. If a genie from one of her old fairy tales came and asked me, "I can grant you one wish. You can nave a father who is kind, who loves you and your mother and even your grandmother. But this father would be poor. Do you want him, or do you want the father you already have?" I would not know what to say. Being poor would be so very hard.

Except for the people of my grandfather's village, I

only knew one person who was poor. All the girls at the Academy come from well-to-do families. Even in grade school, in my class, there was only one poor girl, Yoko Takemoto, who lived in the attic of another classmate's house, where her mother worked as a live-in maid. At the beginning of third grade, when our teacher, Miss Sato, said we could sit with anyone we liked for the whole month of April, no one wanted to sit next to Yoko. After we had all sat down in the seats we had chosen and Yoko was left standing, Miss Sato asked for a volunteer. No one raised a hand for a long time. Finally, I offered to give up my seat next to Keiko Yamasaki to sit with Yoko, because I thought of the Bible stories about Jesus eating dinner with people no one else liked; my mother always told me that being a Christian meant being kind. If I had been proud of myself for being such a good Christian, my pride didn't last very long. I hated sitting next to Yoko. In the last half hour of every day, Miss Sato held a contest in which we wrote stories with our seatmates, each of us contributing a sentence in turn. Yoko and I always had the least written, because she would sit there saying nothing for five or ten minutes. When she finally came up with a sentence, it was something stupid like "The sky was blue," "The princess was very pretty," "The bird flew away." I couldn't believe how long a third-grader took to come up with those kindergarten sentences. While I was mad at Yoko for being so stupid, I was mad at Keiko and my other friends, too, because during recess, they would talk about how Yoko always wore the same brown dress, how her hair smelled funny, how stupid she was.   was mad at them, I realize now, because I looked down on Yoko as much as they did but was unwilling to admit it. What a hypocrite I was; I cringe to remember it.

116

No one knew what had happened to Yoko's father—whether he was dead, or her parents had been divorced or never been married. But Yoko was the person I thought about later, when my mother told me that growing up poor and fatherless means growing up in shame. When I think of being poor or fatherless, I imagine a big room where a crowd of people are sitting down. As the only person without a seat, I have to walk around, looking for a chair. But as soon as I find one, the person sitting next to that chair would glare at me; or else, two or three people would get up to leave, just to avoid sitting near me.

I'm imagining that room again, when my grandmother snaps at me.

"Don't just stand there like that. Do you have something to say? Go upstairs to study if you don't."

I wait a few more seconds, till my father, too, is staring at me, his paper half-lowered. Then I announce, "That woman from Hiroshima called."

The newspaper goes all the way down, making a rustling sound. My father continues to stare at me, his mouth open, while Grandmother glares at him.

"She left no message," I continue. "Just that she called."

My father cannot scold me for rudely referring to her as "that woman from Hiroshima." He can't insist that I call her "Miss Hayashi," as though she were a respectable woman. My grandmother won't scold me, either. Our dislike of Tomiko Hayashi is one of the few things we have in common, though of course we never talk about it. Much as she dislikes my mother, Grandmother must be relieved that my parents won't embarrass our family by getting an official divorce. Maybe she even wishes that my mother were still here, if only to save

117

face. Ever since my mother's departure, Tomiko has been calling our house at least once a week. Before that, she never called Father at home, except very late at night, sounding too drunk to care.

"I'm going upstairs to study," I say, and leave the two facing each other in silence.

Soon afterward, I hear my father's footsteps downstairs and the noises he makes while packing his suitcase—one of the few things he will do for himself. A cab pulls up into our driveway. As I watch from my bedroom window, he leaves without a good-bye. A door slams downstairs. My grandmother has retired into her bedroom.

The blank paper is still on my desk, but I am in no mood to write. Behind me, on the oak dresser, the owl clock keeps moving its yellow eyes side to side. It's a little after ten. Except for the dresser, the desk, the bookshelves, and the bed, my room is bare and dismal. I used to have two big posters on the wall—one showing the snow-covered Swiss Alps and the other, a meadow in Germany in front of an old castle. The posters were taller than I was and glossy with bright colors. My mother bought them for me a few years ago and tacked them up on the wall; she wanted me to take a break from studying every hour and imagine myself in one of the pictures. "No one should study nonstop," she said. "It's bad for your eyes, and your mind, too. Take a five-minute break every hour and think of something pleasant." I made up stories about skiing down the snowy slope or having a big picnic with friends on that flowering meadow. It was just like my mother to give me two big posters when my room already had the best view in the house—of the backyard and the flowers she had planted. It used to make me smile, the way she worried about me. The week after she left, I ripped down the posters. They were just another example of her make-believe. I felt pathetic sitting alone in my room, daydreaming about places I would never in my whole life be able to visit.

For half an hour I sit doing nothing, having one depressing thought after another, till my room feels small and suffocating. By then, everything is quiet. No noise comes from Grandmother's bedroom. When I sneak downstairs, the crack of space underneath her door looks completely dark. Taking my shoes from the foyer, I slide down the hallway into the kitchen and then out the back door. I put on my shoes on the back porch and stand around for a while. If Grandmother wakes up and comes outside, I can pretend that I am out looking at the stars. She doesn't come out. Quietly, I climb over the fence into the Yamasakis' yard, walk across it, and scale the fence into the next yard. After a few more backyards and fences, I am on the street a block away from home. Nobody has seen me. I bolt down the hill.

Back in February, I snuck out of the house three times to go to the Katos', always on the nights when my father was away. It wasn't because I was upset and needed to talk to someone right away. I was just lonely. I couldn't bear to sit by myself in my little room, night after night. I had to go to the Katos' to watch TV in their family room, drink hot chocolate that Mrs. Kato had made, or listen to Kiyoshi's stereo while he did his homework. The Katos didn't ask me what I had been doing out so late. They acted as though my stopping by was the most normal thing in the world. After midnight when I was ready to go, Mrs. Kato sent Kiyoshi to walk me home. He got quiet as soon as we were on my street. From half a block away, he stood and watched as I pulled out the key I had stuck into my pocket and opened the door. With the door open a crack, I looked back and waved at him before he turned and sprinted down the hill. My grandmother never heard me, as far as I know.

Halfway down the hill, I realize I can't very well go to the Katos' house now. How can I sit in their living room like part of the family when I plan to stop going to their church? I keep walking, a little slower. I am a block away from the street in front of the commuter train station. "I'm glad to be here for you," Toru had said, standing in our old schoolyard on Sunday. It's a little past eleven. He might still be working at the bar. If he's not, I will turn around and walk back up the hill, and maybe just that—the fresh air, the walk—will make me feel better. Better anyway than being stuck in the little room like a prisoner.

In front of the jazz club, the neon signs are lit. The place is still open. I walk around to the parking lot in the back.

Toru's blue car is there, alongside a few others in the lot. I try the passenger's door. It's open. I slide in. Closing the door behind me, I sit in the small sliver of space between the slanted windshield, the blue ceiling, and a darker blue seat. It is absolutely silent. I turn sideways with my back against the door, knees drawn up to my chest. Except for a faint smell of cigarettes, I am reminded of sitting in my mother's closet a long time ago. I used to hide there, hoping to surprise her. I sat very quietly, her long dresses and skirts draped over my back, slippery and cool like big leaves of jungle trees after a rainstorm. Once, I fell asleep for a couple of hours, not knowing that my mother was looking for me, worried that I had gone outside on my own and gotten lost. Waiting for Toru now, I close my eyes and lean my head against the cool glass of the window.

* * *

I open my eyes just in time to see Toru's long, thin face framed in the driver's window. Brushing his hair away from his forehead, he is already beginning to smile. When he opens the door, the orange interior light goes on; it stays on for a few seconds before he sits down and pulls the door shut.

"How are you, Megumi?" he asks.

"All right."

"You don't look all right. Are you upset about something?"

I nod.

"Want to talk about it?"

"Not right away."

"We'll go for a drive, then. Let's go down to the water, okay?" He starts the car.

We head south, driving in silence past a park where we used to play. In my album, there is a picture of me with the Uchida boys and Kiyoshi, standing next to a pine tree that looks like a horse with a very long neck. My face in profile, I am blowing into an empty soda bottle, holding my fingers in position as though I were playing a Japanese flute or an oboe. All three boys are looking at me and laughing. It is too dark to see that tree now.

We park near the breakwater in front of an old bait shop. The moment I open the car door, I can hear the waves crashing on the other side of the tall embankment. After climbing up and descending a steep stairway, we stand on the sand beach. The water booms as it comes in; it hits the beach and then drains back into the bay like a long sigh.

"Let's sit down." Toru plops down on the sand.

A few feet away from where we sit, a line of algae and black mussels marks where the tide last stopped. I once found a small dead crab tangled up in a rope of dried

121

algae along the tide line. The crab was bleached white, no larger than my thumbnail. Because there was a tiny hole on its back, between the pincers, I added it to the necklace I was making with the pink and yellow oysters that also had little holes in them. I meant to give the necklace to my mother, but she thought the dead crab was creepy. So did Mrs. Kato. Toru's mother, Mrs. Uchida, was different. "How beautiful," she exclaimed, touching the crab's back with the tip of her index finger. I can still see her walking on the beach wearing that necklace, her long hair blowing around her face.

"Are you warm enough?" Toru asks me. He is lying on the sand, so I lean back and do the same. The sky is dark, with stars I cannot name, except for the Big Dipper.

"I'm not cold."

We don't speak for a long time. The white lamp behind us on the other side of the embankment makes the sand look lighter, except around Toru's white shirt. There, in contrast, the sand looks brown. The waves continue to crash and sigh. It's almost as if all the water in the bay was longing to come to us, to touch the shore just once. It makes me sad.

"So, you want to talk?" Toru prompts me.

Listening to the sad waves, I suddenly don't know what to say. How can I sit on this beach, where we used to walk with our mothers, collecting seashells and laughing, and talk about my father's girlfriend? I feel too embarrassed even to say those words, *my father's girlfriend*. It seems wrong to bring that up in the same place where Mrs. Uchida praised the necklace I had made, insisting that even the dead crab was beautiful. Grandmother Kurihara used to caution me not to make any disrespectful comments in the room where the Buddhist altar was kept. Even if I wasn't speaking about them, Grandmother

122

said, our ancestral spirits would be upset to hear bad words spoken in their presence. For the first time, I understand what she might have meant.

"You don't have to," Toru says.

But I do want to talk, to say something. So I mention the next thing that comes to mind, the second on my long list of grudges.

"I tried to write to my mother," I tell Toru. "I didn't know what to say. I'm mad at her because she won't let me call her on the phone."

"That must be hard. I'm sorry."

"My mother writes me chatty letters about Grand-father's embroidery business and about flowers and the weather. I'm mad at her for writing letters like that. But I have no way of telling her without upsetting her. I know she worries about me."

"But how can you help being angry? You have every right to be."

I sit up to look into his face. He is still lying down, but he raises his head a little. "You don't think I'm being un-fair?" I ask. "Would you be upset if you were in my position?"

Sitting up, he holds his knees against his chest. "Sure. Why shouldn't your mother agree to talk to you on the phone? She shouldn't write a superficial letter when you miss her so much."

"You really think so? Kiyoshi says I'm being selfish and impatient. He got mad at me for complaining."

Grimacing, Toru waves his hand. "What does Kiyoshi know about it? He has no idea what it's like for us. He has his mother." He stares straight ahead at the water in the dark.

I scoop up a handful of sand and let it slide slowly through my fingers. When all the sand is gone and he has

123

not spoken, I say, "I am so sorry. I shouldn't complain to you about my mother."

He takes his eyes off the water and turns back to me. "Why not?" he asks, looking into my eyes, his lips drawn tight.

I don't know what to say. I must have offended him by sounding stupid and patronizing. Bracing myself for his anger, I stay quiet.

After a few moments, Toru shrugs his shoulders. "Look," he says, his face relaxing a little. "I wasn't saying you had no right to complain about your mother— like you should be thankful to have a mother when mine is dead. I would never say a stupid thing like that to you."

"No, of course not." I shake my head, hard. I imagine Mrs. Uchida smiling at us, glad that we didn't get into a fight. I remember her strong potter's hands, her long, thin fingers like Toru's.

Until the last year of her life, when she became too weak from cancer, Mrs. Uchida worked at the potter's wheel set up in her basement. I loved watching the clay rise between her fingers, turning into bowls, vases, teacups. It reminded me of a photograph I saw in a science magazine, of a drop of milk hitting a plate and shattering into a perfect white crown. I liked to think about that photograph when I was drinking milk out of the cups that Mrs. Uchida had made—I could feel all the perfect white drops going down my throat. The thought amazed me and made me happy. Sometimes at the beach Mrs. Uchida dug a handful of sand and brought it back in a plastic bag to mix into her clay. If it was a hot day, a mist of moisture would cloud up the inside of the bag, almost as though the sand were breathing. Mrs. Uchida would hold out the bag, and we would all touch it in awe. When I was with her, I knew that every grain of sand was a

124

miracle waiting to happen, to be turned into something beautiful.

Toru and I lie back down and watch the sky. "I miss your mother, too," I say, sending my words up toward the dark sky.

He reaches out and puts his hand over mine. I continue to stare at the sky in silence, my fingers curled between the dry sand and Toru's warm palm.

A few minutes past one, Toru steers his car around the corner onto my street.

"You should stop here," I say, a block away. "I don't want my grandmother to hear me."

Stopping the car, he tilts his head sideways.

"She's hard of hearing. My father's gone to Hiroshima. My usual curfew is nine o'clock."

He shakes his head and smiles. "Did you tell them you might stop going to church on Sunday nights?" he asks.

"No."

"That could be our usual meeting time—unless you *are* going to church after all."

"I'm not going."

"Want to meet me in the parking lot at seven, then?"

"Sure," I say, without thinking.

"Seven o'clock, then," he repeats.

"Wait." I hesitate. "I can't meet you unless I lie to Grandmother—an indirect lie, that is. She'll think I am going to church."

"Of course. That's the whole point."

"It doesn't bother you? You'll be part of my lie."

"Come on." He laughs. "Nobody is completely honest with their parents or grandparents. Lying to them is a little different, don't you think, from lying to other people?"

He is right. I would never lie to my friends or teachers.

125

If my grandmother and father didn't make up so many stupid rules about what I couldn't do, I wouldn't have to lie to them, either.

"Okay," I say. "It doesn't bother me. Not a lot."

"Good. Of course, you can always come and find me at the club or at my house, if you need someone to talk to. You don't have to wait in my car. My boss won't mind if you come in for a second to let me know you're there."

"Thanks."

"I'm going to wait here and make sure you get into the house." He leans forward and gives my shoulder a light squeeze. "Good night."

I get out of the car and walk up to my house. Turning the key quietly in the lock, I open the front door and wave toward Toru's car. As I step into the house, I hear him driving away, backward for a block so he won't have to drive in front of our house.

I close the door carefully, take off my shoes, and step up to the hallway. Any second, I expect my grandmother's door to fly open, but nothing happens. Suddenly, I have a great idea. I go into the kitchen, open the fridge, and pour myself a glass of juice, still being quiet, but not as much as before. After drinking the juice, I leave the glass on the counter where my grandmother will see it in the morning. If she hears me going up the stairway now, she will assume that I have come down in the middle of the night for juice and left the dirty glass on the counter in my usual inconsiderate way. She will mumble, irritated, but she won't know the truth. I leave the kitchen and go up the stairs, which creak a little no matter how careful I am.

Back in my room, the blank stationery is still on the desk. I sit down, careful not to scrape the chair legs against the floor, and turn on the desk lamp. "Mother," I write with my fountain pen. "I am lonely and miserable. I miss you. I'm mad at you. Please let me come to see you."

As soon as I write the last sentence, I begin to cross out the whole thing, surrounding each word with a black box and filling it in until nothing is visible except a row of black boxes; it looks like a train I would have drawn as a child. The tip of the pen has jabbed some small holes in the paper. I hold the paper in front of the lamp and look at the pinpricks of white light, the way we used to observe an eclipse of the sun. Then I crumple the paper and toss it into the wastebasket across the room. It falls on the floor a few inches away.

Walking across the room to the wastebasket, I see a light flash across the Yamasakis' yard. Repeatedly, a cone of orange light wavers across the dark cluster of bushes. I walk up to the window. When my eyes get used to the dark, I can make out Mrs. Yamasaki, Keiko's mother, standing by the row of hydrangea bushes with a flashlight in one hand. Leaning over the bushes, she picks out something and drops it into a pail at her feet. After a while, she goes to the next bush and starts the same thing over again. I know what she is doing; I have seen her do it many times, though usually earlier in the evening. She is picking the snails and slugs that infest the hydrangea plants, drowning them in salt water. She must have waited till now—one-thirty in the morning—because she had been too busy.

My mother often told me that she felt sorry for Mrs. Yamasaki. Her husband, the doctor, was a rich man, and yet he refused to hire a cleaning lady, a cook, or a receptionist for his clinic because he considered all these things to be part of his wife's job. "I can't believe he expects her to slave away like that," Mother said. "Every day she cleans their house and then his clinic next door. Then she works at the clinic, comes home, and cooks for everyone." Because Mrs. Yamasaki came from a poor farming family in northern Japan, she never complained about the hard work. Not only her husband but even Keiko and her two older sisters treated her like a maid— they were always busy with their piano, flower arrangement, and ballet lessons; I never saw them help clear the dishes, set the table, dust the furniture, or anything. Thin and wrinkled, her shoulders stooped, Mrs. Yamasaki looks at least ten years older than her husband, a plump man with a ruddy face. Tonight she will stay up another half hour picking off the slugs, and then she will get up at five or six to start her endless job all over, cooking, cleaning, bookkeeping. I shudder. Being cooped up in my little room and feeling like my grandmother's prisoner is nothing. I would rather die than to live like Mrs. Yamasaki, doing the same chores day in and day out, a slave in my own house.

It dawns on me then that my mother must have thought her life was even worse than Mrs. Yamasaki's. She had to leave our house because life with Father was making her too unhappy to stay alive. She is gone, while Mrs. Yamasaki is still here, slaving away: My mother considered her life to be worse than picking slugs off hydrangea bushes at one-thirty in the morning. I imagine the soft, pink snail bodies squished between my fingers—how horrible it must be to stand in the dark yard, watching them writhe in the salt water. To be worse than that, my mother's life must have been completely unbearable.

Flicking off the light, I lie down on the bed, not even bothering to change my clothes. Small jagged shapes float in the dark before my closed eyes, afterimages of the light. When I was young, I used to think they were

128

like islands floating in the sea, islands full of secret treasures and beautiful birds. Now they remind me of something broken—colored shards of glass or porcelain.

Trying to fall asleep, I think about the girl in my mother's fairy tale, the girl who had to carry the upside-down bowl on her head for years till she met a kind prince. How relieved she must have been to hear the bowl crack and fall away from her face. She must have laughed to see the pieces scatter on the street along with the coins and gems her mother had so carefully stacked on her head. Surely she must have been happy to be rid of the foolish spell after all those years, no matter what else did or didn't happen. Maybe it would have been all right even if the prince had not fallen in love and married her, or if thieves had come and stolen her treasure. She would have been happy just to lose the weight that she had been forced to carry, to feel the wind ruffling her hair and the warm sunlight touching her face.

7
Easter Sunrise

Halfway up the hill to Dr. Mizutani's, I stop and turn around to look at the sea. The water foams dark blue, the color of the indigo vats at the dye shops in Grandfather Kurihara's village. Only in the far east, on the edge of my vision, the small waves glitter under the sun. I wonder if Kiyoshi got up to watch the sunrise alone. Pastor Kato decided not to hold the Easter sunrise service this year because so few of us had attended last year. "I'm going to get up early, watch the sun, and pray," Kiyoshi told me last week. He didn't ask me to come along.

It's a few minutes before ten. At church, Mrs. Kubota must be playing a prelude on the organ, a series of Easter hymns with *hallelujahs* climbing the scale. People are sitting with their eyes closed, heads bowed, reviewing the past week and talking to God in silence about the things that worry them, the things they regret. I can almost see the three or four rows of thin hands clasped tight in prayer. In the front row, Kiyoshi is wondering where I am, but he won't turn his head to check the door even if he hears footsteps. He is too serious and grown-up to fidget in church. Maybe this once, he and Mrs. Kato will assume that I had overslept or been ill. But before the week is out, I will have to tell them so they won't keep looking for me. I have to write to Mother and ask her not to send her letters to their house. That means telling her that I stopped going to church, that I don't believe in God. The thought makes me queasy. The white buildings along the coast remind me of teeth. The blue sea looks cold and rough. I picture my mother sitting up in bed, her back stooped, her hands clasped so tight in prayer that the veins stand out. She will ask God to forgive me for my faithlessness and protect me all the same; she will panic, thinking that I am completely alone now without the Katos, without God.

Last year on Easter, the sun came up while Pastor Kato was reading the passage in the Bible about the two disciples meeting Jesus on the way to Emmaus. Though the disciples walked with him, they had no idea who he was, till a few hours later when Jesus blessed the bread before dinner. Seeing him in this familiar gesture, the disciples suddenly recognized the way he held the bread, the tone of his voice, the expression on his face. At that moment, Jesus vanished; overcome with joy, the disciples rushed back to Jerusalem to tell the others. Standing between my mother and Mrs. Kato in the early morning light, all of us hearing the familiar story one more time, I wanted to believe again. Jesus seemed like an old friend, someone whose gestures and words I, too, would recognize. But as soon as we got home, I changed my mind. When Jesus caught up with them outside Emmaus, the two disciples were very sad about his death. They told him about the crucifixion, believing he was a newcomer who did not know about the tragic event. It seemed unkind of Jesus not to reveal himself right away, to reassure his two friends. Instead, he tested them, waiting to see what they would say, trying to judge the strength of their faith. That was unfair and cruel. The Son of God shouldn't have to spy on his own friends. Thinking back on it now, a year later, I am still angry at the story. I am not sorry that it is Easter again and I am skipping out of church, once and for all. Turning back up the hill, I hurry to Dr. Mizutani's clinic.

Dr. Mizutani has left the door open for me though I am two hours earlier than usual. She is already in the back room of the clinic. As soon as I walk in, I can hear the chirping and peeping noises from the countertop. The doctor puts down the syringe she was holding over a tiny box, the kind strawberries are sold in; the box is set on a heating pad. I get a glimpse of the little heads—smaller than my thumbnail. I can't help recalling the crushed seedlings underneath the camellia tree in my yard, the broken planters beside them. Who am I to help the doctor take care of birds? I couldn't even water my mother's plants.

"You are just in time to feed the baby sparrows," the doctor says, handing me the syringe and pushing a cup of thick brown food—like cold soup—toward me.

The three birds in the box look nothing like sparrows. Eyes bulging out of pink, naked heads, they could be sick frogs that have sprouted a few quills. Dry peeping noises come out of their open mouths as they reach up and flail their bony arms—their wings, I suppose, but right now they are just tiny bones covered with skin. Though these birds are among the ugliest things I have ever seen, something catches in my throat and in my chest. They remind me of very skinny swimmers treading water and crying out for help.

"Don't be afraid to stick the syringe way down their throats," Dr. Mizutani says, guiding my hand. "You need to get the tip past the trachea opening so they don't inhale the food into their lungs."

132

With the tip deep in the first sparrow's mouth, I pump the syringe and pull it out. The bird clamps his mouth shut and swallows, his neck weaving from side to side with effort. A tiny bulge forms along his throat. Through the thin skin, I can see the brown color of the food. The bird opens his mouth again, peeping, while the other two cry out louder.

"Go ahead and feed the others. Then you can come back to that first one and give them another round."

I fill the syringe and stick it into the gaping mouths. The birds keep swallowing the food and opening their mouths again, flailing around, making their hungry noises. Soon, food is bulging out along all their throats, and dark blue veins stand out. I'm afraid of their thin skin bursting open.

"When should I stop?" I ask the doctor, who is making more food in the blender—pellets of cat food and vitamins and water and things that might turn my stomach if I thought about them too much. She spoons the mixture into an ice-cube tray to freeze.

"They'll stop gaping with they're full," she tells me.

"They won't choke or explode?"

"No." She laughs. "Trust me."

I continue to feed the birds, my hands trembling because I can't stop picturing them with their thin necks splitting open like flimsy balloons. After the third round, all three birds close their mouths and slump down. Dr. Mizutani gives me a cotton ball and some warm water to clean their mouths and feathers so the spilled food won't dry on them. In my hand, each bird is warm and bottom-heavy. Their stomachs are completely naked and distended; the thin legs are pink and smaller than flower stems. I change the tissue-paper lining of the strawberry box, put the birds back in, and place the box on the

133

heating pad. In a few minutes, the birds are sleeping, piled up on top of one another.

"Someone brought them yesterday. She found the whole nest fallen from a tree—one dead bird in it and these three. There's something else, too."

Dr. Mizutani leads me to the other corner of the room, where another berry box has been placed on a heating pad. The bird inside this box is larger than the sparrows, though he looks just as naked except for the white down on his back. Eyes closed, the bird continues to sleep, his body heaving up and down with each breath.

"What kind of bird is it?" I ask.

"A Japanese grosbeak, I think. They are much rarer than the tree sparrows. An old woman found this one in the woods, fallen from a nest she couldn't find. She brought him in this morning. He's about the same age as the sparrows but bigger because he's going to grow up to be a bigger bird—if he grows up at all."

The doctor picks up a book from the counter and opens it to a picture of a grayish bird with a black head, a bright yellow beak, and small patches of white and blue on his black wings. It doesn't look anything like the skinny thing in the berry box. When the doctor taps the side of the box with her index finger, the bird wakes up but does not stretch his neck to beg for food. The doctor sighs.

"We need to make a decision. This bird may have a better chance if we put him in with the sparrows for the first week. They're about the same age. Being with them will keep him warm, and it might make him want to open his mouth and eat. But he might grow up thinking he is a sparrow. He could spend the rest of his life wanting to live in a flock of sparrows."

"Will they chase him away?"

"I don't know. He's going to be bigger than they will.

The sparrows might feel threatened and chase him away or even try to kill him. It's also possible that they will accept him—sometimes birds feed or move around in mixed flocks. But I have never seen just one bird in a big flock of another kind. In a way, it isn't right to raise this bird unless we can raise him to live with other grosbeaks. But then again, maybe we should give him the best chance to survive. I want to know what you think about it. I want you to make the decision."

"Why me?" I ask, wishing she hadn't told me all the particulars. If she had simply announced, "We have to keep these birds separated. There is no other way," then I wouldn't have known any better. If the bird dies, I won't be thinking that I should have done something else to keep him alive.

"You have to decide," the doctor says in a low, patient voice, "because you are the one who will feed these birds. I can't give you that responsibility unless you know everything I know. I would be lying to you otherwise, holding back an important truth. I can't do that." She purses her lips and shakes her head. "It wouldn't be fair."

Looking from her to the bird, I know she is right. The bird has gone back to sleep, head slumped down. Just for a moment, I imagine a beautiful gray bird flying in a flock of brown sparrows, all of them chirping happily. But I push that thought away.

"Show me how to feed him," I say. "I'll try my best to make him live."

The doctor nods.

I put the bird in my right palm and pick up the syringe with my left hand. The bird opens his eyes but does not beg for food. He stays limp, except for his tiny feet scratching faintly against my palm. Through the warm, thin skin, I can feel his heartbeat. I open his mouth with my thumb and index finger, just as I had pried open the crow's mouth, only being more careful because the grosbeak is so much smaller. The doctor shows me how to insert the syringe and pump in the food until the bird's neck bulges out. Then I clean him as I did the sparrows, clean the nest, too, and put him back. Dr. Mizutani says nothing, but I know she thinks I am doing a good job, that I have made the right decision.

The crow squawks and hisses when I peel the bandages from his leg.

"He's coming along all right," the doctor says, holding him with her leather gloves and examining his leg. "Last year, I had a black kite whose broken leg got infected. I taped him up and gave him antibiotics, but his leg shriveled up. It looked like a mummy's leg—he could never use any part of it. I had to put the bird down. This crow looks much better."

To be worse than the crow the other bird must have looked pretty bad. The crow has been shedding or picking out his tail feathers until only a few are left. While the doctor holds him, I tape his leg and then put a white envelope around his remaining tail feathers so he cannot pick them out. He looks ridiculous—like a bird made of paper and sticks.

"We'll take off the tape next week and start working with his leg," the doctor says. "He needs some stretching exercises to get that leg working again. But we can put him in an outdoor cage now. Maybe he'll be happier there and won't go on pulling out his own feathers."

Putting the crow back in the pet carrier, we take him down the hallway to the backyard. Though there are no fences between the two yards, anyone can see where her

136

parents' yard ends and hers begins. Theirs has hedges and clusters of low, groomed pines and dwarf yews. A flagstone path winds around the raised beds overflowing with pansies, spring mums, tulips. In the back, there is a little pond surrounded by yellow daffodils. Her yard is nothing like that. Her trees—maples, ash, rhododendrons, cedars—have never been groomed or trimmed. Instead of a lawn, she has wildflowers sprouting everywhere, and about ten bird feeders, several birdbaths, and a few brush piles scattered around the place. Under the tallest maple tree in the back, there are two walk-in cages with their tops covered with a tarp. Each cage is at least half the size of my bedroom.

We bring the crow into one of the cages and let him out of the carrier. The cage has many branches rigged up at different heights, but the crow stays on the ground, pecking at the grass, his head like a hammer going up and down. We fill the water dishes and bring him food: cut-up fruit, pieces of meat, cat food soaked in water.

"I'm going to cut up one of those frozen rats for him," the doctor says, "but only after you're gone." She winks. "He's ready to tackle that. Crows are great scavengers in the wild."

We walk back to the clinic, where I feed the sparrows and the grosbeak again. The doctor shows me how to mix the food in a blender.

"I have another blender, so you can have this one." She begins to fill a big box with everything I might need—syringes, ice-cube trays, a little ice chest for carrying the food. "I'm going to drive you to school and back every day," she says, "so you can bring the birds and feed them. For the first week, you'll have to bring them to your classes and feed them every twenty minutes or half an hour. Will that be a problem?"

I shake my head. I can sit in the back row of the classroom, the heating pads plugged into the wall. Whenever I have to, I will quietly get up to shoot the food down the birds' throats.

"My teachers won't mind," I say. It's true, they won't. Most of them will think I am doing a good thing. Though I have just stopped going to church, stopped being a Christian, I am glad to be going to Christian Girls' Academy. At the public elementary school I attended until sixth grade, my teachers made me stand in the back for talking out of turn or failed me on tests because I forgot to put my name on top, even though I had a perfect score. They never allowed any of us to leave our chairs during class, unless we were really sick. Even then, we had to first raise our hand and ask. That was their idea of discipline. My teachers at Christian Girls' Academy let me do almost anything because I am a good student. They don't stress discipline all the time. The three words they use instead are *freedom*, *respect*, and *love*. We can act on our own free will, they tell us, so long as we respect God and love our neighbors. Except for the God part, that still sounds like a good idea to me.

"Once the birds are a little bigger," the doctor says, "you can take away the heating pad, and you can feed them once an hour."

"You don't mind driving me to school?"

"Of course not. I don't expect you to take the train with birds in boxes. You'll still save me a lot of time and work. It's hard to feed these birds every half hour while I'm trying to look at someone's yapping dog."

I imagine arriving at school every morning in Dr. Mizutani's red truck and meeting her outside the gate at the end of the day. None of my friends gets a ride to school. Even the twelfth graders don't drive to school

138

because only the teachers and the college girls are allowed to park their cars on campus.

"Thank you," I say, starting to smile. "This is going to be great."

On the way back to my house, I ask Dr. Mizutani the question I've been waiting all morning to bring up.

"Do you mind if I ask my mother to send her letters to your clinic instead of to the Katos'?"

She takes her eyes off the road momentarily to look at my face.

"My father doesn't want me to hear from her," I explain, "so she's been sending her letters to the Katos'. It's a secret—a lie, even. In a way, it's wrong."

"I suppose it is," she frowns. "But your father has no right to forbid you to see her, much less to hear from her."

"Will you help me hear from her, by accepting her letters?"

Dr. Mizutani sighs. "What about the Katos?" she asks. "They don't want to keep a secret for you and your mother?"

"They don't mind. But I don't want to ask them because I'm not going to their church anymore. That's why I came earlier today. I stopped going to church. I won't be seeing much of the Katos from now on."

"Do they know that?"

"Not yet. But they'll know soon when I go to tell them. Maybe tonight."

"You decided to stop going to church because—"

"Because I don't believe in God."

We don't speak for a while. In front of my house, the doctor parks the truck and turns off the engine, but neither of us moves.

139

"Do you believe in God?" I ask her.

"No," she says. "I never have."

"Are you a Buddhist?"

"No. I'm nothing." She pauses and then smiles a little. "Maybe you'll laugh, but watching birds fly is about the closest I ever come to belief. When I see a rare bird in the woods—a paradise flycatcher, say, which has a long black tail and blue rings around his eyes—I can almost believe in miracles. I feel blessed to be at the right place at the right time, just to catch a glimpse. But even common birds make me happy. I love the black spots on the tree sparrows' cheeks and the white bars on their wings. Each bird is so beautiful and perfect. That makes me believe in something, though I'm not really sure what. I believe in everything and nothing, in a way."

I remember the waxwing flying out of our pet carrier in the woods, swirling up into the air and disappearing among the trees. "I think I know what you mean."

"You do? My father thinks I'm crazy when I say that birds are my religion. He and my mother are Buddhists. They believe they'll join the ancestral spirits when they die. They'll never tell me this, but I think they are sad because when they join the spirits, there won't be anyone for them to watch over." Though she tries to smile, a sigh escapes from her lips, and her eyes look sad. "There won't be anyone in my family's family after them—after me. We are the last three. I think that bothers my parents, especially my father, when he thinks of his own death."

"Are you ever afraid of dying?" I ask. "Do you wake up in the middle of the night worried about it?"

She shrugs her shoulders. "Sometimes. Not enough to want to believe in God or Buddha or the ancestral spirits. Besides, people are afraid of dying even if they believe. They are sad to see their friends die even if they be-

140

lieve that the friends are in heaven or with the ancestral spirits or whatever."

I nod. "I know. Both my mother and Mrs. Kato cried at their best friend Mrs. Uchida's funeral though they believe she is with God. They cried almost as much as my friend Toru, Mrs. Uchida's son, who doesn't believe."

The doctor lays her hand on my arm lightly. "I'll be more than happy to have your mother send her letters to my clinic."

"It doesn't bother you that I'm disobeying my father and grandmother and lying to them?"

"No, not really. I only wish you didn't have to lie to them. But maybe that's none of my business."

"Well," I say, "I'm relieved you don't think I'm a big liar or a bad person, somehow."

"Just promise me one thing," she demands, looking into my eyes. "If you decide that you want to see your mother, you'll tell me. You'll ask for my help."

"I will," I assure her, though there is nothing she can do to help me. Even Dr. Mizutani wouldn't be able to get my father or my grandmother to relent. If she tried to talk to them, they would think of her as a pushy woman, the spoiled daughter of a rich family who should mind her own business. She wouldn't get very far trying to persuade my mother, either. Of course, my mother, unlike Father and Grandmother, would understand the doctor's good intentions; still, she would go on believing that I am better off with Father. How can she help it? She is right. She doesn't want me to quit school at fifteen to work in Grandfather's embroidery shop or to go to another house where I might spend my whole day—my whole life—stirring indigo vats, threading looms, or making purses out of loom waste.

* * *

141

Toru is already waiting in the car when I arrive at the parking lot at seven. We drive to a park near his house and sit on the swings. The Emperor's Forest is only a few blocks away. The tops of pine trees rise above the apartment buildings that went up a few years ago while Toru was in Tokyo. I think of all the sparrows and thrushes that must be sleeping in those trees. The sky is completely dark. We have been talking about my baby birds.

"I only have to feed them during the day," I explain. "Except when they're eating, they just sleep. The sparrows sleep piled on top of one another. I feel sorry for the grosbeak. He's all alone in his little box."

"You were always so tenderhearted," Toru says, smiling.

"No, I wasn't," I protest, my cheeks feeling warm.

"Sure you were. Remember how you made me bury my butterfly collection?"

In spite of myself, I shiver at the memory of Toru—he must have been thirteen or fourteen—holding a large yellow butterfly in one hand and a long needle in the other. The butterfly squirmed for a second and then went limp. I had been thinking that it was sick and he was trying to make it well, giving it some medicine with the needle. When I realized what he had done, tears filled my eyes. I cried until he said, "I'm sorry." He showed me the big glass case of the butterflies he had collected, and the two of us went to the backyard to bury them.

"Until that day, I really loved my collection," he said.

I shrug. "I don't see much point in sticking pins into things."

"It wasn't about right or wrong. I just didn't want to see you cry. I liked you too much for that."

In silence, we ride the swings back and forth. Their blossoms gone, the ornamental cherry trees in the park

142

are leafing out. The new leaves make lacy patterns against the white lamplight. Now and then, cars pass on the street in front of the park, their headlights snaking through the dark. Except for that, the neighborhood is completely quiet. When I was younger, on quiet nights like this I used to worry that the Second Coming had already happened and everyone but me had been lifted up to heaven. I would sneak downstairs to peek into my mother's room. She never closed the door all the way, so I would see her sleeping under the covers and be relieved. It wouldn't be so bad, I think now, if everyone else in the world had been lifted up to heaven or onto some spaceship, leaving the two of us here. I continue to move back and forth, dragging my feet now and then to keep from swinging out too far or too fast.

"If I tell you a secret," Toru asks suddenly, "will you keep it to yourself?"

"Of course."

He stops his swing, takes a deep breath, then blurts out, "There's a girl in Tokyo—I think about her a lot."

I pulled hard at my chains, making them squeak. A sick, chilly feeling starts in the pit of my stomach and spreads fast, as if my heart were pumping ice water through me instead of warm blood. In a voice that I scarcely recognize—a tight, polite voice—I ask, "What is her name?"

"Yoshimi," he says. "Yoshimi Sonoda."

The way he stops after her name, he doesn't have to say anything more. He just sits there as though he is watching the sound of her name float around, little glittering stars only he can see. After a while, he smiles at me and says, "In a way, you remind me of her. She is very kind and tenderhearted, but strong, too. And intelligent."

143

I don't say anything.

"She is studying to be a pianist and composer. Her family is well-to-do. After she finishes college next year, they might agree to send her to Europe to study, if they don't decide to marry her off."

A little warmth comes back into my cold hands at the mention of her going to Europe or being married off. But I have never met this girl. I shouldn't be so happy to hear about her going away. I clench my fists around the swing chains, wishing I could get up and walk out of the park— to be alone, at least, to feel miserable in private.

"Yoshimi doesn't know how much I care for her," Toru continues. "She probably thinks we are just great friends. She doesn't know—" He trails off, so I finish the sentence for him, trying to keep my voice level.

"She doesn't know that you are in love with her."

"That's right."

Another car passes by, throwing a net of orange light onto the road.

"You're probably wondering why I haven't told her."

I nod, although I wasn't.

"Just before I left Tokyo, I had a feeling that maybe she liked me, too, that she was waiting for me to say something, to ask her to be my girlfriend. But I couldn't."

"Because you were leaving?"

"Partly. But more than that, I didn't want to stand in her way. She already knows what she wants to do with her life. She's going to be a famous pianist and composer. I don't have any plans for the future. All I have are some goofy ideas about traveling around. Those ideas don't go with how I feel about her. How can I travel all over the world alone and be with her at the same time? It's ridiculous. Some days, I want to spend the rest of my life with Yoshimi, and other days, I daydream about being all alone in some desert. That's how confused I am. So you can see why I couldn't ask her to be my girlfriend. I hate being such a good-for-nothing, confused guy." Toru pauses and sighs. "The last time we saw each other, I put on a happy act about how nice it was for us to be friends. I said we would write to each other, we would read the same books and talk on the phone about them. It wouldn't matter if we never saw each other again, I claimed, because we would still be great friends. I feel sick when I think about the stuff I said to her, all of it dishonest."

"I'm so sorry," I offer. Out of the corner of my eye, I watch him slump down in the swing, a big frown on his face. I want to put my arms around him and tell him that things will work out—that's what he would do for me if I looked like that. But I don't. My gesture would be false, just like the things he must have said to Yoshimi.

"We do write letters and talk on the phone, but we don't say anything serious. What you said last week about your mother's letters reminded me of that." He tries to smile. "Besides, you two have a lot in common. Most pretty girls I know are stuck-up, silly, or nice but boring. You and Yoshimi are different. You are the two most serious, most thoughtful girls I've ever met in my life."

"But I don't think I'm so pretty," I protest. I am not being modest. Sometimes in the mirror, I recognize my mother's large, pretty eyes and long eyelashes, but they peer out at me from under my father's very dark eyebrows. My face, unlike my mother's smooth oval face, is sharp and thin like my father's.

"Yoshimi doesn't, either. She laughed when I told her that she was beautiful."

I'm not laughing, I want to say, but I feel too sad to be making a flippant comment.

"I didn't mean to go on so much about this," Toru apologizes. "I hope you don't think I'm being sappy or pathetic."

"Not at all," I assure him. "You can tell me anything, anytime. I would never think you were sappy or pathetic. You know that." A little more emphasis goes into my voice than I intended, and I have a tight feeling in my throat. All the same I mean every word I say. Every word.

Our drive back to Toru's bar takes us through the neighborhood of the church.

"You should let me off at the Katos' church," I suggest. "I'm going to tell them the truth. I have to say I'm not coming to church anymore. I think I'll do it now."

"I'll go with you."

"No, you won't." My voice sounds determined, almost annoyed. I imagine Toru standing behind me as I stutter my explanations to Pastor and Mrs. Kato. They will think that I am a big coward who can't tell the truth by herself. "I'm going alone," I insist.

Toru shakes his head and laughs. "I'm not going up to their house with you. You don't need my help, I know that. I just want to wait in the car, outside."

"You don't have to do that, either."

"But I want to."

He drives into the church parking lot, turns off the headlights, and cuts the engine. I still want to tell him I'll be all right without him, but as I look out the windshield, I see something that takes up all my attention. Two people are sitting on the bench by the sandbox, directly in front of the car, about twenty yards away. It's the

146

bench where mothers often sit while their children are playing. The two people sitting there now, though, are Kiyoshi and Keiko. They are both staring at us, their necks held stiff and self-righteous.

"I'll be right back," I say to Toru and get out.

The rectory is across the yard, to the left. Instead of veering that way, I walk straight ahead to the bench.

"So who's the boy?" Keiko asks. She doesn't use the giggly voice in which she talked about boys when we were friends. "Who's the friend you go driving around with in the dark?" she demands, sounding icy.

Now that I am standing before them, Kiyoshi looks down and stares at his own shoes, the same brown oxfords he's worn for years with his church clothes. Keiko is dressed in a different way from two or three weeks ago. Instead of a thin dress or tight skirt, she is wearing a long, pleated black skirt, a starched white blouse, and a gray cashmere sweater.

"That's Toru Uchida," I tell her. "Kiyoshi knows him, too. We all grew up together."

I expect Kiyoshi to look up and nod, however begrudgingly, to acknowledge that this is so. But instead, he turns sideways and seems to be examining the slide a few feet away.

"I don't think it's ladylike or wise to be driving around with an older boy like that, do you?" Keiko asks.

"Oh, come on," I say, disgusted. "We were just talking. No different from the two of you sitting here."

Keiko sucks in a short breath and spits out, "How dare you?" She screws up her face, making the same sour face my grandmother often makes. "We were sitting here after our Bible study class, talking about the Holy Spirit. I bet you weren't doing that. You want to tell us what you talked about?"

147

What we talked about is Toru's secret. "I can't tell you," I announce.

That's the moment Kiyoshi turns his head and looks at me. Suspicion and disappointment are written all over his hard-set face.

"It's not what you think," I say, my cheeks turning hot.

"And what is *that*?" Keiko taunts in the same sticky-sweet voice she used as a child when we fought. "What do you think we suspect?"

As Keiko stares at me and Kiyoshi turns away, I begin to worry about Toru. He is directly behind me; I can almost feel his eyes on my back. He must guess that Keiko is taunting me and that Kiyoshi is snubbing me, trying to hurt me with his silence as if I were too lowly for words. What's to stop Toru from coming out of the car and yelling at them? When we were kids, I could beat either Kiyoshi or Takashi in a fair fight, one against one, but sometimes the two of them would gang up on me and pull my hair or kick sand in my face. Toru always came running to my rescue, shaking his fists and shouting to scare them. That was all right then. But I don't want him doing anything like that now.

"This discussion is stupid," I spit out at Keiko and Kiyoshi. Without waiting, I swing around and run to the rectory.

Running up the steps and pushing open the door, which is never locked, I stand panting in the Katos' kitchen, where the pastor and Mrs. Kato are drinking tea. He smiles and nods as if he hadn't noticed my absence from church or Bible study. Maybe he hasn't, or he has forgotten about it already. But I can tell that Mrs. Kato has been worrying about me.

"Megumi." She calls my name, getting up from the

148

table and walking toward me in her gray wool dress. She puts her arms around my shoulders. "Are you all right? You look terrible."

Standing there, trying to catch my breath, I suddenly want to hug her, cling to her even. She will hold me and comfort me. Assuming that I am upset about my mother, she won't ask me any questions, and I won't ever have to tell her that I don't believe in God. Next Sunday I can come back to church and go on pretending as before. It would be so easy.

But I can't do that. I have already made up my mind and have told Dr. Mizutani and Toru. I should have told the truth a long time ago. So I step back, lightly shaking off her arms.

"I can't come to church anymore," I announce, trying to sound calm. "I don't believe in God."

Pastor Kato puts down the teacup and stares at me with his mouth open. That doesn't bother me so much. What gets to me is the expression on Mrs. Kato's face: Her kind, broad face crumples up with worry and hurt. Then she takes a deep breath. After that, her face is full of sadness and pity—she has the look all our mothers had when we were kids and one of us had been hurt while playing. She reaches out toward me just as she did back then, as if to say, "There, let me look at that cut. Let me make it better." Without thinking, I raise my hand and put it in front of my face, in the small space between her and me, warding off her kindness. Immediately the hurt look comes back into her face, and her eyes widen. I can't bear to see that. Taking two steps backward and then spinning around, I run down the steps without even closing the door.

Sprinting down cross the churchyard, I tumble into Toru's car and start bawling. Toru leans forward and

149

holds me while I sob onto the shoulder of his white shirt. He keeps patting my back and telling me that everything is all right, though we both know that nothing is all right. Finally, when I stop crying, he rummages in the glove compartment and pulls out a flat box of tissues. The box looks beat up, its colors faded as though it was very old. As he sits holding out a piece of pink tissue, the thought comes to me that I am not the first girl to cry in his car. I know that Yoshimi Sonoda has cried sitting in this very seat, maybe the first time he told her that he planned to leave Tokyo. He must have shrugged and smiled and tried to console her, just as he is trying to console me. This thought makes me want to cry again, but I don't. In a way, it's also ridiculous. Everything is. I look up out the windshield, wondering what Kiyoshi and Keiko would make of the scene—but they are gone.

"It was very hard," I say to Toru, trying to keep my voice even. I have to take big, deep breaths between words to swallow the small hiccups and sobs that keep wanting to come back. "But I told the truth," I manage to say.

Nodding, he lays his hand over mine. Even after he starts the car and we leave the church, he drives one-handed, holding my hand in his.

"We're going to drive around for a while before I take you home," he says. "I won't let you go home until you are less upset."

I don't protest or ask him if he will be late getting back to work. We drive around for a long time in silence, watching the old neighborhoods and parks zip past us in the dark. The white streetlamps fly backward, as if we were not moving but everything was peeling back behind us. I don't ask Toru if he really has the time, if his boss will be upset. I don't ask because we know the same truth. For us, home is no place to be when we are upset. We have no one to go home to.

8

By the Fountain

A few steps outside the chapel, my friends Noriko and Mieko are cackling about something they saw on TV last night. They are still talking loudly and laughing as we go down the hallway, through the door to the quadrangle. When our Bible study teacher, Miss Yamabe, comes running after us, the two girls clam up, looking sheepish.

Our teachers often ask Noriko to be quiet, because she bursts out laughing at the wrong time and can't stop, or else she whispers too loudly during class. Noriko is the tallest girl in our class and also the thinnest—not big-boned thin like me but beanpole thin, with sharp elbows and knees. She would stick out in a crowd even if she were a shy, quiet girl instead of the troublemaker she is. Noriko is strong-willed and opinionated enough to tell our teachers that they are unfair or wrong. Last year she stalked out of our math class because the teacher said that all the math and science geniuses in history, except maybe for Madame Curie, had been men. If we attended a public school, Noriko would spend most of her time standing in the back of the classroom or staying after school to write letters of apology. Our teachers just sigh, shake their heads, and ask her to be patient or quiet— they know she is a good student; she always gets the highest math score in our class. Still, it's a little embarrassing to be with her sometimes. I brace myself and wait for Miss Yamabe to scold her and Mieko.

Instead, Miss Yamabe puts her hand on my shoulder and nods for Noriko and Mieko to keep going. All around us, girls are hurrying to their classes. Miss Yamabe and I walk a few steps and stop in front of the fountain in the center of the quadrangle. It isn't much of a fountain. The water bubbles up slowly instead of shooting out in a big spray. The sprinkles scarcely disturb the surface of the small round pond where white lily pads float, a few tiny goldfish swimming among their roots.

"I wanted to talk to you about the service at Pentecost," Miss Yamabe says. "Some of the twelfth-grade girls want to lead the Pentecost service. Maybe you would like to participate, too."

When I say nothing, she goes on. "Two of the girls want to play the piano and sing. Another one said she would read from the Bible. I thought maybe you could give a short talk about what Pentecost means to you. That way, the whole service can be led by students, instead of Pastor Miki or me giving the talk."

"I can't," I say. It's been almost two weeks since I stopped going to church, but I haven't told anyone at school. None of my friends are believers anyway; we all attend the morning chapel because it is mandatory. For most everyone, it's a half hour to stare at their fingernails and show off their good voices when we sing the hymns.

"You don't have to worry about being younger than the other girls," Miss Yamabe says. "You are an excellent writer. I'd like you to give the talk." She shifts her weight from one foot to the other. She is shorter than most of us, and plump. The brown suit she is wearing makes her look like an overstuffed koala bear. Her shoes could be a child's—beat-up brown penny loafers at least

153

a size smaller than mine. I have always gotten mad at my friends for making fun of her behind her back, implying that she is religious because she is an old maid with no one else to love, nothing else to believe in. All the same, I myself have never liked talking to her; I hate the way she trains her beady eyes on me and sighs, standing a little too close. I want to take a few steps backward to get away from those eyes. With my back to the fountain, I can't, unless I want to fall into the water.

I look around, hoping to find help. But by now the quadrangle is deserted. All the students and teachers have gone to their classes. The bell will ring in a few minutes.

"Think about it," Miss Yamabe says, patting my shoulder. "Come see me during lunch break, and we'll talk some more."

I nod and then bolt away.

Inside our first-hour classroom, Noriko has saved me a seat by the wall, next to the birds in their pet carriers. Having left their nest two days ago, the sparrows are hopping around inside the carrier, perching on the twigs and branches I have rigged up. One of them is pecking at the seeds scattered on the bottom of the cage, though he is just picking them up and dropping them, not really eating. All three peep and hop toward me as soon as I open the door and hold out the syringe. They open up their mouths and gobble up the food, fluttering their wings the whole time. They are fully feathered now; their backs are brown and their bellies are streaked white and brown.

Nobody pays much attention while I feed them. Two weeks ago, when I first brought them to school, a few girls wanted to see them up close, but many thought they were scrawny and ugly. "Oh, I don't want to see them.

They give me the creeps," one said. She ran away shrieking when I took the grosbeak out of his nest to feed him. "Don't let me see that thing," she screamed. She is one of the many girls at school who cower at the slightest things—a spider crawling on the floor, a gust rattling the windowpane, even the loud noise a soda can makes as it drops from the chute inside the soda machine. These jumpy girls are not my friends. I like the girls who are proud of being bright and funny, even if they are sometimes too loud, like Noriko.

Mr. Okada, our Japanese literature teacher, comes in while I am feeding the grosbeak. He nods to me and starts the class while I pry open the bird's beak and cram the syringe inside. Unlike the sparrows, the grosbeak spends his day slumped inside the nest, sleeping with his head down. He, too, has grown bigger and is now covered with gray feathers, but he does not stand up in the nest or preen his feathers the way the sparrows did before they hopped out. He has never peeped or clamored for food. All I have ever heard from him is a dry, scratchy whistle. Sometimes I feel as though I am simply torturing him, that I should let him die if that's what he wants. Still, I keep stuffing food inside him and cleaning him up, putting him gently back inside the nest to rest.

Mr. Okada is talking about Sei Sho Nagon, the twelfth-century essayist we have been reading for the last two weeks. He asks one of the girls in the front row to read aloud from today's essay, in which Sei Sho Nagon goes on about good manners and bad manners, about how wide the window of the palace should be opened to capture the best view of the snow-covered mountains; she makes lists of things that are in good taste and those that are in bad taste. Noriko passes me a note. It is a caricature of Mr. Okada. She has made his plaid tie look

155

bigger and drawn arrows over it. "Bad taste," she has written on the bottom. I almost start laughing, because Noriko is right—Sei Sho Nagon would surely have included his tie on the list of things that are in bad taste. I wonder why our male teachers can never dress right: Mr. Okada's ties and socks are always wrong for his outfits; our math teacher, Mr. Shimoda, wears his gray winter coat in June because he has never thought to buy a raincoat for summer; and Mr. Sugimoto, the biology teacher, often wears his rugby shirt inside out, with the tag sticking out and the seams showing. Noriko has a big collection of caricatures, showing the teachers' various mismatched outfits. It's too bad, I think on the verge of laughter, that Noriko can't ride in a time machine and travel back to the twelfth century to meet Sei Sho Nagon—the two of them could have written an encyclopedia of bad taste. But my laughter evaporates when I think about how I will have to visit Miss Yamabe during lunch, to tell her that I have lost my faith.

On the wall of Miss Yamabe's office behind her desk there is a large black-and-white photograph taken in 1944. It shows fifteen young girls in white dresses, and two teachers, both women, in dark suits—all of them seated in a semicircle around the fountain in the quadrangle. They were the middle school and high school girls who met for morning services even after the government had banned Christian Girls' Academy from holding them. Back then Christianity was considered American and therefore unpatriotic; at public schools, they held *shinto* ceremonies every morning before classes, worshipping the Emperor. Anyone who belonged to a church was suspected of being a spy.

In spite of the ban, the fifteen girls at Christian Acad-

156

emy met every morning in the chapel with the president and the Bible study teacher, Miss Fujimoto. They gathered, read from the Bible, sang hymns, and prayed for peace. Miss Fujimoto—who still goes to the Katos' church—was thrown into jail for two weeks and released after her family had paid a fine. She went right back to meeting with the girls and praying for peace. When she retired in 1960, she left the photograph on her office wall, passing it on to Miss Yamabe.

But I knew this photograph long before I came to school here. Mrs. Kato, Mrs. Uchida, and my mother all had smaller copies of it in their albums. Ever since I was six or seven, I have been able to point them out in the photograph, each looking unmistakably like herself, though younger. My mother is seated at the very center, her long hair framing her perfectly oval face, her large eyes staring right at the viewer as if to say "Come and arrest us all; we are ready." She is the prettiest girl in the picture, except maybe for Mrs. Uchida, who is second from the right—a willowy girl with a pageboy haircut, a thin chiseled face, narrow but long eyes. Mrs. Kato, who is seated next to my mother, has her hair in thick, long braids. Her face is sensible and determined-looking, her square jaw set hard. Anyone can tell that she was the leader, destined to marry a minister and to carry on her faith. The girls are about the age I am now. I wonder what we would look like—Noriko, Mieko, and me—in white dresses seated by the fountain. In twenty years, would someone know that Noriko was the quick-tempered, funny girl and a math whiz, Mieko was a reliable and kind person, and me—what would they say about me, a girl who fed baby birds in her class, a girl who lost her faith? What would show on my face?

Miss Yamabe motions for me to sit down. I take a

chair across the big desk from her so that I am facing the photograph and Miss Yamabe has her back to it. She knows that one of the women is my mother, who no longer lives with my father and me.

"So have you thought about it?" she asks me in a cheerful voice.

I nod.

She tilts her head and waits for me to go on.

"I can't," I say. "I can't give a speech about Pentecost, Miss Yamabe, because I don't believe in God."

Miss Yamabe doesn't say anything for the longest time. She sits there, her face completely blank, as if she is trying to hide her shock. Maybe she is wishing that I am playing some stupid joke on her.

"I am not joking," I tell her. "I have lost my faith." I look down, avoiding the eyes of the girls in the photograph.

"Is this—" Miss Yamabe falters. "Is it because of your mother?"

I don't answer.

"I know it's none of my business. I only want to know because maybe I could help."

How could she help me? I am not sick or poor or in trouble. I don't want to be helped in the way she means, which is to have my faith back. But I can't tell her that. It would be rude.

"It isn't because of my mother," I reply, "or any one thing." There is nothing more to say, so I rise from my chair. In the photograph, Mrs. Uchida's face reminds me of Toru. He has always looked more like his mother than his father. I wish it were already Sunday and I could sit in his car, telling him about my troubles, including this one. If I told him that Miss Yamabe looked like a koala bear, he would laugh, and that would make me feel better. "Megumi," he would say, "I don't know anyone quite like you. You are so funny." I won't mind about his being in love with someone else. At least I'm the only person who knows about it, the only person he has trusted with his secret. If I'm not his girlfriend, I am still his best friend, and that is important. Sitting in his car, I would feel our words filling up the empty space in the dark, our good thoughts about each other floating in the small distance between us. But it is only Friday, and I am in Miss Yamabe's office, having given her the shock of her semester or even the whole school year.

I turn my back to her and head for the door.

"Wait," she calls me back.

I turn around.

"I want you to give it a chance," she says. "I don't want you to give up on faith."

I stand there saying nothing.

"Everyone has moments of doubt," Miss Yamabe explains. "Especially at your age, there are all kinds of things that seem confusing, that make you doubt God's existence. I can imagine."

I nod, being polite.

"I was lucky," she continues. "I came to faith much later in life, in my twenties. I haven't been tested very much. All the same, I understand. There are moments when nothing seems fair, and a person starts questioning God."

"Miss Yamabe," I say, "it's more than just moments."

She nods vigorously. "Of course. Of course you wouldn't base an important decision on a few moments of doubt. You are smarter than that, I know. Even so, you might change your mind again someday. Isn't that possible? God may make things clear to you. Don't you think so?"

I don't. How can God make things clear to me when he doesn't even exist? The first few days after I quit going to church, I was half-waiting for something to happen—I thought God might kill all my baby birds or make me fall down the stairs, to punish me. Nothing happened. Now more than ever I know that he doesn't exist, just as I know that my grandmother Kurihara is really dead. Right after she died, because she lived far away and I did not see her more than once a year, I kept on feeling as if she were still around and I could call her on the telephone. I would see something, a certain kind of pottery or kimono, and think, *Grandmother would like that*, and then have to remind myself that she was dead. But after a while I got used to the idea. I knew it to be true. It's the same way with God. There are times when I think he's around, too, but then I realize, as clearly as I know about Grandmother, that this is not so. What is the good of explaining such a thing to Miss Yamabe? She means well. She is worried about me—just like Mrs. Kato, who came to school the day after I told her and left a note taped to my locker. In the note, Mrs. Kato said that she loved me and that I could come to her house anytime, whether I believed in God or not.

I try to smile at Miss Yamabe. "I suppose it's possible that I will change my mind," I tell her. It isn't a lie, exactly. It *is* possible, like being hit by lightning on a clear day or winning an overseas trip in a raffle—not at all likely, but all the same, not impossible.

"Good," she says. "You will come and talk to me anytime you want to talk about your faith, won't you? I only want to help."

The way she looks at me, her beady eyes shining earnestly, I want to run away. Still, I say, "Of course, Miss Yamabe. Thank you." When she says nothing

160

more, I open the door, step out, and close it behind me very quietly. But as soon as I am a few steps down the hallway, I sprint to my fifth-hour classroom.

In the classroom, a girl named Reiko is talking to Mieko and Noriko. My two friends glance at me when I come in; their faces look worried. I haven't told them why Miss Yamabe wanted to see me. I shrug and smile, letting them know that I am all right, while Reiko goes right on talking. After feeding the birds and then sitting down, I listen to her story about the boy she sees on the train every morning.

"I think about him all the time," Reiko says, turning to Mieko to smile. "I know he goes to your brother's school because he wears the same uniform. All your brother has to do is to ride on the same train just once. Then I'll know his name."

Mieko sighs. "How am I going to explain that to my brother? If I say 'Please ride on the train with me so you can tell me the name of the boy who always stands by the door. My friend has a crush on him,' my brother will think that I have a crush on him myself and am using you as an excuse."

"But I can't come and explain anything to your brother. I don't know him. He's your brother, not mine."

"Are you going to ride on the train with them?" Noriko asks.

"No," Reiko shrieks. "On Monday, I'll quietly point out the boy to Mieko. Then on Tuesday, she can ask her brother. I'll take a different train. I would die of embarrassment if *he* noticed me pointing him out to another boy."

Mieko shakes her head. "There is no guarantee that my

161

brother knows this boy." She takes a deep breath, puffs out her round cheeks, and slowly blows out the air.

"But he can find out," Reiko insists. "Once he sees which boy I mean, he can ask around if he doesn't already know him."

"Great," Mieko says. "You want my brother to go around asking about some boy—saying to his friends, 'My sister's friend has a crush on this boy, and I was wondering what his name is—' "

Noriko bursts out laughing, her whole beanpole body shaking.

"It's not funny," Reiko pouts. "What would you do if you were in my position, Mieko? If I had a brother who might know a boy you had a crush on, wouldn't you ask me?"

Mieko is stumped, because she is kindhearted. Furrowing her forehead, she thinks hard, her little button-mouth scrunched. I know she will go home and ask her brother, who will tease her about it for a long time.

"But Mieko would never have a crush on a boy she only sees on the train," I suggest. "Not everyone is like you."

Reiko turns to me with a big frown.

"It's true," I insist. "I don't see how you could really like this boy when you've never talked to him. You have no idea what kind of person he is. All you know is what he looks like."

"I can tell by seeing him every morning. He is intelligent and considerate. I know it."

"How? Just by the way he stands next to the door? That's ridiculous." Out of the corner of my eye, I see Noriko making a face—her lips drawn down and eyes rolled up. *Now you've gotten her started*, she is trying to caution me. *Shut up before it's too late.*

162

But it's already too late. Reiko taunts, "What do you know, Megumi? You've never had a boyfriend."

"So what? That doesn't mean I don't know what is reasonable and what is not. It isn't reasonable to like someone you don't know. I don't like half the people I know. I can't imagine liking—much less falling in love with—people I don't even know."

"You can't imagine falling in love because you're just a kid," Reiko says.

"We are the same age," I point out. "I'm no more a kid than you are."

"Age has nothing to do with it. I consider you childish because you've never had a date. You've never liked a boy, and no boy has ever liked you. That makes you a kid."

"You don't know anything," I snap back. "My best friend is a boy—a boy I grew up with." I stop, realizing that I mean Toru. Six months ago, I would have said the exact same thing and meant Kiyoshi. It would have been a statement of something obvious, just like saying "Today is Friday." I wouldn't have felt the sudden rush of worry and happiness I feel now, mentioning Toru even though I haven't said his name. I'm staring into the air the same way Toru did after saying Yoshimi's name in the park, telling me about his secret love. So much has changed since six months ago, when Kiyoshi was my best friend. I pity Reiko for thinking that I am just a kid, when she is herself a silly girl who has a crush on a stranger. Instead of saying anything more, I shrug my shoulders.

"If Megumi doesn't have a boyfriend, it's not because she can't have one," Sayuri, a girl who's been listening, chimes in. "My older brother saw our class picture from last year and pointed her out. 'That's the best-looking

163

girl in your class,' he said. 'If she weren't so young, I'd want to date her.' "

"Your brother said that?" another girl asks, immediately beginning to giggle.

Reiko shakes her head and gets up to find a different seat. I wish Sayuri hadn't said anything about her brother, though she was only trying to defend me. I don't like the idea of some strange boy picking me out of the class picture, his fingernail hovering over my face.

The bell rings, and Mrs. Fukushima, our writing teacher, comes in.

"I have an announcement," she says. "We've read all the essays that were turned in for the time capsule contest. Somebody from this class is one of the ten finalists. The other nine girls are in eleventh and twelfth grades." The way she looks right at me, I know what she is going to say. All the same, my heart beats a little faster as she continues, "Megumi, congratulations."

Mieko reaches across the aisle to ruffle my hair; Noriko, who is behind me, pats my back. Everyone applauds, even Reiko. Mrs. Fukushima explains the next stage of the contest—an outside judge will be invited to read the ten essays. I am happy for a while but I know I won't win. My essay was all about myself, my family, my mother's going away. I'm sure the judge will think it too personal, just like everyone except Dr. Mizutani's father thought my peace essay was. So I don't dwell on the contest. Instead, I begin to feel bad about having spoken so angrily about Reiko's crush. If Reiko wants to fall in love with a perfect stranger, it is her business. Why did I have to get so mad at her for that? Why didn't I just keep my mouth shut? Even if someone is being silly, my mother used to tell me, I shouldn't go out of my way to point it out and hurt their feelings—because being silly, unlike being inconsiderate or unkind, is harmless. I guess she was right. I wish I had said nothing at all.

Dr. Mizutani is waiting in her red truck in the parking lot. I wave good-bye to Mieko and Noriko, put the birds in the truck, and then climb in.

"The sparrows look wonderful," she says, peering in at them. "In a few days, if the weather's good, we can put them in the outdoor cage. They can practice flying and eating on their own."

"With that crow?"

"No, in the other cage. That crow is a little too big and mean for them. Most birds get along fine with each other, but I don't trust him. Maybe we can let him go in a week or two, anyway. His leg is almost completely healed."

We have been working with the crow, getting him to grasp our fingers with his toes and slowly bending and stretching the hurt leg, which is a little thinner than the other one. His tail feathers are growing back uneven and scruffy but getting longer all the same.

"That crow will be all right," Dr. Mizutani says.

"Not like this bird," I point to the pet carrier that holds the grosbeak.

"Don't take it to heart, Megumi," the doctor says. "You've kept him alive this long. That's quite an accomplishment, even if he doesn't live to leave the nest." She smiles. "Besides, he might still make it. He may be a little younger than the sparrows; not all birds develop at the same rate."

"Like people?" I ask, remembering how Reiko called me a kid because I have never had a boyfriend.

"I guess," she says. "Though with birds it has something to do with species or seasons. Sparrows usually have several hatchings through the summer. These babies," she says, pointing at the sparrows' carrier, "are probably from the very first brood. They'll take a long time learning to fly and eat, compared to the birds born later in the summer. The later birds grow up much quicker."

"Because they know there's less time left before fall?"

"Maybe. Or else the mothers lay better eggs because by late in the summer they've been eating better food. I don't know." She laughs. "I want to think it's because of the mothers. With most birds, the fathers look better, so I want the mothers to be important in another way."

As we drive onto the highway, I tell her about my fight with Reiko. "I don't know why I was so bothered by her stupid crush. It's none of my business. But she made me so mad; she was so silly."

Dr. Mizutani shakes her head. "That's the curse of being an intelligent woman, Megumi. You can't stand silly women." She shrugs, her mouth turned down at the corners. "I used to be the same way—still am. I can't stand to see women being giggly and stupid and incompetent. It burns me up. I feel like saying to everyone, 'All right. What you see before you is a very foolish woman. But please, please pay attention. We are not all like that. Some of us are intelligent, me for instance. I would never giggle in front of you like that. Please make note of it.' I could go on forever like that."

I remember walking downtown with Keiko, who kept giggling, whispering, and playing with her hair. What Dr. Mizutani says is true—I didn't want everyone to think I was like Keiko.

"I think I lost a friend a few years ago because she started acting silly. I couldn't stand it. I couldn't forgive her."

"I understand." The doctor nods. "I know all about

that. When we were in college, most of my friends started pretending to be frivolous and dumb. School was too difficult, they said; they were tired of studying. They skipped college classes to take cooking lessons and to go out on dates. One by one, they got engaged and stopped coming to school. They were busy buying clothes and planning their weddings—they did just enough work to squeak through the last classes. I felt quite out of place, my nose buried in science books. I had no interest in getting married back then. I wanted to be a famous scientist, not someone's wife." She falls silent and concentrates on the road, a deep frown between her eyebrows.

I watch her serious face and wonder what happened to those friends. Did Dr. Mizutani have to stop being friends with them, as I had to with Keiko? But Keiko is just one person. To have no friends from school is something different. Though my mother was always cordial to the neighborhood women, she would never have confided in them the way she did in Mrs. Kato and Mrs. Uchida. Nobody my mother met later could take the place of the women she had grown up with. Watching Dr. Mizutani drive, I wonder if she has any special friends.

On Sunday after I come back from Dr. Mizutani's clinic I open the first letter my mother has sent me there. The sparrows are still with me because it has been raining for the last few days. Before I unfold the letter, I pull open the door of their pet carrier. Hesitating for only a second, the sparrows fly out and circle the room, their wings making whirring noises like windup toys. While I read the letter, they flit around from wall to wall and perch on the windowsill just as the waxwing used to.

167

Dear Megumi:

I am glad to hear that you are well. I am sending this letter to Dr. Mizutani's office, as you requested.

I hope you will visit the Katos now and then, even if you have decided—for now—not to go to church. Mrs. Kato is worried about you. She would like to see you regardless of your feelings about church or God. Back in January when she drove me here, she promised to watch over you, to do anything for you. Please go and see her from time to time. It would make both you and her feel better. And Kiyoshi, too. You two have been close friends all your lives. It would be a shame to lose your friendship.

As for you not going to church—Megumi, I wish I were there to talk to you. Not because I want to change your mind or convince you of God's existence and love, but because a person who is grappling with doubt needs a friend. Yuko Uchida's death tried my faith very much, too. If Mrs. Kato and I hadn't been able to talk to each other, we might have lost our hope and faith. We were fortunate to be friends with each other, and also to see how Yuko herself never doubted God's kindness. She showed great courage in the face of death, in the uncertainty of having to leave her two children.

Megumi, if you will let me, I will pray for you. More than anything else, I hope that God will comfort you and give you happiness, though I also pray, of course, that your faith will be restored. Perhaps this is wrong of me, but I would rather that you be happy, even more than that you believe in God. I know Mrs. Kato feels the same way. Both she and I will love you always, regardless of your feelings about God.

My father sends his love. As you know, the anniversary of my mother's death is in two weeks. It's hard to believe that she has been gone three years now. My father plans to invite my mother's two sisters, their children, and a few of the neighbors for a small gathering to remember her.

Take good care of yourself. Please write soon. I miss you.

Your mother, Chie

Reading the letter the first time, I am relieved that my mother sounds much less upset than I expected. But as I read it twice, three times, I am not so sure. How do I know that what she says is what she really feels? Maybe she is very upset but is not telling me, pretending to be calm and reasonable, as she often does. Besides, even if she were sincere, I don't know what she means by wishing me happiness more than faith. If she really believed in God, if she thought believing in Jesus was the only righteous way to live and go to heaven, shouldn't she want me to have faith more than happiness? After all, Jesus always told the disciples that those who believe in him will be persecuted, poor, or unhappy in this life. Shouldn't my mother want me to be unhappy and faithful?

Folding the letter, I put it away in my desk drawer. Words are cheap. It's easy for Mother to wish in a letter for my happiness. If she really thinks that I shouldn't be alone in my time of doubt, why doesn't she demand to see me? If I were sick and dying, surely she would ask my father to make an exception, to let her see me. Isn't my loss of faith just as serious as being sick—at least for her, who still believes? Isn't that a reason for her to talk to me in person? Instead, all she says is that I should visit

169

Mrs. Kato, as though visiting one or another were the same thing.

On the windowsill, the three sparrows are crying out for food. I get up to feed them with the syringe and then pick them off the sill with my hands. When all three are inside the carrier, I take out the grosbeak, pry open his beak, and pump in the food that keeps him alive against his intentions.

In the evening, sitting in the car with Toru, I keep thinking about his mother. She didn't lose her faith even while she was dying and leaving behind her children. Maybe her faith gave comfort to my mother and Mrs. Kato, but to me, her believing is the saddest part of it all. She died believing in a kind God who didn't even exist.

The raindrops collect on the windshield and then trail down like silver tears. We are in the park near Toru's house, the same place as last week and the week before. The rain keeps us from getting out this time. The small space inside the car is like the inside of a tent in a storm, dry and safe. I start thinking about all those desert-island questions. If you were going to be shipwrecked on a desert island, which one book would you bring, which one record would you want to hear over and over for the rest of your life, which one person would you want to live with? Maybe Toru would be that one person for me, but I know I wouldn't be for him. He would choose Yoshimi Sonoda. If she couldn't be with him, he might even ask for his brother before me. But that's all right, I tell myself. If I could have any wish granted in the world, it might be to have Toru talk about me the way he does about Yoshimi. But I am determined to get over feeling that way about him so I can still be his best friend—the person he might choose after Yoshimi, after his brother.

Those desert-island questions are stupid anyway. In real life, most people would bring a how-to book about building tools and shelters rather than the Bible, or the *Tale of Genji*, or the complete Shakespeare, or whatever they say. Most people would not want to spend the rest of their lives seeing only one other person, either. Given the choice between that and being completely alone, people might even choose the latter.

"I got a letter from Yoshimi," Toru says, staring into the windshield.

"What does she say?" I ask.

"She told me that one of our friends, Michio, is going to paint houses this summer. He wants a partner."

In silence, I watch the raindrops trailing off.

"Yoshimi thought I should write to Michio or call him and ask him if I could be his partner. I can probably get a place to stay for the summer."

"That's good," I manage, sounding blank and stupid. "Will you go?"

"I don't know." He turns sideways in his seat to face me. "I can't decide what she means by inviting me. Is she telling me to work with Michio so I can spend the summer in Tokyo and we can see each other? Or is she just thinking that I must need a job?"

"She must want to see you."

"How do you know?"

"I'm sure she loves you. How can she not?" My voice trails off weakly, and suddenly there is absolute silence in the car. In the dark, small space, we can almost hear each other breathing. Toru is looking straight at me. Something comes into his eyes—an understanding, a kindness, but I'm not sure. I might be imagining it.

"Megumi," he says, his voice softer than usual. He leans forward a little, as if to touch me.

I don't let him. I pull back toward the passenger's door and shrug, almost knocking my shoulder against the window. "Look at it this way," I say in the chattiest, most reasonable voice I can manage. "You are an intelligent and considerate person. You are fun to talk to, and thoughtful. Most of the girls in my class would have the biggest crush on you. I would, too, if we hadn't grown up together. So why would Yoshimi be different? You said she is an intelligent girl. Well, she is bound to see your good points."

Toru tilts his head and smiles. The concerned look is gone from his eyes.

"Anyway," I add, talking fast and businesslike, "it doesn't matter if she is just telling you about the job out of friendly concern. Once you are in Tokyo, you'll be able to see her and decide for yourself how she really feels." Taking a deep breath, I smile—feeling terrible, but better in a way, too. As my mother taught me a long time ago, if you keep doing the right thing even if you don't really feel like it, you'll soon begin to feel right about it, too. When Kiyoshi and I used to fight, my mother convinced me to apologize to him even if I was still mad, even if I thought the fight was as much his fault as mine. I would grit my teeth and say, "Listen, I'm sorry," and then, seeing the relieved look in his eyes, I would feel genuinely forgiving. What I'm doing now is no different.

"You should go," I tell Toru. "You know she wants to see you."

"But I don't know what I should do if she *does* like me. I still don't want to stand in her way. I haven't given up my dream of traveling around the world by myself. So I might not tell her how I feel after all."

I shrug. "Maybe you will and maybe you won't. You

172

can decide when the time comes. After spending the summer with her, you'll have a clearer idea. No matter how it turns out, it would be better than wondering about her from far away."

He nods slowly. "I guess you are right," he says. "I should give Michio a call."

"If you don't," I continue, "you will always wonder what might have happened if you had called him." I smile encouragingly, in spite of the cold, sinking feeling in my chest. I try not to think of the summer I have been envisioning—the two of us walking on the beach at night, talking and laughing while the waves crash in.

When we drive by the church on our way up the hill, I notice the light on at the rectory. Keiko and Kiyoshi would not be sitting in the playground, in the rain. Maybe she is inside the rectory, drinking tea with his family and asking Pastor Kato questions about the things he said at the Bible study meeting. I picture her in a white blouse and a dark skirt, with a lacy cardigan buttoned up to her throat. She would smile in such a pretty and earnest way at the pastor. When she laughs, she would cover her mouth delicately with her hand so that even Mrs. Kato would think what a nice girl she is.

Toru lets me off a block away from my house, and I walk back, holding my umbrella above my head. At the Yamasakis' house, Keiko's window is dark, so I know she must still be at church. I'm angry at her, especially when I remember the self-righteous way she berated me last week after not having talked to me for two years, but suddenly, as the cold wind makes my umbrella nearly sway out of my hand, I miss her, too. I miss the days when she and her older sisters played hide-and-seek with me in their house—Keiko and me hiding together in the

173

dark oak cabinets and holding our breath. Their mother always gave us snacks at precisely three o'clock in the afternoon. Every fall, Mrs. Yamasaki's family sent a box of huge pink apples from their farm in northern Japan. They were sweet, juicy apples—nothing like the hard Red Delicious and sour green Granny Smiths we bought at the store. Keiko and I ate the cold, quartered apple slices and drank her favorite drink, lemon tea with just a touch of sugar. Had we continued to be friends, we might have gone to the movies downtown and then stopped for tea afterward—she would have sat bolt upright, curling her fingers just-so around the cup, in that delicate way of hers. It all could have been so different.

In our house, my grandmother is working in the kitchen and my father is away. Because she believes that I have been to church, she does not come out to greet me as I take off my wet shoes in the foyer. Even when I go into the kitchen to say hello, she says nothing; pretending that I am just a speck of dust or an insect, something unworthy of her attention, she continues to wash the wineglasses in the sink. Once a week, she takes all the unused wineglasses out of the cabinets and washes them because she believes that dust gets inside the cabinets. Rinsing them one by one, she stacks them next to the sink; they look like an outcropping of glaciers.

"Can I help you dry them?" I ask, standing behind her. If I tried to be kind to her, maybe I would start feeling that way, at least a little.

She looks at me for a brief second and then turns her back. "No," she says.

"It would be no trouble," I offer.

"You don't dry them the right way," she pronounces.

"Maybe you could show me how."

She shakes her head. "I want you to go upstairs and

take off your wet clothes and hang them up. You must have some studying to do—some homework you didn't finish because you spent your Sunday going to church and helping that spinster doctor up the hill."

What more can I do? I know Grandmother is mad at me for being gone all day, never spending time with her. She must think it's insincere of me to come back late and offer to help her with the dishes, as if I really cared. Maybe she is right—I don't care about her. But that isn't my fault. I wouldn't be trying to avoid her all the time if she were nicer to me.

I turn around and march up to my room. My father is in Hiroshima again. He has not come back even once in the last week. More and more, I think Dr. Mizutani is right. It isn't fair that my mother had to give me up, that she had to go so far away. If my father was going to leave our house and get Grandmother to care for me, *he* could have left in the first place. My mother and I could have stayed here, and he could have given us money, just as he gives Grandmother now.

My grandmother is wrong about one thing—I had finished all my homework on Friday night. Closing the door behind me and turning on the light, I change into my pajamas. While I'm pulling my pajama top over my head, a rustling noise starts up in the corner, where the birds are in their pet carriers. It goes on a few seconds, stops, and then begins again—a dry, scratching sound as though some animal were trying to dig through paper. I finish changing and go to the corner to see.

Inside the carrier, the three sparrows are sleeping, lined up side by side on a branch, their beaks tucked under their wings. It still amazes me how they can sleep perched like that and not fall off. One sparrow opens his eyes for a second and then shuts them again. The rustling noise starts up again.

Afraid to look, I bring the other pet carrier over to my desk and sit down first. I imagine a disaster—the grosbeak flapping around in agony, trying to dig his way through the plastic, or worse still, some other animal, maybe a mouse or a rat, eating his bloody carcass. My heart beating hard, I look in.

The berry box is empty. The bird is perched on the box's edge, his two feet grasping the cardboard. While I watch, he turns his head and slowly runs his beak through his wings. He is preening his feathers, combing them with his beak till every feather and down is aligned exactly the way he wants it. Only then does he turn his head to look forward again, shifting his weight a little. He doesn't want to stay still. Raising his right foot, he leans sideways to scratch his head with his toes; losing his balance, he falls back into the nest. Immediately he crawls back out, his claws digging furiously through the tissue paper. Perched again on the rim of the nest, he leans on his right leg and stretches his left leg backward. His left wing fans out gradually till every feather is spread out. He holds the stretch for a few seconds and brings the left leg forward again. The wing folds up as neatly as a fan. Looking straight at me with his brown eyes, he shakes, ruffles his feathers, and peeps just once.

I am sitting in front of the pet carrier with my mouth wide open. How do I thank a bird for leaving the nest, for not giving up and dying? The first thing tomorrow, I will give him more branches to perch on, scatter seeds and berries in the cage for him to peck at. I watch him for another minute—my grosbeak perched on the nest he has just left, getting ready to sleep on his feet. "Go to sleep," I say to him as I rise to turn off the lights. For just a moment in the dark, with wild birds sleeping only a few feet away from me, I believe that in spite of everything I am happier than I have ever been.

9

Wooden Dolls

In my dream, I am sitting alone in a big drafty house, waiting for my family to arrive. My mother and father, Grandfather Kurihara, and Grandmother Shimizu have all promised to come, but everybody is late. The house is cold. I have been waiting for a long time.

The room is empty except for a big cabinet in the corner. Through its glass door, I can see the four thumb-sized dolls arranged in a row in front of a gray ceramic bowl. Mrs. Uchida, I remember, had a doll her mother had made from scraps of old kimono and her own hair, which she had cut after her husband's death. Mrs. Uchida kept that doll in a glass case with two tiny ceramic bowls—one holding water and the other some grains of rice—because that was how her mother had instructed her to keep the doll, feeding its spirit. Kiyoshi, Takashi, and I used to dare each other to sit alone in the room with the doll. I was the only one who was never afraid, though none of us had reason to be. Unlike Mrs. Uchida's mother, we were Christians. We didn't believe that dolls had spirits.

Standing in front of the cabinet, I realize that the four shrunken figures, though they look nothing like them, are my mother, father, Grandfather Kurihara, and Grandmother Shimizu. They have agreed to be turned into dolls

178

so that I will be spared. The bowl in the back does not contain grains of rice. It holds Grandmother Kurihara's ashes, the only thing left of her.

You didn't have to do this, I say to my family through the glass door. *You are stuck inside a cabinet together, and you never even liked one another.*

The dolls say nothing back to me. Their faces have sad expressions permanently carved in wood. The evil spirit they've bargained with has no intention of keeping its promise. Soon it will find me here. I must make my escape now. Picking up my coat from the floor, I go out the rickety front door. Outside, the ground is shaking from an earthquake. I step carefully, paying attention to the cracks that keep forming all around me.

When I wake up, my face is wet with tears even though I don't remember crying in the dream. The windows are gray with early light. I remember what day it is—the first Sunday in May. Today, my grandfather is holding a small gathering at his house to commemorate the third anniversary of Grandmother Kurihara's death. My mother must be up already, working in the dark and drafty kitchen of their house, preparing tea, rice balls, dumpling soup. I picture her tired face. While steam rises from the kettles on the stove, Mother would roll out a thin floury skin on the cutting board, spread a spoonful of minced herbs and meat, wrap and seal each dumpling with her strong fingers, as carefully as she would an important letter. Thinking about her makes me so lonely.

Grandmother Kurihara has been gone for three years already. The last time I saw her, almost four years ago, I had no idea that I would never see her again. Both of my grandparents were in good health. My mother and I spent our August with them, just as we had done every year.

179

The only thing different about that summer was me—I was irritable with Grandmother even though she was the same as always. All her life, Grandmother Kurihara was a great worrier. Sometimes in the middle of dinner she would turn to my mother or me and insist, "You are getting too thin. Eat more." If we talked to her on the phone and our voices sounded even the tiniest bit wrong, she would ask, "Are you catching a cold? You sound like your throat is sore." Half the time it was just a bad phone connection. Until last year, my mother and I used to laugh about Grandmother's unnecessary worrying; I never thought much about it.

That August, for the first time, I kept snapping at Grandmother. No matter how often I reminded myself that she meant well, I couldn't help shooting her mean looks or ignoring her when she spoke to me. One night near the end of the visit, Grandmother told me to put on a sweater because it was cold in their old house. She reminded me at least ten times, but I refused to get one; shivering from the cold, I continued to read my book. Finally, Grandmother brought her quilted jacket and handed it to me. I didn't accept it. Worse than that, I tossed it clear across the room and screamed at her, "I don't want a jacket. It's August. I'm not cold. I hate your ugly jacket. Why can't you leave me alone?" Grandmother stared at me, her whole face crushed into a big, hurt frown. She didn't say anything. The next moment, even though I was the one who had hurt her, I got up and ran out of the room, pretending that the whole thing was Grandmother's fault. I went to bed in a great sulk. When I apologized in the morning, Grandmother said, "No, you don't have to apologize. I shouldn't have nagged you." Her voice was very quiet, and her eyes looked almost as if she were afraid of me or my temper.

I regretted that incident—and all my mean looks and words—when she died from a stroke the following spring. She had no time to see us, no time to hear how much I loved her in spite of my bad manners and moods. Now I will never be able to tell her about my love or regrets or anything.

Staring at the ceiling above my head, I worry that someday, my mother or Grandfather Kurihara will be gone, too, before I have any time to spend with them. If one of us were to die now, my mother, especially, would not know how much I loved her in spite of my angry words and lukewarm letters. Instead, she would remember the last thing I said to her when we were alone: "You didn't have to lie to me." Unless I see her again face-to-face and tell her something else, those words will be the last words between us. At the time I thought I was telling the truth, but my words have become a terrible secret. I am too ashamed to tell anyone—even Toru, Mieko, or Noriko—that I said such a cruel thing to my mother on our last day together.

I think sometimes that the truth isn't just one thing. On the day my mother left, it was true that she was leaving never to come back and that she had been lying to me about her intentions. But it's also true that I was angry at her and wanted to see her cry. I kept bullying her to be honest with me, not because I believed in honesty or truth as Kiyoshi believes in God, but because I wanted to see my mother lose her composure. I wished she would break down and tell me how sad she was to leave me. I wanted her to say how much she loved me, how hard it would be to live without me. I was trying to make sure that she felt as miserable as I did. That's a truth I didn't know then.

Downstairs, Grandmother Shimizu is beating on her

181

samisen, making angry music at the crack of dawn. If she or my father were to die suddenly, I would not worry about what they thought about me, whether they knew that I loved them. I am not sure myself whether I love them. Even though I behave no better to them than I did to my mother or Grandmother Kurihara, I don't think I would regret anything if they were to die.

Arriving at Dr. Mizutani's later that morning, I walk straight to the outdoor cage in the backyard. The sparrows fly down to a low branch and beg for food, flapping their wings. They have been outside for almost two weeks, eating seeds and fruits from the dishes; even so, they line up to be hand-fed as soon as I come in. Having had their fill, they swirl up to the highest point of the cage and land side by side on a branch. From another corner, the Japanese grosbeak watches me. I put a few dabs of liquid food on a branch not too far from him. Cautiously he hops over and pecks until all the food is gone, eyeing me the whole time. Once in a while he spreads out and closes his wings, balancing himself. The edges of his dark wings flash white.

I refill my syringe while, on the ground, a brown-eared bulbul screeches and hisses. He is opening his mouth wide, as if to say *Hurry up. Feed me.* As soon as I approach him and hold out my hand, he lunges, snapping his beak to bite me. I flinch and pull back—long enough for him to flop backward a few steps and then dash across to the other side of the cage, where he hides behind a log. I have no choice but to corner him and pick him up in my hand while he continues to screech and hiss. He must think I mean to kill him. All the same, he opens his beak at the sight of the syringe. Quickly stuffing the tip into his mouth, I pump in the food and gently drop him to the ground, where he looks dazed, almost satisfied for a moment, before he begins to back away from me, hopping backward and hissing. He is this way every time I feed him.

Dr. Mizutani got him last week; he had been sitting in a fallen nest with another baby. Both birds were already feathered and beginning to stand up in their nest—something they do a few days before they can hop out—so we thought they would have no problem. From the beginning, one of them was mean, snapping at me while I fed him, gaping and hissing at the same time. The other bird was sweet, always peeping at me with a wide-open mouth. I named the mean bird Rie and the nice one Haruko—after my two grandmothers. Maybe that was what jinxed the nicer bird, being named after my dead grandmother. One morning I got up to feed the birds and found him slumped over, his body already stiff, his legs held straight and brittle as two twigs.

"It isn't anything you did," the doctor said, holding the dead bird in her hand. "Baby birds just die sometimes. This one might have had a small infection or maybe he couldn't digest his food. It could have been anything."

"You don't think the other bird killed him?"

"No," she said, turning the bird around, under the lamp. "I don't see any abrasions or cuts."

I didn't tell her about naming them after my grandmothers. That same afternoon, the mean bulbul left his nest and began to hop around. He didn't seem to mind being alone at all.

Dr. Mizutani comes out while I am raking the floor of the cage and refilling the water dishes.

"Good job," she says, coming inside. "Everyone looks good."

Inside the other cage, the crow begins cawing.

183

"We should let him go," the doctor says, pointing in his direction. "He is as ready as he is going to be."

"Where will we take him?"

"We'll just let him out in my yard. I thought about bringing him back to the mountains, near the house where he was found. But it's been a long time. I don't want him to get caught in a trap again or go to those people's house where they were going to kill him."

The crow, who has been pecking at the ground, flies up to a branch as soon as we walk in. His wings make a sound like a heavy coat being dropped on the floor. He caws and eyes us suspiciously, no doubt thinking that we are going to catch him again to hold him and make him stretch his legs. He turns his head sideways and begins to preen his feathers. The leg he broke looks a little thinner than the other, but not much. Dr. Mizutani and I notice it only because we know what happened to him. He isn't favoring that leg anymore. Because he has had plenty of food, he is fat and his wing feathers are glossy. Anyone else would think he was just an ordinary crow—maybe a little ragged around the tail, but sometimes they are like that.

Dr Mizutani picks up his food dish, walks out of the cage, and sets the dish on the ground several yards away. I follow her, propping open the door with an extra branch. We back away to the middle of the yard and sit down at the picnic table, where the doctor eats lunch during spring and summer.

After a while, the crow comes down from the branch and walks around on the ground. He stands in the doorway but does not come out. Instead, he goes back up on a branch. Repeatedly, he flies up and down, forward and sideways, always veering away from the open doorway. It takes him almost ten minutes to figure it out. Finally, he swoops down from a branch and then flies up through the door, flapping his wings hard and circling higher and higher. With great commotion, he flies around the yard a few times and lands in Dr. Mizutani's maple tree.

"He'll probably hang around here for a while," the doctor says, shading her eyes as she peers at the bird. "When you feed the other birds, make sure there's some food in his dish and the birdbaths have water. He'll come back to eat."

The crow is still in the tree, going *kaah, kaaah, kaaah,* when we go inside.

As I turn the corner onto my street, I catch a glimpse of someone coming out of my house. Even from a block away, I recognize Keiko in a long gray dress, her hair put up in a bun. Her back is toward me as she closes the door. Turning around quickly, I retreat around the corner and run down the hill. She wouldn't have seen me or heard me.

What is she doing at my house? I wonder as I slow down to a walk and enter a small park. Sitting on a bench by the drinking fountain, I wait for ten minutes before heading home again.

There is no trace of Keiko when I come back to the house. Going into the foyer, all the same I know that something is wrong. My grandmother is in the kitchen. I hear the pots and pans clattering. Usually she does not make that much noise doing housework. My heart begins to beat faster, and I feel sick to my stomach. For just a moment, I consider going outside again. Maybe Grandmother has not heard me come in. I can still run away. But where would I go? Sooner or later, I will have to come home.

Taking off my shoes, I walk down the hallway to the

kitchen. Grandmother stops the water and begins to dry her hands. Even after her hands are dry, she keeps rubbing them with the towel. On the kitchen table there is a crystal bowl full of strawberries—the bowl in which Keiko's mother sometimes sends over fruit, cookies, or flowers, sharing the gifts that her husband's patients have sent to their house. When my mother was around, she gave back the bowl in a few days filled with homemade cookies or cakes, returning the neighborly gesture. My grandmother just brings back the empty bowl, cleaned and polished to perfection. I think it's rude, but it hasn't discouraged Mrs. Yamasaki. She usually sends one of Keiko's older sisters with these gifts; I'm sure Keiko ordinarily doesn't volunteer to come to my house.

Grandmother Shimizu finishes drying her hands and then, to my surprise, tosses the towel in the sink instead of hanging it up. "Sit down, Megumi," she barks at me.

I sit down, but she doesn't. Dizzy with worry, I want to lean forward and hold my head in my hands.

Standing a few feet away from me in her gray kimono, my grandmother says in an icy voice, "I have just called your father and asked him to come home. Do you know why?"

I shake my head no, already wanting to cry. I know that Keiko's visit had something to do with my grandmother's anger. For her to call my father at his girlfriend's house on a Sunday afternoon, Grandmother must be very, very upset. Still, it is unfair of her to ask me if I know why. Of course I don't.

"I've asked him to come because you are a liar, Megumi." She clamps her mouth shut and breathes hard through her nostrils like an angry horse.

Avoiding her eyes, I look again at the strawberries in

186

the bowl; the ones on the bottom are squashed against the glass. They might as well have been poisoned.

"You don't go to church anymore," Grandmother continues. "Instead, you go driving at night with a boy—an older boy."

I wish I could march out of my house into the Yamasakis' and grab Keiko by the collar of her prim long dress. What a hypocrite she is, to come to my house pretending to bring a gift from her mother, when all along, she must have been looking for the perfect chance to tell on me. I regret all the years I spent thinking of her as my best friend.

"What do you have to say for yourself?" Grandmother demands.

Nothing, of course. She is right—I have lied to her. What I have done must look completely wrong to her. It's no use explaining that Toru is my childhood friend. Grandmother doesn't care about my childhood friends. I look down at the polished wood of the kitchen floor, wishing I could just disappear.

"That is not the only thing," Grandmother hisses. "You have been receiving letters. Letters we specifically forbade you to receive." Reaching inside her *obi*, she pulls out the six letters my mother has sent to me. "You were scheming to talk to her on the telephone."

I jump up from my chair. Suddenly, I am so angry that I can hardly breathe. Grandmother had no right to take and read my mother's letters. She shouldn't have gone into my room looking for them even if she suspected me of lying. And Keiko, too—how dare she talk about those letters, repeating a secret she must have heard from Kiyoshi, getting me in trouble and ruining my chance of ever hearing from my mother again? Even God, if he existed, would tell her to mind her own business.

187

I step forward and snatch the letters out of my grandmother's hands. She winces; a dark red spreads over her face and neck as she stands, glaring at me. I can hear her breathing harder. If she were younger, she would try to grab me or hit me. Maybe she would try even now, but I am too fast for her. I back away from her reach.

"You have no right," I scream. "My mother never meant for you to read her letters."

"You lied to me," she repeats.

"That makes no difference. You gave me no choice." I am clenching two tight fists, the fingers of my left hand squeezed around my mother's letters. I want to step up to Grandmother and punch her. I imagine her doubled over with pain, her shriveled hand clutching her broken jaw. It would be so satisfying to see that. But the thought frightens me, too. What if I caused her to have a heart attack and to die? She would keel over, gasping for breath. I turn the other way and walk quickly to the back door.

Standing with my hand on the door, I remember that my shoes are in the front foyer, but it's too late. I run out to the backyard in my socks, then jump over the fence into the Yamasakis' backyard. Keiko must be in her room, doing homework or maybe reading the Bible. I want to shake her and yell at her until she has to cry and beg me to stop. But that won't change anything. Besides, just the thought of seeing her face sickens me. So I run across the yard past her mother's shrubs and flowers, jump over the fence into another backyard, then another, until I come out on a street. It is a mild spring day, but the pavement feels cold through my thin socks. I start running up the hill toward Dr. Mizutani's, moving too fast to avoid the small pebbles that hurt the soles of my feet. As I run, I think about the narrow, winding mountain paths my mother and I used to walk on. No matter how careful we were, we couldn't help kicking some stones and pebbles behind us as we walked—causing them to slide off the steep cliff to the side. I feel as though I am falling headlong down the cliff in an avalanche of gray pebbles and dust. I will never see my mother again. My life will never be the same.

Dr. Mizutani is reading a book in the small study inside her clinic, in the back of the examination room. "Megumi. What is wrong?" She gets up from her big maroon chair and walks toward me as I stand in the doorway.

"I need help," I tell her. "I'm in trouble."

Putting her hand on my back, the doctor guides me to the maroon chair. "Sit down," she says, gently pushing me down into the seat. She goes out and comes back with a glass of water, which she hands me, and pulls up another chair for herself. "Take a sip of water first, all right?"

I take a drink and then start telling her everything. Halfway through, I realize that I am clutching my mother's letters in one hand and the glass of water in the other. I put them down on the carpeted floor and continue talking.

"Grandmother said my father was coming home to talk to me. They'll never let me see Toru again or hear from my mother. Maybe they will forbid me to see you, too. I'll be all alone." I have to pause, to keep from crying.

Dr. Mizutani doesn't say anything for a while.

"It's not fair," I add, "the way my grandmother and father can order me or forbid me to do things. They can take away anything from me. Anything I like—my mother, my friends, even my school."

"But it doesn't have to be like that," the doctor says, her eyes wide with sympathy.

"It is like that," I insist. "Now that they know I've lied to them, I'll never see my mother again, and my grandmother will talk my father into making me change schools, too. She'll say I became a liar because I wasn't getting enough discipline at my school. She hates my school because my mother went there. She'll send me to a public school now. She's been nagging him about it for months."

"You don't have to do anything your father says, if you believe that he is wrong and you are right. You can protest if you are truly convinced." The doctor looks into my eyes, as if to impress me with the truth of her statement.

"But I have to live with him and Grandmother," I explain, suddenly irritated with Dr. Mizutani. How can she think everything is so simple? "So long as I live in their house, I have to do what they say."

"I get the feeling," the doctor says, frowning, "that you don't even like living with them."

"Of course I don't," I yell, forgetting that I haven't told Dr. Mizutani much about my father or grandmother. "I don't like living with them," I repeat in a softer voice, trying to calm down. "My grandmother is always in a bad mood and my father is seldom home. But I have nowhere else to go. My mother and grandfather would worry more about me if I had to live with them. So long as I am with my father, they know that I have a good future. They gave me up so I won't be poor and fatherless, but now, I've ruined it all. Maybe my father will even disown me." I take a deep breath and try to sit still without beginning to cry. "He will send me away to live with my mother and grandfather, and be a burden to them. Or maybe he will keep me with him but forbid me to ever see them again. I don't know what he will do. All I know is I'm in trouble. No matter who I live with, I will never be happy."

"What would happen," the doctor asks, "if you asked—if you insisted—that every year you live with your mother during the summer and your father during the school year? Doesn't that seem more reasonable?"

"My father would never allow that," I answer, irritated. Doesn't the doctor understand what I've been saying?

"What choice would he have if you insisted?"

"He would say that I could live in his house and obey his rules, or else I could stop being his daughter. He would disown me."

"Your father is never going to disown you," the doctor says. "It would mean losing you forever, never seeing you again."

"I don't know if that would bother him. I don't think my father loves me very much." The doctor doesn't say anything, so we sit in silence for a while. What I said isn't exactly true. I remember the finches Father bought me after inadvertently killing my canaries. I picture his stiff smile and hear the thin voice in which he asks me, "So how are you, Megumi?" On the few occasions when he is home and Grandmother begins to criticize me or talk about making me switch schools, Father changes the subject or ignores her, pretending to be too tired or distracted to continue the conversation. That is the only way he knows to defend me or take my side. His weak attempts anger me; all the same, I can't say he does nothing or he doesn't care. "Well, that isn't true," I am forced to admit to the doctor. "My father doesn't love anyone very much, not the way my mother does, or Grandfather

191

Kurihara. Even Grandmother Shimizu loves him more than he loves her. Still, Father probably loves me and Grandmother Shimizu as much as he can love anyone—of course, that isn't a lot."

Dr. Mizutani thinks that over for a while. "If he does love you," she says finally, "he isn't likely to disown you and risk losing you forever, is he? If the only way you will live with him is to see your mother—to live with her for the summer—then he will have to accept that in the end."

"I'm not sure," I say, completely confused. I don't know how we got from talking about the big trouble I am in to my making demands on my father. But the doctor looks so calm and reasonable. Anything she says, I think, is worth considering.

"Besides," she says, "think about how he would look, disowning you and forcing you to grow up in poverty."

"My father doesn't care much about appearances," I have to point out. "As soon as Mother was gone, he went to live with his girlfriend in Hiroshima. That's why he's never home. Everyone he works with must know about her. He's not embarrassed by that." I look down, ashamed even though my father's affair isn't my fault.

But the doctor just shrugs. "A man is never criticized or shamed for having mistresses. That's why your father doesn't care. If anything, he wants everyone to know that he has a girlfriend. Now that your mother is gone, he doesn't want to look like a poor deserted man; having a girlfriend helps him save face. If he disowned you, it would be different. He would come across as an irresponsible man who lets his own daughter live in poverty while he makes a good living and stays with his mistress. He wouldn't want to look like that."

She may be right. My father does care about appear-

192

ances enough not to marry his girlfriend. He might not want to embarrass Grandmother Shimizu by seeming irresponsible any more than by having a big divorce trial.

"I think you would be safe to make your demands," the doctor continues. "He is not going to disown you. You can insist on seeing your mother, on going to your school. You have every right. He can't forbid you. He will never go to court to try and keep your mother from seeing you. Going to court means publicity, bringing shame on the family. He'll never do it. I know about these things, Megumi. The man I was married to gave me a divorce in order not to embarrass his family. At first he and his family thought our divorce would make them look bad. They wanted me to pretend that we were still married and I had come back to Ashiya to take care of my parents. I insisted I wouldn't live with a lie like that. I didn't want to be connected to his family at all. He had to agree in the end because going to court would bring him and his family more embarrassment than getting quietly divorced, so he settled with my family's lawyer in a private mediation. Your father, too, will do whatever he can to avoid lawsuits."

"But what if he decides to disown me or go to court anyway? What can I do then?"

"You won't have to face that alone, Megumi," she says, "because I'll do what I can to help you." She leans forward and looks into my eyes. "If your father wants to go to court, I'll get my family's lawyer to help you. If he disowns you, then you can come and live with my family, go to Christian Girls' Academy, and spend summers with your mother. I won't let you be poor. I know how lucky I was to have money, how much shame I was spared because of that. No one will insult me to my face because my father is a rich man. I can't just stand by and watch you and your mother suffer or be humiliated."

The way she tries to smile, I know she means every word. She will indeed take me in if I have nowhere else to go. She will look out for me and make sure that I won't live in shame or poverty, just as she didn't have to. Suddenly, I am so relieved that I want to cry again. I am not falling off a cliff after all. Dr. Mizutani is telling me that she is my friend—and my mother's friend, too. "I don't know how to thank you," I say. My voice sounds choked up.

"Don't worry, Megumi," Dr. Mizutani says, smiling. "I'll always be there to help you, but you won't even need my help. Your father won't disown you or stop paying your tuition. If he is anything like most other people, he cares a lot about his reputation. He won't do anything that will cause him to lose face or look stupid. His concern about appearances is your best advantage."

"Maybe you're right."

"It's worth calling his bluff. If that doesn't work, we'll come up with another plan. Trust me."

"Thank you."

"No need to thank me." She shrugs. "It would be no imposition, even if you were to need a place to stay. My father and I helped some of my cousins—my mother's nieces—go to college because they had no money and we did. I didn't know them that well. Helping you would be a pleasure, not an obligation. I enjoy your company, Megumi. The minute you showed me that waxwing, I knew I'd enjoy getting to know you."

That bird is in Siberia, pecking at the early spring berries, building a nest. By now the week he spent in my room eating cut-up grapes and chirping on the window-sill must seem like another lifetime to him.

My father and grandmother have locked the door even though it's only five o'clock. I pull the key chain out of my pocket and open the door; I want to laugh at their stupidity. How can they lock me out when I'm fifteen and I have had my own key for more than three years?

I enter the house and go straight to the kitchen, where my father is drinking tea and, as usual, my grandmother is hovering over him. Both of them glare at me in silence. My father is in the brown suit he usually wears while traveling. I remember what Dr. Mizutani said about everyone caring about appearances. Maybe she's right. My father does not want to scold me in his usual relaxing-at-home outfit of an old kimono and long underwear.

"I'm sorry I lied," I admit right away. "I should have told you that I was getting letters from Mother and talking to Toru on Sunday nights. I was doing nothing wrong. I had no reason to hide anything from you or to be ashamed of myself."

The two of them glance at each other. She sticks her chin out toward him and then nods.

"You and I will talk in my study," Father announces to me as he slowly rises from his chair.

I follow him down the hall while my grandmother stays behind, pretending to clean the kitchen. In his study, Father sits down in his large leather chair. There is no other place to sit, so I stand near the door. Around us the walls are lined with his books, all of them about money and banking and insurance.

"You have disappointed me, Megumi," he declares in his extra-deep voice. "Your grandmother has told me everything."

"No, she hasn't," I snap back. "She can't tell you everything because there is a lot she doesn't know."

Completely ignoring my point, Father says, "I have specifically told you not to visit or write to your mother. You have disobeyed me. You made me look like a fool by involving the Katos and your veterinarian friend. As if that weren't enough, you lied to Grandmother and went driving around with a boy at night."

"The boy was Toru Uchida. You remember him. I wasn't sneaking around with some strange boy."

"You know nothing about men," my father raises his voice. "This boy is twenty or twenty-one. You have no idea what boys think about, sitting in a dark car with a young girl. You were lucky nothing happened."

If I weren't so mad, I would laugh. Most of the time that Toru was sitting in the dark car with me, he was thinking about another girl. My father has no right to assume the worst about Toru and make him sound like a bad person.

"Toru would never hurt me," I declare.

"You don't know."

"Yes, I do. He cares about me more than you do." I picture Toru taking the dead butterflies out of the glass case, holding them delicately by their wingtips and burying them, one by one. If my father owned something that hurt me, the way Toru's butterfly collection had, he wouldn't give it up—he wouldn't bury it or throw it out and say, "I just didn't want to see you cry." More likely he would keep explaining in his dry and reasonable voice about how wrong I am to be hurt, how right he is to do what he wants to. "Toru would never hurt me," I repeat, "because he is a kind person. He cares about me more than you do. That's the truth."

My father says nothing for a long time. He narrows his eyes, as if concentrating on some important thought. He drums his fingers on the arm of the chair and sighs, still saying nothing. Finally he mutters, "I work hard for you." His voice is low and weak; he swallows hard. I have never heard him sound so pitiful before.

Maybe I should feel sorry for Father. He can't help not caring for me the way Toru does. Father has never cared about anyone enough to give something up for them. Even when I was very young—before Father had a girl-friend—my mother was often unhappy because he worked late every night and then went out with his work friends on weekends. He never gave up an hour of work or a day on the golf course to make Mother happy. Now he must know that Grandmother is unhappy because he had asked her to give up her house and live with us, only to abandon us himself. He will never give up his girl-friend, or even any of the time he spends with her, for Grandmother's sake or mine. He is different from every-one else in that way. Not only my mother and Toru, but all of my friends—Mieko, Noriko, Dr. Mizutani—would give up things for me if they had to, and I would do the same for them. Maybe he can't help being different. That is a reason to feel sorry for him, just as I would feel sorry for someone who couldn't appreciate beautiful colors or music because they were color-blind or tone-deaf.

"I work hard for you," he repeats. "I send you to an ex-pensive school, a school I don't approve of, only because you want to go there."

As I stare at him, my anger comes back. He doesn't have to remind me of all the things he pays for.

"When your mother left, I thought about taking you out of that school," he continues, his voice getting louder with every word. "Your grandmother thought I should. But I didn't. Do you know why?" He stops, waiting for me to answer.

"No, I don't know why." My voice sounds stiff and

197

wary. I can't help feeling suspicious. My father never asks questions because he wants to know the answer. He is only trying to trick me.

"Because I felt sorry for you," he says. "I thought you would feel bad enough with your mother leaving the way she did. I didn't want you to have to change schools, another thing you had to adjust to. To be honest I didn't think you would be able to handle so many changes, psychologically. That's why I kept you at your school. I didn't want you to fall apart."

He is saying that I should be grateful. He is reminding me that he did think about me after all. But the way he says it, the way he keeps squinting at me, doesn't inspire gratitude at all. His eyes have a small gleam of satisfaction. He sticks out his chin a little, as if to taunt me. What he said is rude and unfair. He didn't have to make me sound like a pitiful character, a girl about to fall apart. None of my friends would talk about me in that way, to my face or behind my back.

"I don't care how hard you work to send me to school," I say. "You are my father. You are supposed to send me to school, it isn't a special favor you are doing for me. It doesn't give you an excuse to act the way you do. You are the most selfish person I know. I'm ashamed to be your daughter."

My father stares at me, his eyes bulging out. I'm not sure if he is too angry to speak or just surprised.

"You gave me no choice except to lie to you about Mother's letters. You had no right to forbid me to hear from her."

"Your mother left you," he says in a quiet voice. "If she truly loved you, she would have stayed, no matter how unhappy she thought she was. You are better off without her. We are both better off."

He sighs as if he truly believed that. And maybe he does, but that makes no difference.

"How can you say that, when you were the one making her unhappy? You have no right to say that she should have put up with the unhappiness you were giving her."

"But she made me unhappy, too."

Maybe that is true. "I don't care," I insist. "If my mother had made you leave and I had wanted to see you, she would have allowed me to. No matter how she felt about you herself, she would have let me hear from you because she loves me."

My father is silent for a long time. I think he must be trying to come up with an argument to prove me wrong. But when he finally speaks, he asks me something completely different. "If I had left you and you were living with her, would you have asked to see me?"

I look down at him slouching in his chair. For the first time I notice where his hair is looking brittle and almost gray along his temples. His face looks pale and pasty; there are circles under his eyes. Even those people who used to say that he was good-looking, if they saw him now, they wouldn't think that anymore. Just like my mother he is unhappy, if not for the same reasons. I should feel sorry for him. But I don't. I can't help telling him the truth. "I don't know," I reply, "probably not."

For a second, he slouches even more, looking as if I had punched him. But then he straightens out. His back goes rigid and his face hardens, thin and determined. In his sternest voice, he says, "I forbid you to receive any letters from your mother. Because you lied about them, you can no longer see the Uchida boy, the Katos, or the veterinarian."

"You can't forbid me," I retort. "I don't have to do what you say just because it's your house. You don't even live here. You live upstairs from a bar with a girl-friend who wears orange lipstick."

"Don't you ever talk to me in that way," he threatens. Hard, thin lines ridge his neck—he is gritting his teeth, but I'm not afraid of him anymore. Dr. Mizutani is right. He can't make me do anything I don't want to do, when I am in the right and he is in the wrong.

"I'll talk any way I want to," I reply as calmly as possible. "When school is over, I am going to stay with Mother and Grandfather Kurihara. If you don't want me to come back here after that, I'm going to live with Dr. Mizutani. She already told me I could live with her and go to Christian Girls' Academy. She knows the whole story. I don't care if you disown me. I have a place to go to."

Before my father can say anything, I walk out of the study, slamming the door behind me for good measure. Down the hallway, the kitchen is absolutely quiet. My grandmother must have been trying to hear the conversation; she would have had no chance, especially with her bad hearing. Grabbing my shoes from the foyer, I go out the door.

The sun is just setting behind the mountains to the west, but the sky is still a dark blue instead of black. In the east, the three-quarter moon looks pale and thin, like the lemon slices Keiko and I used to put in our tea. Her mother could slice the lemon so each piece was a whole circle, paper-thin. Keiko and I were clumsy, or maybe we were distracted by the fear of cutting our fingers; we could never get the knife to go down straight. Our slices looked like that moon—crooked, imperfect circles.

From the end of our block, I look back at the Ya-masakis' house. The light is on in Keiko's room. She must be getting ready for the Bible study meeting, making up her face so it looks as though she had no makeup on, choosing a dress or a blouse that will show off her figure yet look modest. It will be a long time before I can forgive her for telling on me—and Kiyoshi, too, for giving away my secret to her, for thinking of her as someone he should trust.

I don't want to spend any more time thinking about them. I walk down the hill toward Toru's bar. It's only a little after six, so I will be early. Maybe I can go into the bar and call Dr. Mizutani from there and tell her that everything will be all right.

Toru will be happy and surprised to hear of my new summer plans. The first time we talked, he told me how he got his way with his father and grandfather. They threatened to disown him if he didn't go to college, but backed down as soon as he moved out of the house on his own. Our first talk was only early last month, but it seems like a long time ago. Back then, I had thought he was more resourceful than I, or luckier in being older, being a boy. I know differently now. Being a girl or being younger wasn't the problem—what matters is having someone to count on: Toru had an older friend, I have Dr. Mizutani. Calling a bluff is like being a circus acrobat, I suppose. Though we don't expect to fall off the wire, we can't climb up there unless there's someone holding a net underneath just in case—someone we can trust. Laughing to myself at the thought of Toru and me on a circus wire, I stop walking and look down the hill.

The lights are coming on fast in the city. They glitter white, orange, red. I think about my mother in the countryside, in a drafty house next to a pampas field, which is pitch-dark after sunset. Moving from the living room to the kitchen and back again, she would collect the cups and plates the guests had left—trying to balance as many as possible on her strong hands but being careful. She must be so tired, and sad, too, remembering her mother's death. I try to send her all my love. *Wait for me*, I think to her. *It won't be long now.*

10
The Pink Rose

At four-thirty in the morning, the sky is dark outside my windows. Even my grandmother is still asleep. I walk quietly down the stairs and the hallway to the kitchen, pour myself a glass of orange juice, and sit down at the table. Without the light on, I can feel my grandmother's silent anger floating around in the dark.

In the week since she found out about my lies, she has said about twenty words to me: *Dinner is ready; Lock the door; I am going to bed; The telephone is for you.* Every night we ate in silence except for the clicking of our chopsticks, the occasional scraping of a spoon or a fork against the plates. Last night, as I was bringing my dishes into the sink after supper, I stacked my glass on top of the dirty plates in a clumsy way. I dumped the potato skin, which she thinks we should eat because of the vitamins, into the sink instead of scraping my plate carefully over the garbage can. Grandmother didn't scold me. She glared in such a cold way that I knew never to try that trick again. I can't irritate her out of her angry silence and make her talk to me.

I have not seen much of Father since our argument. By the time I came home after talking to Toru on Sunday night, Father had already gone back to Hiroshima. He came home only once, late Wednesday night, when I

203

happened to be downstairs making a cup of tea. In his usual stiff voice, he asked me how I was. "Fine," I said, picking up my cup to bring it back to my room. He made some small talk about the trains being crowded, about all the rain we have had even though it isn't the rainy season yet. I couldn't tell whether he was talking to me, to my grandmother, or to both of us. "I broke my umbrella," he said. "I should go and buy a new one." Then he disappeared into his study and I didn't see him again; he went back to Hiroshima the next night after work. He never mentioned our argument: He didn't ask me if I really meant to spend my summer with my mother; he didn't say whether or not I could live in his house afterward.

I used to get angry with my mother for pretending that nothing bad ever happened in our family. But at least my mother didn't just clam up; on the contrary, she talked a lot. Whenever my father, grandmother, or I said or did something inconsiderate, Mother found kinder, however mistaken, interpretations and reasons for our actions. That's how she tried to make us sound or look better than we were. She never pretended that we hadn't said what we said, that certain conversations had never taken place. I had plenty of opportunities to contradict her instead of silently resenting her for being falsely cheerful. With my father and grandmother, there is no talk, no chance for me to say anything. All I can do is to sit there, worried about what they are really thinking.

Maybe my father and grandmother are doing what Keiko and I used to do in grade school, when one of us was very angry. We would pretend that the other person didn't exist. Once, she walked the ten blocks from our school to our houses, staring at me without any expression as if I had become invisible. I kept asking, but she wouldn't tell me why she was angry. She showed no sign of hearing me. My voice might as well have been the scarcely noticeable stirring of hot air, not even a breeze. Finally, I broke down, cried, and begged for forgiveness though I had no idea what I had done to offend her. If my father and grandmother are trying to do the same thing—biding their time till I am so lonely for conversation that I'd agree to say and do anything—they might as well stay silent for the rest of their lives. I am too old now to fall for that trick.

It's almost time to go. I put my empty juice glass on the table and stretch my arms over my head. I'm still stretching, feeling sleepy, when the door of my grandmother's room slides open and she comes walking down the hallway in her mud-brown kimono. She flicks on the kitchen light and grabs my glass while I am sitting dazed in the sudden brightness. At the sink, she begins to rinse the glass.

"I was going to do that," I protest. She doesn't have to pretend that I am irresponsible about the dishes.

Without a word, she washes the glass in steaming hot water and soap, scrubbing hard as if the orange juice—or maybe I—had contaminated it.

"I am going to visit my mother," I announce while she is drying the glass with a dish towel.

No answer, of course.

"Dr. Mizutani is driving me there in her truck. I told her I would meet her at the clinic."

I am just getting up when Grandmother says, "Wait."

I sit back down, irritated. Why does she have to choose this moment to say something when she has had the whole week? It's nearly five o'clock. I told Dr. Mizutani that I would be there at quarter after.

My grandmother doesn't speak. She pulls open the refrigerator door and stands scowling at the contents. After a while, she pulls out the two eggs I boiled last night for the birds—once a week, I feed all the baby birds mashed-up boiled eggs mixed with yogurt to give them a protein boost. My grandmother peels the eggs at the sink, letting the shell fall into an empty bowl in jagged pieces like paint chipped off a wall. In another bowl, she mashes up the eggs, the potato masher coming down hard and steady in her hand. By the time she puts a dollop of mayonnaise into the bowl and looks for the salt, I know that she is making my lunch. *Don't bother,* I can tell her. *I don't want lunch.* But I keep my mouth shut. Her face has an irritated and put-upon look—her bottom lip sticking out, the corners of her mouth wrinkled. It isn't the icy, silent glare she has shot at me all week. In the bowl, the egg salad is a pale golden color, not very different from what I offer the birds. I remember the herb tea and the broth she made for me at her house in Tokyo, when I was sick. I can almost hear my mother saying, "Grandmother Shimizu is a good person at heart. She is from another time. Being strict is her way of showing love." There must be a better way of showing love and kindness. What I want is an apology, not a sandwich. But I know an apology is never coming. I can accept the food she offers—or I can throw it in the sink, make a scene, and leave the house feeling angry and self-righteous.

My grandmother finishes making the sandwich and wraps it in wax paper; she puts it inside a paper bag with an apple and a can of soda. She brings the bag to the table and puts it down with a thunk.

She doesn't say *Have a good trip; Give my regards to your mother;* or *It's nice of Dr. Mizutani to bring you there.* She hasn't made any food for Dr. Mizutani. But Grandmother Shimizu cannot be who she is and still do any of those things. To say or do something so normal

206

and polite, she would first have to be turned into someone else, by one of the genies or good witches in my
mother's fairy tales. Even when my mother was trying to
be cheerful, she had to admit that Grandmother didn't
know how to show love or concern. As I put my hand on
the bag lunch, I let myself imagine throwing the bag
against the wall—the apple would bruise, the soda can
might explode. In a way, it would be satisfying to stay
angry. But that's what I've been criticizing Grandmother
about—how she prefers to complain and stay mad. I
can't do the same when she is trying to make a kind
gesture.

"Thank you," I say, trying to keep the begrudging tone
out of my voice. "I'll be back in the evening. It won't be
very late."

No words come out of her mouth as she stands between the sink and the table, with a frown on her face.

I get up to leave. "Please don't worry," I offer before
turning away.

While the doctor is getting ready, I go out to the backyard with a flashlight to change the water inside the
birdcage and fill the food dishes. All the birds are
asleep—the sparrows perched side by side on a high
branch, the grosbeak alone on a middle branch, and the
brown-eared bulbul ruffled up on the piece of wood that
sticks out above the door. Each bird has been flying well,
eating on his own, getting ready to leave. Dr. Mizutani
and I are watching the weather forecast and waiting for
the first stretch of mild days without rain or strong winds.
It could be any day next week.

Stepping outside the cage, I drop a few pieces of cut-
up meat and berries into the crow's dish. He must be
asleep in one of the maples, his black wings folded up

against the new green leaves. He has been flying around with the other crows in the neighborhood, sometimes chasing them away from his dish. Every week we give him a little less food. By the end of next week, Dr. Mizutani says, we will stop altogether. She puts out a lot of food in the yard for all the birds in our neighborhood— seeds, fruits, corn, suet. If the crow wants to eat here he can, without having his own special dish. He is looking better these days, much less ragged. In a month, his tail feathers will grow out completely and even we won't be able to tell him apart from the other crows.

When I come inside, Dr. Mizutani is putting food in a cooler—bread and cheese, apricots, cherries, cans of juice. I take out my lunch and put it in, too.

"I'll trade my sandwich for an apricot," I joke. "My grandmother made me a sandwich, after not talking to me all week."

The doctor raises her eyebrows. "Your grandmother should have been a Trappist monk."

I laugh, thinking of the monks up on a hill in a suburb near my school. My mother used to buy tins of the butter cookies they baked. They are the monks who never speak. When I was in grade school, I used to get them confused with vampires, probably because of their black robes. I believed that the monks who baked the cookies slept in coffins and turned into bats at night. I didn't realize then that not speaking would be much harder in a way than sleeping in a coffin or even turning into a bat.

"Grab that Thermos, all right?" the doctor asks me.

We load the car in the gray light before sunrise. There is a faint band of orange across the water and along the eastern sky. The trees are coming into focus. As we pull out of the driveway, I remember the first all-day field trips I went on from school, back in first and second

208

grades. My mother would get up before dawn to pack a special lunch for me and to walk me to the schoolyard, where the bus was waiting. We were always the last ones there. While I boarded the bus, she stood with the other mothers, all of them trying to look happy with tight, scared smiles on their faces. The way they waved to us when the bus started moving, no one would have thought we were only going to be away for ten or twelve hours at the most. Back then, being apart for the whole day was a big event. Now, after four months of separation, I am coming to see her, and she doesn't even know it. She has no idea.

Somewhere north of Osaka, as we drive on the highway past the small suburban factories and offices, the sun comes up. I have been telling Dr. Mizutani about how I tried to provoke my grandmother into talking last night.

"Your grandmother sounds a little like my mother-in-law," she says.

I glance away from the gray factory buildings toward her. It's so hard to picture her with a husband or a mother-in-law. Sitting behind the wheel in her denim jacket, white linen blouse, and jeans, she looks like someone who has always been young and carefree—not at all like an unhappy wife or daughter-in-law. In spite of the early hour, she doesn't look tired, sleepy, or grumpy in the slightest. Her eyes look wide awake and happy; beaded peacock feathers dangle from her ears, catching the morning light. I've come to think of her as the prettiest woman I have ever seen, except maybe for my mother and Mrs. Uchida.

"My *former* mother-in-law," she corrects herself.

"What was her name?" I ask. "Was she very mean, like my grandmother?"

With a shrug she answers, "Her name was Etsuko Hamanaka. She was mean, all right, in a silent, sullen way. When she wanted to, she could also turn vicious and loud. My husband, Masao, and I lived with her. He had had his own apartment, but we went to live with his parents after our wedding because his father was ill. Masao was an only child." She stops speaking and concentrates on the road, stepping on the gas to pass a slow car.

"Is that why you left?" I ask. "Because your mother-in-law was mean?"

"In a way, but it was more than that. I don't think my husband and I understood each other very well in the first place." I say nothing, and she goes on. "When we moved into his parents' house, I assumed that my husband was going to take care of his father or help his mother with housework. I was a graduate student in ornithology, working on my master's thesis. I stayed in our tiny room studying all day, trying to stay out of everyone's way.

"After a month, my mother-in-law started complaining to my husband about how I never did anything around the house. She said I was a coldhearted and spoiled girl. The thing is, she had never asked me to do anything. My husband didn't help much, either. He was a professor at the university where I was a student. He drove to work in the morning and came home for supper. About all he did was clear the dishes and clean our room now and then.

"Seeing that, I thought that Etsuko had everything under control. I assumed that she had asked us to live with her because she just wanted moral support and maybe someone to drive her husband to the hospital in case of an emergency. I had no idea that I was expected to help more than my husband because I was a woman." She shakes her head. "That sounds naive, but I didn't know.

210

My father always did some work around the house—not as much as my mother, but quite a lot. My parents never expected me to help with chores if I was busy studying. I suppose I should have known better all the same. My mother had often talked about her friends having problems with their mothers-in-law, who lorded over them and made them miserable. These mothers-in-law claimed they had sacrificed so much for their husbands and sons, now it was their turn to have someone slaving for them. Though I had heard these stories, I never thought something like that would happen to me. I was young and stupid."

"No," I say. "My grandmother was mean to my mother in the same way, always criticizing her about housework and bragging about how hard she used to work. I never thought my mother should put up with that. Grandmother doesn't have a right to be mean just because she's had a hard life. That isn't my mother's fault, even if it was true."

"My husband wouldn't have agreed with you," Dr. Mizutani says. "He never stuck up for me, not once, while his mother made my life miserable. After I put my thesis aside and started helping her, things only got worse. All day she would find fault with me, hinting that my mother had not raised me right. She would send me to the store with a grocery list, only she would forget to write down one or two things. When I came home she would scold me for not having thought of things she'd forgotten to write down. 'If you had been paying attention,' she would scream, 'you would have known what I really needed.' A couple of times, I bought some extra things that weren't on the list, just in case. It was no good—Etsuko scolded me for wasting her money. 'I never wanted my son to marry a rich, spoiled girl,' she

211

said, 'a girl who never learned anything but study, study, study.' "

Dr. Mizutani screws up her face and speaks in a nasal tone, mimicking her mother-in-law. I imagine her as my Grandmother Shimizu's identical twin. I can see exactly how this old woman must have screamed in the kitchen and written out incomplete lists so she could complain about how she never got what she needed. But I can't fit Kumiko Mizutani into the picture.

"I don't understand," I blurt out. "I can't think of you putting up with someone so mean, going to the store and worrying about what she was going to say. That isn't how I think about you."

"You can't imagine me being so wishy-washy?" she asks.

"Well, I didn't say *that*," I protest, my face feeling warm because that is exactly what I meant.

Dr. Mizutani turns to me momentarily. Her eyes look darker and larger, and her lips are slightly parted in concentration. "Believe me, Megumi. Sometimes people can break our will. They can make us feel so low that we don't even know how to defend ourselves." She turns back to the road and falls silent.

Outside, the small factories near Osaka have given way to the black-slated farmhouses and rice paddies.

"I was lucky to catch myself in time," she continues. "After two months, one day I came home from shopping and was about to unlatch the front gate of their house and go in. But I couldn't. My hands couldn't be lifted; my feet felt frozen into place. I couldn't make myself go into that house, to face that woman. 'Now or never,' I kept repeating to myself. I must have stood there for five, ten minutes, saying that. Finally I held my basket upside down, dumping all the food on the ground. Then I ran to

212

the train station. When I got there, I realized I didn't have enough money to get home. I was in northern Honshu, hours by train from Ashiya. I called my mother collect from a pay phone and all I could say was, 'Help me. I need to come home. Come and get me.'

"I must have sounded terrible. Neither of my parents knows how to drive, but they called one of their friends who had a car. I took the train to Nagoya, which was as far as my money would go, checked into a hotel, and waited for them. I never went back. My parents hired a lawyer to get me a divorce and to arrange for my things to be sent back to Ashiya. I already told you that. I never saw my husband again, or his mother."

She shudders, narrowing her eyes a little as if remembering her marriage has stunned her with pain. *I'm glad you got away,* I want to tell her. *You are the most remarkable person I have ever met.* But I feel too shy to say such a thing.

"I didn't finish my master's thesis," she adds. "Instead I enrolled in a veterinary school so I would have an occupation—and nobody would say that I was just a rich-man's daughter." She smiles dryly. "People still say that anyway, but I have an occupation, and I know it. Besides, I didn't want to continue at school because my husband was an ornithology professor there. I had originally gone to study botany, but during my first month, I met Masao and became an ornithology student, and later married him. I know that sounds stupid. All through college I was determined never to fall in love or be married. The only women I knew who were important—who were professors or doctors or politicians—were single. I wanted to be a famous scientist. But I fell in love with Masao because of a bird."

I wait for her to go on.

213

"One day at school, I saw a sign asking for volunteers to help Professor Hamanaka band some warblers that were coming through the mountains. I didn't know him, but I went because it sounded like fun. I stood in a clearing in the mountains with six or seven people, holding a tiny willow warbler I had taken out of the mist net. The professor smiled and asked me if I knew how to tell birds' ages. I shook my head no. He leaned over and blew very lightly on the bird's head—as if he was going to whistle, only no sound came out. Instead his breath parted the feathers and the down on the bird's head. He guided my hand so we were holding the bird in the light. The bird's skull looked almost clear in that light, like soft, clear plastic. 'You are holding a one-year-old bird,' he told me, 'last year's baby.' It takes a long time for the birds' bones to ossify. As they get older, their skulls get more white spots, and that's how you can estimate their age. I fell in love with Masao for showing me that. It's stupid, I know."

"No, it's not stupid," I say.

"I was making a foolish assumption," she insists. "What he did with the bird—it was such a tender gesture. Because of that, I thought Masao was wise, gentle, kind. I suppose in a way he was. He never was cruel on purpose, but when his mother was mean to me, he complained to me instead of to her. 'Why can't you do what she says and make peace?' he would ask me. Later, when things got really bad, Masao started taking long research trips, avoiding his mother and me so he wouldn't have to get in the middle. He left me alone with his parents." She grimaces. "Still," she says in a brighter voice, "I did learn about birds from him. I don't mind not having become an ornithologist. I do know about birds; I work with them."

Watching her drive, I remember the way she examined

the dead bulbul—the one I had named after my grand-mother. "I hope you won't find this outrageous," she had told me as she put the bird inside a plastic bag. "I'm going to donate this bird to the ornithology museum in Kyoto. They are always looking for specimens. This way, somebody will learn something from him." Sealing the bag and putting it in the freezer, she turned to me and smiled in a worried way. "You're not upset, are you?" I shook my head even though I wasn't sure. I should have shown more enthusiasm. She believes that no catastrophe is too terrible to learn from.

The trip to my grandparents' house used to take my mother and me a good part of the day. We would change trains in Kyoto, getting on a local with only two cars, and travel along a single track to the last stop. Then we had to ride a bus that went up the winding mountain paths for two hours, stopping every twenty minutes or so. But this time in Dr. Mizutani's truck, the small cities and villages fly by. We stop once to check the map, drink our coffee, and eat some bread and cheese. When we start up again, driving past the shelved plots of tea, grape arbors, lettuce, spinach, and wheat fields, we don't have very far to go.

It is only three hours after we left Ashiya, and we are already in my grandfather's village. The road takes us past the little bus depot, the general store, the town hall where a doctor visits twice a week in case someone is ill, an old bathhouse that has been closed but never torn down because no one has the money to hire a crew. The long hill that goes up to the house is unpaved. From the mountains around us rises a chorus of harsh, rhythmic whirs, as though many angry women were whispering together.

"What is that sound?" Dr. Mizutani asks me.

"Looms," I tell her, "from the weaving cottages nearby. Most people around here are weavers, yuzen-dye, or indigo-dye craftspeople. They're all in the kimono business. My grandfather is the only embroidery man left. All the others went out of business a long time ago."

"It's beautiful here," she says, pointing to the forests of cedars and pines.

We pass only a few old houses hidden behind trees. I imagine my mother and Mrs. Kato driving up this hill in January. The road must have been covered with ice and snow.

"Here," I tell Dr. Mizutani. "We have to pull over and park on the side." I point to the bamboo grove on our right. "The house is on the other side. See the footpath? This is as close as we can come in a car."

She is staring, looking completely surprised. "Everyone has to walk?" she asks.

"My grandfather didn't want a road to cut across the grove—or across the field behind his house, which has pampas grass. That was a long time ago, before the war. Now the village has no money to cut a road even if he wanted one, but he doesn't regret it. If people want to visit him, he always says, they won't mind the walk."

"What about the people who deliver things for his business?"

"He never gets such a large order that he can't carry it himself."

We fall silent. I slouch forward, feeling nervous all of a sudden. What if my mother doesn't want to see me? My grandfather is an old man. Perhaps surprising him isn't such a good idea. I should have written first. I had wanted to come and see my mother in person, to tell her that I would be spending the summers with her, because it seemed too important to write in a letter. But now I'm not so sure. What if she's not home—or worse still, if she isn't happy to see me?

It's too late to change my mind; I put my hand on the door. "I'll be back as soon as I can," I say.

"No need to hurry," Dr. Mizutani replies, reaching into her glove compartment and pulling out her binoculars. "I'm going to walk around for a couple of hours and look for birds. I'll come up the path and find you when I'm done."

"You won't get lost?"

"No," she laughs. "I know how to find my way in the woods."

"Okay." I open the door and lean out. "Thank you for bringing me here."

"You are more than welcome."

I step down onto the dirt road, cross over to the other side, and enter the path. Just before it curves out of sight, I look back at the truck. The doctor is still sitting inside, watching me as intently as she had watched the waxwing and the crow when we let them go. I smile even though she probably can't see my face. Then I turn my back and walk on.

The path is like a narrow green tunnel, fifty yards of trodden grass and roots. Under the trees, there are violets and white anemones. My footsteps flush out small sparrows, which disappear into the yellow-green hair of the bamboo. Toward the end the path veers to the right, and suddenly I am in the clearing looking at the one-story frame house, sprawled flat and sagging in the corners. All the wood looks weather-beaten and gray.

My grandmother's peonies by the front door are just

about to bloom. The bushes hold up large buds like loose pink fists. Along the side of the house, her irises have shot out their long flower spikes—the lower buds are almost open, so I can tell which flowers are going to be purple and which are going to be yellow. Because my mother and I always visited in late summer, I have never before seen these flowers in bud or bloom, except in the pictures Grandmother sent us every spring.

The yard is deserted, and no noise comes from the house, but that is not unusual. My grandparents' home was always quiet during the day; they didn't own a TV, a radio, or a stereo. In the embroidery workshop inside their house, they worked holding their needles on the low worktable, listening to silence. At night, however, the darkness was full of sounds—the wind rattling the dry branches and the windows, whispering through the leaves and creeping through the eaves' troughs, mingling with the owls' hoots or the rain. My grandparents were amused that I, who lived in the city all year round, complained about not being able to sleep in the countryside because—I insisted—it was too noisy.

Crossing the yard, I go into the house through the sliding front door. It's cold inside. My footsteps make no sounds in the foyer and the kitchen, both of which have dirt floors. Taking off my shoes, I climb up the low steps to the main part of the house. The first room to my left, my grandfather's, is empty and the door is open. It's a little after nine, the time for his midmorning walk. He must be strolling through the woods just as he has done twice a day for as long as I can remember. He might run into Dr. Mizutani. What would he make of her—a thin young woman in jeans and a denim jacket, a pair of binoculars hanging from her neck? Would he be puzzled to see the long peacock feathers dangling from her ears?

218

With every step I take, the floor creaks under my feet. The floorboards were deliberately laid to creak at the slightest touch, my grandfather told me. All the old houses in the country have the same kind of floors, meant to discourage intruders. *Uguisu yuka*, bush warbler floors they are called, because the noise reminded someone of the harsh calls the birds use to warn one another of threats.

An intruder—that is what I feel like, coming unannounced. I could be a thief, or worse still, a ninja sent as a spy or an assassin. If we had lived in a different time, my mother's and my father's families could have been at war, and I, an only daughter, would have been considered a member of my father's family. *But we don't live in those times,* I tell myself. *I am no intruder. This is my house, too.* The floor keeps creaking. I imagine a flock of warblers chattering with their harsh, scolding notes. It doesn't seem right for me to be here. At best I feel like a ghost come back to life to walk through a familiar but strange place. *Maybe no one will be able to see me,* I think. *Or else this is a dream, and I'm not really here.* I stand on my toes and touch the horizontal wooden beam above my grandfather's door, just to make sure that my hands cannot go through things, as in movies about ghosts. My fingertips come back with a light coating of dust. Grandmother Shimizu would have a fit and say that my mother and grandfather live in filth. As soon as that thought occurs to me, I know I am not a ghost, this is not a dream, I am really here: Housekeeping isn't something a person would think about while dreaming or dead.

The next room down the hallway is my mother's, the room she had as a young girl, where she and I stayed on our visits. From the open door, I can see a pile of her wool sweaters on the floor by the dresser. Maybe she has

219

been trying to put away the winter clothes. I stop and peek into the room. She has pictures of me in frames on her desk, on her dresser, on the windowsill; the three are placed so that no matter where she is in this room, she can see at least one of them.

Standing in her doorway, I take a deep breath to keep from bursting into tears. In every letter she wrote to me, my mother mentioned how much she missed me. But I skipped over those words as though they were meaningless, no more than a standard greeting like "How are you?" or "Take care of your health." The three pictures—my sixth-grade graduation picture, a snapshot from last year in her garden, and a baby picture—make me realize how much she misses me, how she must treasure all the years we have spent together. I stand still for a while, trying to compose myself.

As I begin to walk toward the next room—the family room—I can smell the incense my grandfather offers at the Buddhist altar to pay respects to his ancestors, his son, Susumu, and my grandmother. There is half an inch of incense left; smoke is rising from crumbling ashes. Somebody must be in the house, in the last room past the family room, which is the embroidery workshop. My grandfather would never burn incense in an empty house—he is afraid of fire. He and Grandmother lived and worked in Osaka for a few years during the war, when they had to close down the embroidery business. There, firebombs fell from the sky almost every night. They spent hours crouched in the dark, their windows covered. Because of that time, my grandparents could never even see fireworks in the summer without getting sweaty-palmed and dizzy. They worried about incense and candles starting their house on fire. I quicken my steps; my mother must be here.

The sliding *fusuma* door of the workshop is partially open. I stand in the doorway looking into the narrow, tatami-covered room with windows on one side. The five small worktables are arranged next to the windows, one behind another like seats on a train, all of them facing away from me. Behind each table there is a flat pillow to sit on. My mother is seated at the first table, the farthest one from the door, with her back to me. Sitting bolt upright in her navy blue cotton sweater and gray slacks, she is holding her work a few inches from her eyes, examining her stitches. She must have been too absorbed in her work to have heard the creaking of the floor. She has no idea that I am standing in the doorway. Lowering the cloth a little, she guides her needle through the weave with her left hand—she is left-handed like me. Carefully tugging at the thread, she straightens and secures the stitch.

I take a step into the room. "Mother," I call to her, my voice trembling with everything I want to say to her.

She turns her whole body toward the door. The moment our eyes meet, she takes in a sudden, short breath; then her face freezes, more in surprise than anything.

"Megumi," she calls my name in a choked-up voice.

My mother has gotten thinner since the day she left me. Her sharp cheekbones stick out, making her face look angular like mine. "Mother," I ask, "are you all right? You look terrible."

She stares at me without speaking. After what seems like a long time, she manages to say, "I'm all right." Slowly she puts down her needle and embroidery on the table; then she covers her face with her hands.

The next moment, I am running to her and kneeling down on the tatami floor to throw my arms around her shoulders. She clings to me and starts crying.

221

"It's all right," I tell her. "I'm so sorry to surprise you. Please don't cry."

I hold her tight, rubbing her back with my hand to soothe her. As I make the wordless, cooing sound she used to make to comfort me, I keep thinking of how I wanted to make her cry, in January. How could I have been so mean? I actually wanted to hurt her, to see her suffer. The memory makes me want to cry, myself, but I hold back my own tears and keep patting her shoulders, her hair. I would give anything, now, to see her stop crying, to make her smile.

"It's okay," I repeat, even though she can scarcely listen. "You don't have to cry. I'm coming to stay with you for the summer. We'll be together every summer."

Over my mother's back I can see the work she has put down on the table. It is a mandala for a Buddhist altar cloth. My grandfather once showed me the tiny, knotted stitches that must be used for them—made in silk thread, each stitch smaller than a grain of sand yet luminous as a pearl. On the edge of the cloth, the stitches trace circles within circles like the patterns the monks rake into their sand gardens each morning. In the center, there is a rose that is slowly opening in a perfect bloom. The rose, the circles, all the stitches are the same smoky pink as the silk cloth they are made on. The flower seems to be appearing out of nothing but air; it is spreading wave after wave of beauty back into the same air. The monks, my grandfather told me, believe that a whole world could be contained in a perfect ceramic cup or even in each stitch of an altar cloth. I remember what Mother wrote in her letter, how she and Grandfather pray to the same God although they have different names for him. Looking at the rose my mother has embroidered, I understand what she must have meant, and I am sorry, more than ever, to have

222

assumed the worst about her: When I read that letter, I dismissed her thoughts as strange and crazy—another thing that I could never tell anyone about my family. I take a deep breath and struggle to stay calm.

Holding my mother, rocking back and forth with her tears, I notice my own hands rubbing her shoulders. My broad palms and long fingers look just like hers. Our thin wrists have sharp knobs of bone sticking out from the side. All four hands and wrists are the same. My mother's eyes are scrunched up behind her tears. When she is done crying, when she opens her eyes, she will look right into my eyes, which are hers, passed on to me.

Repeating words of comfort, I wait for her to calm down, so she can understand what I have come to tell her: I am her daughter; no one is going to keep us apart for seven years. There is so much for us to talk about, sitting together in this house where she grew up. Though I will see her every summer now, there is scarcely enough time to tell her everything I want to say. I try to be patient. I crane my neck and press my cheek against her shoulder, just as she is doing, holding on to me. The mandala is like the two of us. I cannot tell which is the flower, which is the air.

11
The Migration of Words

The morning after my visit with my mother and grand-father, I wake up before five, worried about the yellow irises I brought back from their house. Getting out of bed in the near dark, I walk over to the desk, where I have left the flowers in a small pail of water. They look the same as yesterday, no worse. The yellow buds are looser and larger at the bottom, some of them beginning to open.

I take the flowers out of the water and wrap them in layers of newspaper. Then, changing my clothes in the dark, I leave the house before my grandmother gets up.

Outside, the streetlights are on, but the sky is already a pale gray. On my way down the hill, I meet only a few businessmen in their suits, carrying their briefcases. Birds are twittering in the maples along the river, but I cannot see them among the dark branches and leaves.

I get to the Katos' house at five-thirty and climb the steps to the rectory. The door is open, as always—Pastor Kato believes that one day someone may come looking for help or shelter in the middle of the night.

Inside, everything looks the same. The stoneware cups and plates are drying on the rack by the kitchen sink, the placemats and napkins carefully folded on the table. I can find my way around in the light coming through the windows.

Making as little noise as possible, I open the cabinet where Mrs. Kato keeps her good china, crystal glasses, and vases. All three vases are on the second shelf: a crystal bud vase, a stoneware vase that matches her plates and cups, and the large salt-glazed vase Mrs. Uchida made. I reach up and take Mrs. Uchida's vase in both my hands. It is heavy and round, the size of a small watermelon; its pockmarked surface and bright rust color remind me of oranges. Mrs. Uchida made the vase for Mrs. Kato's thirty-eighth birthday, back when Kiyoshi and I were in third grade.

At the sink, I fill the vase with tepid water, hoping it won't be too cold or too warm. Taking an aspirin from my jeans pocket, I crush it with the back of a spoon to dissolve in the water—a trick my mother showed me to make the flowers last, though it has not always worked for me. I bring the vase to the table, put the irises in it, and reread the letter I brought for Mrs. Kato.

Dear Mrs. Kato:

These flowers are from my mother's garden. She sends her love. I went to see her yesterday and am going to stay with her for the summer. We hope you will come to visit us there.

I am sorry about church and about not having come to your house in all this time. I miss you very much and promise to visit soon.

Love, Megumi

It will have to do, though there was a lot more I wanted to say. I put the letter back in the envelope, seal it, and prop it against the vase. I am wiping off the water I spilled on the counter when a door swooshes open down the hallway and someone comes padding down the carpet

225

with bare feet. It's too late for me to leave. By the time I get to the door, whoever it is will be in the kitchen, just in time to see me running away like a burglar. I have no choice but to stay.

Coming into the kitchen in his blue pajamas, Kiyoshi squints into the gray light. His small eyes disappear in the folds of sleepy eyelids. His hair is puffed up on one side and completely flat on the other. I want to laugh, almost forgetting everything that has happened in the last month. He looks surprised, then glad, before his jaw freezes into a square outline, pulling his lips straight and tight. Just for a second he must have forgotten, too, and been glad to see me.

"What are you doing here?" he whispers, not taking another step toward me.

"Leaving your mother a note," I whisper back. We are about ten paces away from each other. I stop whispering and speak in a soft voice instead. "I was just leaving. I didn't mean to wake you."

Though we have nothing more to say, Kiyoshi and I stand staring at each other in the kitchen where we used to play and bicker and make peace. The memory makes me lonely. I will never come here again, except on brief visits to say hello to Mrs. Kato. Those first few nights after my mother left, sitting in this kitchen with the Katos—watching Kiyoshi do his homework, Pastor Kato reading the evening paper while Mrs. Kato made tea— gave me the only comfort I had. I wish we could go back to a time when Kiyoshi and I could be friends. I almost wish I hadn't decided to give up my faith. But I cannot apologize for my decision, so I offer what I hope would be the next best thing. "I'm sorry that I hadn't been more honest all along. I should have told you a long time ago. I haven't believed in God for the last few years—maybe

226

even the last five, ever since Mrs. Uchida's death." I stop, my eyes on the vase. When Mrs. Uchida gave the vase to Mrs. Kato, I thought it was ugly because of its rust color, its texture, its squat shape. Back then, I didn't consider anything pretty unless it was a soft pastel color like pink or lavender and its surface was smooth and shiny. That was a long time ago. I knew nothing. Even in the near dark, the vase is vibrant with color, the rusty glaze burning with the yellow of the irises. Kiyoshi is looking at me, waiting for me to go on. "I'm very sorry," I repeat, wishing I could say more.

He shrugs his shoulders. "You've made your decision," he mumbles. "It's up to you whether you want to believe or not." When he closes his mouth, his neck tightens as if he were clenching his teeth. He doesn't mean what he said—at least not in a forgiving way.

I should turn my back and leave, but I can't. Kiyoshi's blue pajamas remind me of the Nativity play we put on in second grade, when there were more kids at the church. We were all dressed in pajamas and bedsheets our mothers had tried to alter into the robes of shepherds, wise men, Joseph, and Mary. Even the girl who played the angel wore a white nightgown with paper wings taped to her back. Kiyoshi, Takashi, and I were the three wise men. There were only two girls' parts—Mary and the angel—and three girls, so one of us had to play a boy's part. My head covered with a brown sheet, I looked no different from the two boys, my voice only a little higher than theirs. "We come bearing gifts," we were supposed to say in chorus, but one of us always missed the cue. I am sad that Kiyoshi and I will not be remembering the silly play together in the years to come. When we grow up, we will not be like our mothers, who were always bringing up some funny event from the time before we

227

were born. Driving in a car or drinking tea in the kitchen, one of them would mention something, and suddenly, both women would burst into uncontrollable laughter and they would bend over almost choking—floored by their funny memories.

"I'm going," I announce. My voice sounds choked up.

Maybe I am imagining it, but he looks sad. His mouth droops down a little at the corners.

"I'm going to spend the summer with Mother," I tell him. "Maybe we'll see each other when I come back in the fall."

He says nothing. I don't expect him to. Even if we were to see each other in the fall, we will never again be close friends, and we both know it. Walking quickly to the door, I go out and run down the steps into the empty churchyard. A few tears fall from my eyes as I pass the sandbox and the swings, but I take a deep breath and keep moving.

During lunch at school, Noriko and Mieko have to eat in the cafeteria with me because I didn't bring my bag lunch. After going to the Katos' and then to Dr. Mizutani's to feed the birds, I didn't feel like stopping at home again. My grandmother must be mad. She will scold me when I get home about wasting the lunch she had made for me. What she really wants to scold me for but won't is yesterday's visit to Mother.

I didn't get back to Ashiya until eleven last night. My grandfather and Dr. Mizutani took a walk in the afternoon to see more birds while my mother and I stayed home talking and cooking in the kitchen. The afternoon flew by. We were just beginning to really talk—about my decision not to go to church, about Kiyoshi and Keiko and Toru—when the sun set and it got dark. All of us ate supper together. Both my mother and grandfather liked Dr. Mizutani, I could tell. They kept urging her to eat more, commenting on how skinny she is; when we were ready to leave, my grandfather gave her a small framed embroidery he had done of a sparrow perched on a bamboo branch.

When I finally got home, Grandmother came to the door in her brown kimono; she hadn't yet changed into her pajamas even though she usually goes to bed around ten. I knew that she had stayed up, not just to scold me, but because she was worried about me. For a second when she opened the door, her frown went away, her lips loosened, and I could hear the small sigh she made. But before I could say anything, she frowned again and gritted her teeth. "How can you be out all Sunday? You have school tomorrow." She didn't say anything about my mother or Dr. Mizutani or where we had been. She was pretending that I had broken my curfew out of carelessness. I suppose that's the only way she and my father can save face to me and even to themselves. Until the day I leave, they will both pretend that I am not really going to my mother's for the summer, that I have not gotten my way. They may be hoping, even yet, to make me change my mind by being silent and unfriendly. But they must know, down deep, that it will never work. I love my mother too much to grow up without seeing her. They have no choice except to let me go, but they would never admit that to me. In the fall when I come back, my father and grandmother will pretend that I have not been gone all summer long. And if they had worried about me during my absence, they would never show it.

Getting some soup and a hard-roll, I carry my tray and sit down at one of the long cafeteria tables across from my two friends. Noriko and Mieko have both brought

229

sandwiches. Their mothers cut off the crust, the way my mother does when she makes sandwiches. My grandmother leaves the crust because it's wasteful not to eat all of the bread. "During the war," she often lectures, her face in a scowl, "we had nothing to eat but watered-down rice. You don't know what it's like to go hungry. You waste food because you don't know how lucky you are." Though my mother must have gone hungry during the war, too, she isn't mean about wasting food. She used to bake bread and cut the loaf in half so I could eat all the soft part, leaving a brown boat of crust on the table. My grandmother would have lost her temper if she had seen that. I smile, thinking about the face Grandmother might have made.

"What is it, Megumi? What's so funny?" Noriko asks, always eager for a joke.

"Just a private joke." It's not worth explaining. I haven't told my friends about spending the summer with my mother. I know they will be happy for me, but the subject seems too serious to bring up now, while the two are chattering about Reiko's first date with the boy from the train.

"Reiko just raves about him," Mieko says. "They went to an amusement park in Nara and rode the roller coaster all day long."

"Reiko did?" Noriko asks. "I thought she was afraid of heights. She couldn't even stand on the balance beam in gym last semester. She kept complaining and whimpering. She's such a chicken."

"I know. But the boy told her that he loves high speeds. He wants to drive a race car when he turns eighteen."

"I guess Reiko thought she'd better get used to it. Can you imagine *her* in a race car? She's afraid to go down-

230

hill on a bicycle," Noriko says, and the two of them laugh.

I don't think it's all that funny—a girl who hates heights spending the whole day on a roller coaster. Reiko must have been desperate to impress him. I almost feel sorry for her, but I smile at Mieko and Noriko anyway and drift in and out of their conversation.

I won't see them—or any of our school friends—all summer, every summer. Maybe I will feel out of place in the fall, more than I already do. I feel queasy thinking about all the things that have happened to me since January. If I spend every summer with my mother and every school year with Father and Grandmother, will I feel as though I have two homes, or no home at all? Long ago, when I first heard about astronauts, I had nightmares about being locked up in a spaceship that went around and around the earth, never to come down. That is how I feel now, watching my friends across the table.

They keep talking. Noriko is shaking her fork at Mieko, to make some point. When they laugh again, a little too loudly, several twelfth-grade girls glance in our direction. We are the only tenth graders here. Almost all the girls who eat in the cafeteria are twelfth graders, most of whom think it's childish to bring bag lunches to school. I've heard that from the girls in my class who have older sisters; they describe the arguments their older sisters have with their mothers about lunch, about clothes and makeup.

Girls in twelfth grade dress nothing like girls in tenth grade. Anyone looking around the cafeteria can tell that Mieko, Noriko, and I are tenth graders, all three of us dressed in blue jeans and T-shirts. The twelfth-grade girls are wearing dresses or skirts and silk blouses. We are not supposed to wear makeup to school, but every one of them has very light lipstick, a little mascara, a dab of rouge.

There are several girls in our class, too—usually the ones with older sisters—who are beginning to dress more like the girls in the cafeteria. When I pass these girls in the hallway, I can smell a faint whiff of perfume. Their spring coats, if they got new ones this year, are a little longer and slimmer-looking than ours. The colors are purple, pale pink, or slate blue, instead of the red, yellow, and sky blue the rest of us still wear. One by one, I suppose, we are all changing. Maybe in two years, Mieko, Noriko, and I, too, will look like the girls who are now in this cafeteria.

I don't want to. I don't like the way the older girls laugh in thin, choking voices, their hands fluttering up to cover their mouths. They sit at the long tables picking at their food, brushing their hair back from their faces, sighing now and then. When I don't like my food, I just don't eat it. I see no point in stirring the food around with a fork, eating a tiny little mouthful and leaning forward to sigh as if exhausted from the effort.

"Is something wrong, Megumi?" Mieko asks, a slight frown between her arched eyebrows.

"Oh, nothing," I reply, putting down the hard-roll I have been crushing in my hand. Because all the hard-rolls look the same, with their dark, almost-burnt crusts, I have taken the pumpernickel, which I hate, instead of the sourdough. I put the uneaten roll down on my empty soup bowl and push away my tray.

Suddenly, the P.A. system comes on. Someone's scratchy breathing comes through the microphone. Down the table from us, two older girls scowl and squirm, pretending to be horrified. It's just someone—one of our teachers, no doubt—getting ready to speak.

"We have an announcement," Mrs. Fukushima's voice says.

There is complete silence in the room. Everyone puts down her silverware, trying to listen politely; only a few of the girls are rolling their eyes.

"Professor Goto from Kobe University has just phoned us with the results of the time capsule contest. As you know, we sent him the essays of the ten finalists."

Mrs. Fukushima proceeds to read the ten names, stretching out the announcement and building up the suspense. Across the table, Noriko looks kind of pale—nervous, I realize, on my account. Mieko, too, has a very serious expression—her eyes narrowed, her lips pouted a little. *Forget it,* I want to tell them. *I'm not going to win anyway. My essay was too personal.* It would be nice, all the same, to get at least an honorable mention.

"Of these ten finalists, Mr. Goto has decided to give two honorable mentions: Eiko Sakamoto and Sumire Kuroda," Mrs. Fukushima announces.

I should be proud, I tell myself, *just to have been a finalist.*

"The second place," Mrs. Fukushima continues, "goes to Hideko Shibata."

From the way everyone's head turns in the cafeteria, I can see exactly where Hideko is sitting. She is at a table on the other side of the cafeteria from us. At first, her face is blank, then a funny expression comes over her; she can't decide whether to be happy or sad. I suppose I would look like that, too, if I came in second. It would be almost better not to know that you were close to winning, but didn't. Maybe they should give us a choice when we enter contests. "If you come in second but don't win, do you wish to know? Yes or no: Check the appropriate box."

"The first-place essay, of course, will be put into the time capsule, along with the best essays from the other high schools in Kobe, Osaka, Ashiya, Nishinomiya, and Amagasaki. This writing, then, is our message to the people in the future, in the year 2000." Mrs. Fukushima pauses. I look away from Hideko Shibata to Mieko and Noriko, who are sitting with their hands clenched into fists. "I am pleased," Mrs. Fukushima says, "to announce that this honor will be given to a young writer, the only tenth-grade finalist."

My heart almost stops.

The next moment, Mrs. Fukushima is saying my name over the P.A., and Noriko is springing up from her chair and giving a shrill yelp.

"Congratulations," Mrs. Fukushima finishes. "All of you wrote fine essays." The P.A. is turned off, leaving a brief moment of silence.

By the time the buzz of conversation starts up again, Noriko and Mieko are leaning over the table to hug me. I'm still sitting down, stunned. I get up in a daze, hug my friends, and then plop back down on the chair.

"I'm so happy," Mieko says, her eyes shining. She looks like she might start crying.

"Good job," Noriko says. "I knew you'd win."

The two twelfth-grade girls who were sitting a few chairs away from us are getting up and extending their hands to me. "Well done," they say, shaking my hand. "Congratulations."

Because lunch hour is almost over, girls are bringing their trays back to the window and leaving. Those who pass by our group stop for a moment to murmur, "Congratulations, Megumi" or, "Good job." They remind me of Keiko's older sisters, who used to roll their eyes at Keiko and me but were more than kind if one of us cried

234

or got hurt. I am sorry to have thought mean, critical things about the twelfth-grade girls, though I know I will think these same things again.

Out of the corner of my eye, I notice Hideko, the second-place winner, getting up from her table. She is walking straight toward me. When she is about ten steps away, she smiles and holds out her hand, letting me know that she has come to wish me well.

I take her hand, which is slender and smaller than mine. As we shake, I try to imagine my words in the year 2000. By then I might have changed my mind about many things that I think are now true. My handwriting might look different, the way my mother's looks different from the handwriting in her old books and letters. Maybe I will be embarrassed by what I had written while sitting in my room soon after I thought I had lost my mother.

"You should be proud of yourself," Hideko whispers before she walks away.

Her back straight, Hideko steps lightly between the chairs and then out the door. She should be proud of herself, too—for having written a good essay, for being able to wish me well instead of acting like a poor loser, as I often did as a kid and maybe still do sometimes.

Though the bell will ring soon, I sit for another minute, thinking about my essay. After describing my mother's departure and my grandmother's arrival, I talked about how I was always different from my friends.

" 'Look at the positive side,' people often tell me," I wrote near the end. "There is nothing positive about my mother's leaving. There is, however, a small relief. I know that the worst is over. Nothing else can happen to hurt me in the same way, and more than that, I know I can never be like everyone else even if I were to try.

"Ever since seventh grade, I have felt split between two feelings. On one hand, I was proud of the ways in which I was different from my friends—spending the afternoon reading a good book instead of watching television, not acting silly in front of boys. But in another way I wanted to be like everyone else. Even though I liked the blouses and jumper skirts my mother had sewn for me, I insisted on wearing blue jeans and T-shirts, because that's what everyone wore to school. Hearing my friends sigh and complain every time our teachers asked us to write an essay, I didn't want to let on that I actually enjoyed writing, looked forward to it, even. I often felt irritated with my friends or envious of them—I wanted to be just like them and different from them at the same time.

"After my mother left, I realized that I could never be like my friends no matter how much I tried. My family was nothing like theirs; my friends didn't understand what I was talking about when I told them about things that happened at my house. I realized, at the same time, that my friends like me and worry about me even if they don't understand. It hurts me not to be able to explain things to them, but I know that they love me all the same. That realization has given me at least a little comfort.

"As time goes on, maybe each of my close friends will experience something that makes her different, too. When that happens, I think I will be understanding, just as they have been. To me, that is the most important thing about being a high school student in 1975: wanting to be different and wanting to be included, to have friends. It is possible, however difficult. That's what I want to remember in the year 2000 about myself as a high school student. If I were writing myself a letter to be opened in the future, I would remind myself not to be ashamed or afraid of being different, because my true friends will always try their best to love me."

Noriko is getting up and picking up my tray, to bring it back to the counter for me. Mieko is motioning for me to get up. It's time to go. Noriko and Mieko know that I'm stunned by winning the contest; they are trying to make me hurry up without rushing me too much.

Right after I wrote my essay, I felt that I had been falsely hopeful in my conclusion, that my essay was a kind of lie. As I follow my two friends out the door to our fifth-hour class, I see the truth of what I had written: There are many kinds of lies just as there are many kinds of truths. Most lies are inexcusable—the lies we tell to gain an unfair advantage or to avoid punishment—like my pretending to my father and grandmother that I was going to church instead of meeting Toru, that I wasn't hearing from my mother—even those, I suppose, are wrong. But the hopeful lies we tell our friends and ourselves may not be always so bad. They turn out to be the truth sometimes—like my mother insisting that Grandmother Shimizu cared about me, or my writing that my friends loved me at a time when I felt too lonely to really feel that way. When my mother told me she planned to come back in the spring, maybe she was lying to me in that same way, hoping—though in this case, she could never be right—that it would miraculously turn into a truth. That isn't the same as lying to hurt people.

Walking down the hallway to my class, I am sure of one thing: No matter how much I change between now and then, I won't be embarrassed by my own words. If I were to read my essay again in the year 2000, I would remember the waxwing singing in my room as I wrote it, the lonely cricket noise he was practicing, to call a whole flock from miles away. I picture my words flying around

237

inside the dark trunk with the words of the other high school students—students who must be as thrilled as I am to have been chosen. If we could all meet up somehow, we would stand on the shoreline waving, while with the swirl of a hundred wingbeats, our words begin their migration into the future.

12

A Swan's Wing

Of all the stories my mother used to tell me, my favorite
was about a girl whose six brothers had been turned into
swans by an evil stepmother. To free her brothers, the
girl had to gather nettles and sew them into magic shirts;
she could not speak or laugh until she was done. At the
end of the story, her six swan brothers came flying just as
she was going to be burned at the stake as a witch. The
girl threw the finished shirts over the swans, and immediately, the swans changed back into her brothers and res-
cued her. But the girl had run out of time before she
could sew the left sleeve of the last shirt, so her youngest
brother was missing his left arm. Where his arm would
have been, he had a swan's wing.

Though the story ended with everyone living happily
ever after, I used to wonder about the boy with the
swan's wing. I imagined him living in a palace with his
brothers and sisters, dancing to an orchestra every night,
entertaining other princes and princesses. He would
dance with only one arm; inside the left sleeve of his bro-
cade jacket, he would cradle his delicately folded wing.
Only when he was alone, perhaps late at night in the
palace orchard, he would slip off his jacket and slowly
spread out his wing in the moonlight, revealing the white
feathers. I was never sure whether he would be admired

or pitied for being different from his brothers. I wanted to know if he was happy or sad when he looked at his wing. Would the wing remind him of the hardships he and his brothers had suffered under the evil spell? Or would he miss his days of flying? Would he be saddened to re-member the seven years his sister spent gathering prickly nettles and sewing them, being mistaken for a witch but unable to defend herself with words, just to turn him back into a boy when he wanted to be a swan? I know that wasn't the important thing about the story, but I couldn't stop wondering. Often with stories the unimpor-tant parts are the ones I like to think about.

I'm remembering the story again as I walk into the out-door birdcage at five on Tuesday morning. Standing on the folding chair I have brought from the clinic, I reach up to the highest branch where the three sparrows are sleeping. Perched side by side on a branch, they look like three apples or pears and are as easy to pick because they can't see me in this dim light. One by one, I lift them in my hand and put them inside the pet carrier. By the time they wake up and begin to flutter around and chirp a little, I have already closed the door. I throw a pillowcase over the carrier to quiet them.

The brown-eared bulbul screeches at me a few times from his perch near the door of the cage, but in a few minutes, he, too, goes back to sleep. The Japanese gros-beak shifts his weight but makes no noise. Outside the cage, the yard is completely quiet. There are no lights in Dr. Mizutani's clinic or in her parents' house next door.

I sit down in a chair and close my eyes, waiting for the sunrise.

The weather is expected to hold for the rest of the

week. On Saturday, Dr. Mizutani and I will take the bulbul and the grosbeak to the mountain path where we let go of the waxwing in the spring. Till then, they need a few more days to practice eating the berries I tie up to the branches, the seeds I scatter in the grass at the bottom of the cage.

"You can let the sparrows go tomorrow. Take them outside the cage and let them go. You are in charge," she told me. "I'll probably be sleeping."

I thought about asking Toru to come with me. I went to see him at home last night because I hadn't returned in time for our regular meeting time on Sunday. Takashi was home, too, so the three of us sat in the backyard trying to name the constellations we had learned in school long ago. None of us could remember much except the Big Dipper, the North Star, Cassiopeia's Chair. After Takashi went in to do his homework, Toru and I talked for a long time; he doesn't work on Mondays. He told me he planned to head for Tokyo in early June, about a week before I leave Ashiya to stay with my mother and grandfather. At eleven, when he drove me home, I almost asked him if he wanted to get up early and come with me to watch the sparrows fly away. He would enjoy seeing them.

But I thought of the two of us sitting inside the outdoor cage and waiting for sunrise, being quiet together. It wouldn't be right. He would be thinking of Yoshimi, whom he will see in less than a month, while I would sit a few feet away, my heart beating the way it does sometimes when I am with him and we are quiet. It's different if we are talking. Then I can say the right things, regardless. I can tell him how glad I am for him and mean it, too, for the most part: I am his friend; I do want him to

241

be happy even if that means not seeing him all summer. But being quiet is another matter. Then I can feel him thinking about Yoshimi, and that makes me lonely even if he is sitting next to me. I don't want to feel like that. I should be happy, not sad, on the day the sparrows fly away.

Besides, if I were going to be with anyone at all, it should be Dr. Mizutani. Toru had nothing to do with my raising the sparrows. He wouldn't know about those early mornings I would turn on the light in my room to start my first feeding—how my heart would flip over and my stomach would feel queasy when I saw the birds slumped together in their sleep. Each time, I was sure that at least one of them had died during the night. Only Dr. Mizutani would know how I had felt then, every inch of my body tense with worry.

Maybe in the fall, if Toru comes back from Tokyo as he plans to, we will walk in the woods to look for wild birds. Dr. Mizutani has promised to visit me every weekend in the country, to walk with my grandfather and me in the woods to see the birds. She will bring me all the baby birds people might give her, and I can raise them in my grandfather's house. "They have the same birds in the country, and much more," she said. "I'll help your grandfather build you an outdoor cage." If Toru comes back in the fall, I can teach him about birds. And if he doesn't—well, I won't think about that until it happens, except that I will visit Takashi now and then, to make sure he is all right.

At six-thirty the sun is up. The sky has changed from gray to white and then to light blue. The grosbeak ruffles his feathers, stretches, and flies over to the east side of the cage, where the sun is hitting one of the branches.

Perched on the branch, he begins to preen his feathers. Overhead a flock of crows comes flying down from the mountains, cawing loudly. Soon the crow in the yard will wake up and flop down from the maple tree, looking for the few bits of food I have left in his dish.

Getting up from my chair, I uncover the pet carrier and pick it up. The sparrows begin to flutter and chirp inside. The bulbul is watching me from his perch. I shoo him away with my hand, and when he flies to the other side of the cage, I exit quickly, closing the door behind me. The sun is hitting the stretch of grass where Dr. Mizutani's yard borders her parents'. I walk over there, hold the carrier over my head, and pull open the door.

Immediately one sparrow flies out and soars straight toward the maple branches. In just a few seconds the other two swirl up into the air, heading for the maple tree to join the first one.

Putting down the carrier, I shade my eyes with my hand. For a while I can see all three birds in the maple, flitting from one branch to another. Then they take off together, dipping halfway down to the ground and then soaring up. Fluttering their wings a few beats and then pulling them in, the birds dip and rise, dip and rise, in the irregular way all sparrows fly.

I raise my left arm and begin to wave as the birds disappear over the neighbors' houses, and my eyes ache from staring into the sky. I know they will be back among the flocks of sparrows in Dr. Mizutani's yard— eating the seeds from the feeders, splashing noisily in the birdbath. Only I will never again be able to tell them apart from all the other young sparrows, the hundreds of this spring's babies with their streaky breasts and pinkish legs. So even after I can no longer see my sparrows, I keep waving in the direction of their flight. If they could look back, they would see the blurred motion of my arm—a rough, repeated outline in the air, the closest thing I can manage to a wing.

If you loved *One Bird,* don't miss Kyoko
Mori's moving story of a girl whose mother
commits suicide.
For a glimpse of *Shizuko's Daughter,*
please read on . . .

SHIZUKO'S DAUGHTER
by Kyoko Mori

The telephone was ringing in the hallway. Shizuko woke up
and pushed aside her blanket. As she got up from the couch
and walked slowly toward the noise, she thought: In a
month, the cherry trees will be in blossom. It was strange to
think that. Spring was late this year; the first week of March
had been gray and damp. I won't be here to see, she thought.
I wonder if the dead can see or smell the flowers. She
thought of how her mother put fresh flowers on the Buddhist
altar every week in memory of her son who had been killed
in the War.

"Mama, can you hear me?" Yuki's voice sounded anxious on the other end as Shizuko picked up the receiver. In
the background, a stereo was playing a symphony. "I'm
calling from Miss Uozumi's house."

"What happened to your piano lesson?" Shizuko asked.
"I thought you were supposed to be taking it now." She
blinked and tried to clear her head. She was still thinking of
Yuki running around the cherry tree in her dream.

"That's what I'm calling about," Yuki said. "Miss Uozumi's
going to be about an hour late. Her mother let me in and gave
me some tea. Miss Uozumi told her to have me wait. Is that all
right?"

"That's fine," Shizuko said.

"I won't be home until five or five thirty, just in time for
supper. Are you sure it's all right?"

"Of course," Shizuko said. "How was school?" She knew she was stalling. Let me hear her voice just a while longer, she thought. I can't let her go. Not yet.

"So-so," Yuki said. "I scored two runs in baseball. Two of the boys on the other team said I bragged about it, so I had a fight with them during lunch break. Don't worry, Mama. Nobody was really hurt, and the teacher didn't scold anyone. I scraped my knee a little when I fell down, but I punched one of them, right in the stomach. I was winning before the teacher came and stopped us. You're not worried, are you? I'm not hurt, really."

"You should be careful, Yuki," Shizuko said, remembering her dream. "You may get hurt someday."

"I don't think so. Most of the kids won't fight me anymore. They're afraid of me."

"Be careful all the same."

"Sure," Yuki said. "What are you going to do this afternoon? You sound kind of tired. Are you all right?"

"I just woke up from a nap."

"I didn't mean to wake you up. Do you want to go back to sleep?"

"No," Shizuko said. "I'm awake now."

Yuki seemed to hesitate. "You're sure you don't want me to come right away? I can fix supper."

"No," Shizuko said. "You should wait for your lesson. You prepared for it all week."

"But I can practice the same pieces another week. I'm sure Miss Uozumi won't mind. She's always telling me to practice more. I'll tell her mother I have to go home."

"Don't do that," Shizuko said. "I'm only tired. You'd better go now."

"All right. I'll come home as soon as I'm done. Maybe we can eat out—then you won't have to cook. I'm sure Father won't come home for supper. Can we go out to eat?"

"Maybe," Shizuko said. Her own voice sounded strange.

She wondered if Yuki could hear it. "Yuki," she said. "Be good. You know I love you."

"I love you too, Mama. I'll see you later."

Shizuko held the receiver for a moment and waited for Yuki to hang up. When the click did not come, she hesitated for another moment and then put down the receiver. She pictured Yuki waiting on the other end for her to hang up first, her face puzzled and uncertain.

Shizuko went to the den, where she kept her sewing machine, ironing board, knitting basket, and a small desk for writing letters and taking care of the bills. Perhaps I haven't done so badly, she told herself as she thought of her fifteen years of marriage. Then she saw the cloth she had cut out for Yuki's new skirt and pinned to the sewing board. Triangular pieces of white cotton and maroon trimming, they reminded her of butterfly wings. She had meant to finish the skirt. But it was nearly three now; there was just enough time to write two notes—one for her husband, Hideki, and one for Yuki.

Somebody else will finish the skirt for her, Shizuko thought as she sat down at the desk and picked up her pen. She looked at the pad of blank paper and tried to concentrate. There was so much she had planned to do—she had even meant to clean out her closet and drawers, throw away some things and pack the rest to be saved for Yuki or given away to relatives. She had wanted to spare the others the trouble, the unpleasantness. She remembered the rainy morning after her mother-in-law's death, two years earlier. Her father-in-law and her husband had left her and Yuki, only ten at the time, to dispose of the clothes and jewelry and books. "This is an awful thing to have to do," Yuki had said as she poured mothballs into a box of clothes to be given away to charity. "Why don't *they* help?" "It's women's work," Shizuko had told her. It's always women's work, she thought now as she sat at the desk with a sheet of blank paper, to deal with the consequences of other people's deaths, their mistakes, broken promises.

247

Please forgive me, she started to write in large, bold letters, *for my weakness, for the trouble I have caused you.* As I have forgiven your coldness, she thought, all the hours and days you were too busy to spare for Yuki and me, even the nights you have spent with another woman. These things I have forgiven, have had to forgive. *I do not do this rashly,* she continued, *but after much consideration. This is best for all of us. Please do not feel guilty in any way. What has happened is entirely my responsibility. This is the best for myself as well as for you. I am almost happy at this last hour and wish you to be.*

She signed the note and took out another sheet of paper. She knew what she wanted to tell Yuki. *In spite of this,* she wrote, *please believe that I love you. People will tell you that I've done this because I did not love you. Don't listen to them. When you grow up to be a strong woman, you will know that this was for the best. My only concern now is that you will be the first to find me. I'm sorry. Call your father at work and let him take care of everything.* Shizuko stopped to read over what she had written. This is the best I can do for her, she thought, to leave her and save her from my unhappiness, from growing up to be like me. Yuki had so much to look forward to. At twelve, she was easily the brightest in her class; all her teachers said so. The art teacher had been particularly impressed by her watercolors. They reflected, he said, her bold intelligence and imagination as well as her skills. *You are a strong person,* Shizuko continued. *You will no doubt get over this and be a brilliant woman. Don't let me stop or delay you. I love you.*

SHIZUKO'S DAUGHTER
by Kyoko Mori

Published by Fawcett Books.
Available in your local bookstore.